A Rock and a Hard Place

By the Author

Dead Man's Bay (2000)

A Tinker's Damn (2000)

Strawman's Hammock (2001)

The King of Colored Town (2007)

Pepperfish Keys (2007)

Kaleidoscope (2008)

Darryl Wimberley

A
Rock
and
a hard place

The Toby Press

A Rock and a Hard Place

First Paperback Edition 2008

The Toby Press LLC
POB 8531, New Milford, CT 06776-8531, USA
& POB 2455, London WIA 5WY, England
www.tobypress.com

ISBN 978 1 59264 221 2, *paperback*

A CIP catalogue record for this title is
available from the British Library

Typeset in Adobe Garamond Pro
by Koren Publishing Services

Printed and bound in the United States

Chapter one

The sun swelled an angry blister over a bright and empty sea. An abandoned, cypress-framed structure was propped below on a rotting pier, teetering over what was actually a bay that opened out, could you follow the buoys, to the Gulf of Mexico.

It used to be a restaurant, this rectangle of cypress and tin along the water; a lobster painted over screenless doors made that deduction simple, along with a more obvious clue oil-based in block letters beneath, KEY'S REST—. The remainder of the invitation had long since faded away, as had the lobster's once-scarlet pincers. Seagulls still hovered outside the kitchen, though, as if remembering the shrimp heads and fish guts that long-absent cooks once tossed out the building's wide-silled windows.

The windows were boarded up now. It was almost dark inside. But motes of dust drifted in the slender shafts of sunlight that fell like spears through the rusted roof. You could imagine stars shining brightly overhead, arranged in brilliant constellations. Orion over here, say, or over there the Big Dipper. The whole place seemed about to collapse. It was as if the building, long abandoned, was kept erect on columns of insubstantial illumination.

There were few things left to see below the star-studded ceiling, though Rita Hayworth was still glorious in a pinup above the bar. The bar once boasted a brass rail. Not much brass left now, though. A couple of cheaply framed glossies punctuated the walls—Perry Como, Billie Holliday, Sinatra. Elvis never played here. The easygoing young men and women who used to congregate at this place came home from the war listening to the Big Bands and the crooners. They'd lean from booths and barstools upholstered in bright red Naugahyde to drop dimes for "Birth of the Beat" and "Black Magic." That was all before The King.

And now? Only two men inhabited the dining area's sweltering interior. They were seated on backless chairs set to face across a card table. They had not come seeking steaks or seafood.

A Latin American dressed to the nines in a bone linen jacket and white silk tie dripped sweat as if regulated by a metronome. Large, solitary drops. Like from a gutter after a thunderstorm.

A middle-aged American slouched at his side of the table in a baggy, sweat-stained blazer that looked fashioned from polyester and catgut. A single, pencil-thin shaft of light burned a hole dead center in the laminated tabletop that separated Frank Sienna from his better-dressed companion. A gambler's mask set like plaster over the American's deeply lined face. A long silence. Frank retrieved a package of cigarettes from his blazer. A Zippo lighter came next—"Semper Fi," the inscription scrolled beneath an escutcheon embossed on a globe and anchor. Smoke soon coiled sinuously amidst the columns of light. Finally…

The Latin interrupted the perfect rhythm of his perspiration with a handkerchief.

"Next month. You can have the rest next month."

"That was not our arrangement." Frank shook his head.

"It is all I can do." The Latin folded his handkerchief carefully.

"It's not how we've dealt in the past."

"The merchandise was satisfactory. In the past."

"Never had a problem before," Frank observed.

"See for yourself." The Latin man returned the handkerchief to his jacket. And came out with a short-barreled machine gun.

It was an Uzi. The barrel was steady in the Latin's hands and level on Frank's heart…but there was no clip.

Sienna took a careful drag on his Marlboro. The Latin pulled back the Uzi's bolt—breech cleared. Nothing in the chamber.

Sienna kept his attention resolutely on the smoke that writhed, now, in and out of the columns of sunlight that supported the roof. "Looks fine to me," he said, nodding toward the firearm in his companion's well-manicured hand.

"The rifle, perhaps," the Latin agreed too amiably. "But where is the ammunition? One hundred fifteen weapons were to be delivered. And twenty thousand rounds of ammunition. Nine-millimeter, *Parabellum.* Standard load. You can see—we have no ammunition."

"We sent the rounds. I know. Packed 'em myself."

The Latin smiled broadly. "What you see is what we got."

The Latin offered the weapon for examination. Frank took the Uzi, tapped out a Marlboro for his companion.

"You provide twenty thousand rounds of ammunition," the Latin went on unctuously. "We make payment in full."

"And next time, Hernando," Frank said, lighting the other man's cigarette, "what'll be missing then?"

"I do not understand."

"I've played this game before, compadre. This time you stiff me for ammo. Next time you'll tell me we're short on guns."

Frank snapped his Zippo open and shut. Open and shut.

"Perhaps there can be another scenario." Hernando smoothed his silken tie.

"It had better involve payment."

"Suppose I disregard the ammunition I did not receive," the other man went on as if Frank hadn't said a word. "Then for the weapons I owe you…?"

"Forty-one thousand," Frank supplied. "Plus transport, naturally."

"Naturally. How much more for, say, two hundred and fifty thousand rounds of ammunition?"

"Quarter of a million rounds? Nine millimeter?"

"*Parabellum, sí.* How much?"

"Twelve thousand, about, for the rounds. Five to deliver. That doesn't pay for the twenty I know damn well I already got you."

The Latin leaned across the table.

"Two hundred and fifty thousand rounds. Provide me with *that*, we can conclude our business."

"What the hell?" Frank returned the Marlboros to his blazer. And came out with a clip of ammunition. "Why don't we just finish our business right now?"

Frank slapped the ammo home, locked back the bolt.

The Latin stared practically into the Uzi's barrel. A long, long moment passed. And then—

Sienna emptied the Uzi on full automatic into the roof. New spears of light fell from fresh constellations tattooed overhead. The Latin man sat frozen on his backless seat.

"A half million rounds." Sienna popped the clip free.

"That's twenty-five thousand dollars on top of what you owe me. Plus another five for shipping. Make it a half. At twenty-five plus. We've got a deal."

The Latin regarded the poorer-dressed American who sat across from him at the dead diner's last available table.

"Agreed."

Chapter two

Up the coast from Mr. Key's long-abandoned diner was a thriving, contemporary establishment. It was a pretty standard night at Ramona's Restaurant, which meant that business was terrific. People were pouring in out of the heat. Ceiling fans paddled full tilt over customers distributed all the way from the bar that bordered one side of the dining area to the veranda that provided another border facing out to the gulf. Ramona had air-conditioning, of course, but the fans kept up a pleasant, tropical breeze that made things seem cooler right off the bat. It was one of the little things that made people want to come and then come back.

The Baptists were drinking iced tea. Everybody else was drinking.

Newcomers tabled alongside regulars and there was Ramona. Working the crowd. Taking care of business. And there, too, seated by himself on the eve of his seventh anniversary, was Detective Barrett Raines. From across the restaurant you might judge Raines to be a bigger man than he actually was. Older perhaps than he actually was. A smidgeon under six feet, Barrett weighed in after his irregular bouts of belly work, bags, and runs at less than two hundred pounds.

He carried a lot of dignity for a man in his mid-thirties, and a lot of muscle on a chassis that had seen more than its share of bodywork. Barrett was also distinguished, this particular evening, by the color of his skin; he was the only black human being in a room filled with whites.

Ramona winked. Barrett acknowledged with a smile and a nod. You could take most any Friday night, get about a half hour off U.S. 90 toward the coast, and find half the locals at Deacon Beach unwinding over some kind of seafood at Ramona's SeaSide Restaurant. Barrett was not a bona fide regular anymore. He worked too many hours scattered over too many shifts and too much overtime for which, by virtue of his occupation and Florida's Garcia Act, he was not entitled extra pay. It had created a problem at home, this stochastic and exhausting schedule. And Barrett's wife worked, too, of course. So when the detective *did* get some time off, Laura Anne was busy herself, or asleep, or catching up precious time with their boys.

The twins, luckily, were fine, happy little first graders, due in no small part to the fact that Barrett and Laura Anne were righteous about family time. But Barrett knew that he and Laura Anne also badly needed a few minutes to themselves. The first couple of years it had been so easy. Evenings at Ramona's with friends were a big part of their marriage. But that was before Laura Anne started teaching music at the high school and then piano lessons on the side, and before Barrett, pressing hard to get his detective's badge, began taking the shifts and overtime no one else wanted.

He was trying to back off a little. Seven years on the job ought to cut a man some slack. Particularly on an anniversary. In fact, Barrett had actually planned to be with Laura Anne this evening, had planned as would any normal man to relax with his wife on the eve of seven years of marriage. But Taylor Folsom had called in sick, and even though Barrett was already scheduled to work the midnight-till-dawn shift, somebody had to cover Taylor's three-till-midnight.

"Go ahead," Laura Anne sighed. "Friday's never a good night for me anyway. And I've got grades to figure."

"We'll go out tomorrow," Barrett promised and went off to

work Taylor's swing shift and his own graveyard back-to-back. That was sixteen straight hours. Provided nothing happened that generated paperwork.

It was a bad night for Taylor to get the runs, or get laid, or whatever he was doing. Fortunately the rules of the department did allow a man to piss and eat, so around ten o'clock Barrett pocketed his beeper, crawled out of his unmarked sedan and settled in Ramona's for a bite of seafood. He never got tired of the various concoctions of seabass or snapper that Ramona served up on mahogany plates that the health department still gave her hell for. He never tired of the pilau and biscuits and locally concocted mayhaw jelly that Ramona mixed curiously into her menu of otherwise ocean-spawned ingredients. Most of all, like any other red-blooded man in the place, married or otherwise, Barrett never got enough of an eyeful of Ramona herself.

Any banker will tell you that there are more failures in the restaurant business than in any other, and yet Ramona was making a killing. Barrett knew that the success he was witnessing wasn't all due to the food, which was very good, nor to the sea breeze and ambiance that everyone around here took for granted. Nor was it due entirely to the service, which was excellent.

The secret ingredient was Ramona herself. Barrett heard Doc Hardesty say more than once that Ramona Walker wasn't close to being a spring fashion. In fact, she'd just turned forty-two. You walked into her place for the first time, you'd see a woman damn near six feet tall with auburn hair that fell from shoulders wide as a lumberjack's to a waist small enough you could circle it with your hands.

She had long dancer's legs that she liked to show off from a split skirt. She had eyes green as emeralds. And she had one of those Lauren Bacall voices—low, throaty. Barrett traveled with Ramona on occasion on town business. They'd usually forsake Barrett's unmarked sedan for her '64 Thunderbird. (What the hell? The city paid a per diem either way.) Then they'd bolt down the road at seventy or eighty miles an hour with the top down, and as the wind hiked an already borderline skirt even higher up those long, long, long, ivory legs they'd listen to oldies on Ramona's antediluvian eight-track until they reached an official destination in Tallahassee, usually, or sometimes Gainesville.

They'd pull up to a steamy curb. She'd stretch those gams getting out of her T-bird. Take two steps down the street. Heads would whip around as if jerked on a leash. Doc Hardesty used to compare Ramona to Helen of Troy. Faces launching ships. An odalisque in Priam's harem. That sort of thing. But Barrett liked Taff Calhoun's characterization better.

"That woman," Taff would spit a wad of Red Man, "could make a tadpole slap the shit out of a full-grown whale."

Ramona had opened her place a dozen years earlier on a shoestring and a hotplate and now people came from all over to sample her homemade tartars and side dishes and eat the catch of the day. And look, of course. And flirt. Ramona knew how to do that. Even with married men. Nobody ever got jealous, either, which was astounding in a place as small as Deacon Beach.

Barrett was never quite sure where the customers came from. Every conceivable type roamed in. Tourists in cutoffs that chafed below their swimsuits and over their sunburns. Girls in tank tops. Guys in jeans. And then the locals would drop by, the men in their modest, short-sleeved Arrow shirts, the wives in blouses and skirts or sometimes a dress from Penney's.

There was a smattering of professional folks, naturally. Even a place as small as Deacon had to have a few. And so amidst the surfers and catalog dressers you'd see a suit or two drop in with a well-set spouse in an evening dress. One of the first things Barrett noticed when he started coming to her place was that Ramona Walker never spent any more time with those highrollers than with the other folks. She'd smile. She'd flirt. She'd show the moneyed gentleman and his lady to whatever table was available. And then she'd turn away, as though distracted by the dart game which always was going near the bar, and as she'd turn she'd just brush the suit's vest with a hand or sometimes slide over his summer twills with one of those rock-hard, ivory legs.

Even the most homely waitress coming in behind that kind of introduction could report ten-dollar tips.

Ramona was very good to the folks working at her place. Barrett discovered that particular aspect of Ramona's character over supper (translated to "dinner" anyplace else) one evening while discussing his own financial affairs with Ramona's accountant. Ferris Boatwright was a huge hippopotamus of a man, deeply into Southern Baptist politics, which were Byzantine, and deeply into wearing his religion, if not his heart, prominently on his elephantine sleeve.

Boatwright was a man a little too certain of his relationship with God to make Barrett comfortable, but Ramona assured him that the doughboy deacon was a first-rate accountant. And Barrett needed some counsel. He and Laura Anne were both salaried. Both would have, if they stayed healthy, modest retirement benefits. But Barrett was worried it wouldn't be enough. He had supported his mother through a long and expensive illness. By the time Mama Raines mercifully died, her savings were gutted and so were her son's. Barrett worried about aging, dying, and passing along a similar debt to his own children. Cops, after all, could have their careers cancelled early. And even if he and Laura Anne worked another twenty years, Barrett had no faith that Medicare, Social Security, and a modest retirement could outlast a serious illness, an old-folks' home, or a determined Republican.

And so one Friday Barrett met Ferris Boatwright at Ramona's. Ferris explained the various options, including trust funds for the twins, and a Keough for Barrett and Laura Anne which left earnings generated from their salaries tax-deferred until they were actually used. In the course of explaining the details of that arrangement Barrett found that Ramona had set up Keoughs herself. Not just for her personal estate. Turned out that Ramona required even her part-timers to divert a portion of their income to Keough accounts. Even her *black* part-timers.

Not many people in Mr. Raines's neighborhood worried about part-time help at all, much less their *black* part-timers. Deacon Beach occupied a coastal strip of pine and sand west of U.S. 90 about an hour south of Tallahassee. Taylor County was not generally regarded as a region progressive in race relations. The head of the Ku Klux Klan used to headquarter in Perry, which was only about twenty miles inland from Deacon. Even though the school was long integrated, housing laws passed, and voters' rights extended, the white population in North Florida still treated blacks, for the most part, like second-class citizens. Any white businessman, for instance, explaining why he didn't hire many "Negroes," or "coloreds," would tell you that blacks from the Beach were undereducated. That was true. It was also true that many of the whites working for those businessmen were undereducated—many lacked even basic working skills—but those contradictions didn't make a dent in the region's carefully constructed web of denial.

The society which Barrett straddled was divided along a line that was literally black and white. Black men and women at Deacon Beach knew without being told that if they were to get along with their predominantly white neighbors it would be best not to speak too openly about anything that smacked of "discrimination." They didn't complain about jobs or salaries. They didn't advocate labor unions. They knew, most of them, how to keep their place.

Keeping your place—that was something you never really got over when you're a black person in a place like Deacon. "Bear," as Barrett was locally known, was born and raised on the Beach and had worked there seven biblical years with a gun and a badge, but he could still remember the first years, the early years, when he felt as if he were an unwanted guest in a stranger's house. As if the word *nigger* was waiting to be hurled. Hurled at him. In those early years Detective Raines was still a jigaboo to a good portion of the folks whose property, children, and lives he defended.

Truth was, Barrett should have been something of a hero to the folks in his small town-by-the-sea. His history was, after all, familiar to most of the people Bear daily encountered. His accomplishments. White men and women recalled the quiet nigra boy who walked to school welted on his arms and back from straps and belts and peachtree switches. There was talk, particularly after Barrett's father was killed, of closets and smokehouses and goings-on. You would think a boy surviving that legacy might merit respect in the larger community.

And Barrett had done much more than survive. In spite of his violent and chaotic home, the young black man went on to graduate valedictorian in a high school which still prided itself on having resisted integration. There was a party after that graduation. At the Boatwright place. Ferris's mama and daddy did it up nice. Most of the girls in his small-town class got invited to that fling. Half the boys. But not the Bear. Just a mistake, he was assured later on. An oversight.

You couldn't get past your place. Being first in school wasn't enough to make you as good as a white. Serving honorably in the army and the reserves wasn't enough, either, even with Desert Storm. Barrett came home with a diploma *and* field decorations. *That*, he had expected, would make some kind of a splash back home. A bronze star, a double major, top 10 percent in his class—surely that would earn Barrett some kind of respect, even if begrudged, in the community! But it didn't happen. Nobody, black or white, seemed much to care.

What they cared passionately about was football. Football, as had been too often said, was a religion for Southerners whose cavalier past, lost during the Civil War, rekindled each fall Friday on gridirons kept alive with Rainbow sprinklers and ardent booster clubs. Had Barrett run tailback or played linebacker at some Southeast Conference school, *that* would have "been somethin'." Even if he'd been a lineman, even a punter! *That* would have been something to talk about. But Barrett wasn't a football star like his brother had been; he didn't attend Florida State or Georgia Tech or the University of Alabama, as his brother was recruited to do, so whatever else the Bear did as a classics and criminal justice major at some half-ass university in Texas was not important.

Barrett knew for a fact that many of the white faces now slopping down bourbons and seabass at the tables around him had not been happy when the Bear, after pulling a year as a street cop in Jacksonville, came to his hometown applying for an opening at what was euphemistically called the "municipal" police department.

Barrett could still remember Chief Smoot Rawlings grinding teeth over his application.

"You sure you want to do this, Bear?"

Barrett was certain that, had he been a white man, Smoot would have addressed him by his given name or perhaps even as "Officer Raines." But the Bear was black. Born locally. And so his sobriquet was to remain his title.

"You mean apply for the job, Chief? Sure I am. Why I drove down."

"We never had a black on the force before."

"Well, Chief, I'm here. And I am definitely qualified."

His qualifications would not have amounted to a hill of beans had it not been for what came to be known among insiders as Walker's Charge. The city council had been planning to turn Barrett down. In fact, they had gone so far as to consider withdrawing the job opening (for "budgetary concerns") in an attempt to discourage Barrett's application while insulating themselves from any kind of legal complication.

Ramona walked in while the council was still in session to put a hitch in that get-along. Barrett wasn't present at the meeting. Taff Calhoun, the then-newest member on the council, was there and so the Bear's knowledge of Walker's Charge was based on the two or three dozen occasions on which Taff had since related and relished the story.

Seems things were at a lull. Just the usual business of the day. Street signs. A zoning ordinance would mandate parameters for sewage systems within two hundred feet of beachfront property. City Attorney Roland "Fountain Pen" Reed had been asked to comment on the ordinance; Chief Rawlings had just concluded his take, which basically was that the requirement would piss off local contractors and would be a pain in the ass to enforce. Roland cut his comments short by simply seconding Rawlings's assessment. Councilman Ferris Boatwright was in agreement. So was Taff. Mayor Stanford Crosby, delighted to have unanimity on anything, raised his gavel to conclude the meeting. They were all set to let the shit flow downhill as usual when Ramona came strolling in.

"Afternoon, gentlemen." Ramona took a chair nearest the mayor.

"What can I do you for?" Stanford, according to Taff, tried to ignore her legs.

"I want to talk about Barrett Raines's application to our police department, Stanford."

"May not need that slot right away, Ramona." Smoot Rawlings smiled.

And of course Ferris, being an accountant by trade, had to put his two cents in.

"Budget concerns. You know how it is."

"Oh, I know how it is," Ramona replied. "Everybody here knows good and goddamned well exactly how it is. And, boys, I would dearly love to just sit around and shoot the shit with you-all on this situation, but I've got a restaurant's been broke into twice inside the last three months. My *house* has been busted into within the last year, for god's sake, and so I am more than usually impatient."

And with that she dropped a letter into the mayor's lap.

"What is this?"

"Letter I wrote for a lawyer friend of mine." Ramona smiled sweetly. "He works for Connie Mack. That's Congressman Mack? The letter just suggests that you-all need to be taken to court for a civil rights action."

"Ramona, this isn't the way to do business."

"It sure as hell isn't." Ramona's retort was, according to Taff's account, very cool. "You gutless sons of bitches. Barrett's a good man. He's the kind of man, black or white, that we need more of in this pissant little town and I'll be *damned* if I'm going to stand by and watch a gaggle of good ol' boys run him off!"

"That be all, Ramona?" the mayor finally managed to say.

"That depends—" Ramona snitched a stamp off Stanford's own desk. Licked it. "On you."

Couple of days later Smoot called to say Barrett had been hired as a uniformed officer for the Deacon Beach Municipal Police Force. When asked after donning the badge how he and Smoot got along, the Bear always replied, "Just fine."

Seven hard years later Barrett Raines was in street clothes, the senior of two detectives, second on the force only to Rawlings himself. Smoot even called him "Barrett." Now and then. And by then the Bear was not only accepted at Deacon Beach, he was downright popular. A model middle-class citizen. Days went by when the Bear never thought about his first days on the force, when he never thought about difference, or color, or bigotry at all. But then something would invade. Usually from the outside—a race riot in Los Angeles, say. A notorious trial. Or the sight of black teens hauled off by the local John Q. for some brutal, senseless crime. On those days Detective Raines would find himself raising his guard. You never could tell what might destroy a reputation. One drink too many in public. A problem with the boys. A disputed call at a slow-pitch softball game. Barrett felt sometimes he had built a house of cards that could at any moment come tumbling down.

The only cards falling this particular Friday, though, fell at the poker game which Laura allowed in the boathouse out back. This particular Friday found Barrett on the eve of his anniversary thinking only of his wife.

He could remember their first anniversary. They'd been over there. Near the lobster tank.

"You're still the girl from high school I came back to marry," he had told Laura Anne quietly.

"You never noticed till you came back," she had said, blushing.

"Did too!"

"Don't mess with the truth, Bear. You're not a handy liar."

They laughed together. Only a couple of years younger than Bear and still in her early thirties, Laura Anne was probably the best-looking woman in the county next to Ramona. Laura Anne's father, a bitter bastard while he was alive, used to say if Laura'd been white instead of colored she'd have married a lawyer beside the bay instead of a cop by the canal.

Laura Anne was what folks in the region still called a "high yeller." Her skin glowed with the kind of soft, bronze patina that an Egyptian princess would without question have envied. She had light bones, high cheeks. A long, strong back. Her hair was smooth and straight and black as ebony. But her skin was light. Locals who were drunk or sequestered enough might still speculate, at a card table, say, over jacks and queens, as to the genesis of that high yeller's complexion. Would imagine over their whiskeys and cigarettes what white master had humped what darkie to spawn the grandmother who, being freed after the war, must undoubtedly have shacked up with some Frenchman in New Orleans and then whelped the lighter and lighter-shaded nigger girl who was, the genealogy would be concluded with the certainty of science, Laura Anne's mama.

Barrett had in darker moods reflected that nobody ever felt the need, or the rage, to concoct a pedigree for white folks' women. Unless maybe they were Jewish. The Jews, too, had once been less than white. Maybe in some circles they still were. It was not a thought that obsessed Barrett, nor even occupied his thoughts very often. But it was on the backside of the linen of his mind. And if the wind blew just right the linen stirred, like sheets nigger-rigged for some massah's bedroom curtain, and the thoughts would come. And then for a while it was hard to take joy in anything.

But that breeze this evening was calm. Barrett was looking forward to bringing Laura Anne in here tomorrow. They'd have snapper and shrimp. Some drinks. Maybe he'd drop a quarter or two in the jukebox and they'd slow dance on the parquet floor.

Show off a little to the neighbors.

Yes, after seven years Barrett had come to think of those white people with whom he labored and leisured as more nearly neighbors than the people of color who remained uneducated, poor, and sequestered as if behind a wall in corrugated tin shanties and trailer homes east of Canal Street.

The same held true for Laura Anne. Barrett's wife lost her parents even earlier than had her husband. Like Bear, she was not close to the few relatives who survived. Her social and personal life, like Barrett's, became defined by her work. There was only one other black teacher at Deacon Beach's small high school, so Laura Anne's life came to revolve around her white colleagues' in much the same way that Barrett's evolved from time spent with people like Doc and Taff and Smoot.

Barrett nurtured the conviction that his family's assimilation into Deacon Beach's small, white world, while not a perfect state of affairs, was successful. After all, the same folks who once denied Barrett a job or a Christian name now accepted Detective Raines and his beautiful wife as one of their own. Local men of stature deferred to Barrett, sought his protection and occasionally even his opinion on matters of policy not directly related to law enforcement. That kind of thing gave some comfort, at least, on a sixteen-hour shift.

And now, as if to deepen Barrett's conviction, some additional comfort came strolling his way. The woman who stuck up for him when it counted came swaying across the restaurant. It was Ramona. Teasing. Flirting. Working the crowd as she went.

Chapter three

Snake Adders had just speared a lobster from the tank kept fresh beside the bar. Sometimes a customer, usually a lady customer, was a little squeamish about grabbing a lobster even though Ramona cheerfully told them that the little beggars' claws were firmly wrapped in the finest Trojan rubbers.

Snake's idea of flirting was to pull one of the beasts up for some cotton-topped local. Snake had other attractions. One of his overlarge eyes was a cerulean blue. The other was brown as a dog's turd. Ramona leaned onto the bar to interrupt Snake's latest romantic interlude.

"Snake."

"Yes, ma'am."

"Here's a test. Just a little something to see if you're on your toes."

"All right." He dropped the lobster onto an outlawed hardwood plate.

"A little chore." Ramona paused to give the gear in Snake's mind time to engage. "Somethin' you're s'posed to do every Friday. On the way in to work."

"Oh, dammit." Snake smacked his forehead with the heel of his hand.

"Snake. Did you walk my dog?"

"I loped my mule. Does that count?"

"Tell you what," Ramona sighed as one in grief. "I'm tired of coming home to piss on the floor. You walk my puppy three weeks straight *I'll* lope your mule. How's that?"

Even Snake had to allow a smile.

"Fair enough."

"Give your boss a drink."

"Yes, ma'am."

He pulled a fresh bottle of Wild Turkey. Ramona would have taken it if Doc Hardesty hadn't intercepted it first.

It was a gauge of the town's tolerance that Hardesty was still addressed as "Doc" even though he hadn't peered down a living throat in twenty years. The throats he did examine were now frequently slit. It happened more often than Barrett wanted to admit and more often than Doc wanted to see.

Doc held Ramona's bottle in one hand now. And a handful of darts in the other.

"Doesn't leave a hand for me, Doc."

"I only got two."

"'Minds me of a joke."

"I was sure it would."

"Sheriff comes up on two young ones necking in a car." Ramona licked her lips as if already in approval. "They're doin' over eighty. Boy's got one hand in the girl's pants. Other one he's got on the wheel. Sheriff pulls 'em over. 'Now, son,' he says to the boy. 'Don't you think you'd be better off with two hands?' "

"'Yes, sir,' the boy agrees right off. 'But I need *one* to drive!'"

A grin split Doc's leathered face like a pumpkin.

"Why don't you get old with the rest of us, Ramona?"

"I don't know. It's either the booze or the ballin'. I haven't figured out which."

"Stick with sex." Doc reluctantly surrendered the bottle. "It's safer."

Ramona left a laugh. A kiss. And turned to the nearest table. "Evenin', Martha. Ferris."

Ferris Boatwright copied his wife's smile over a small mountain of grouper and home fries. Ramona ran a finger down Ferris's tie.

"You'll have sauce all over that thang."

"I try to tell him," Martha whined. "We go through two, three ties a week."

"Here." Ramona freed his tie from the Mason pin that bound it to his hippo belly, arranged it like a doily over his shoulder. To Martha—

"I hear you've got a brand new home."

"Oh, yes. We're gonna have a housewarming, too."

"Are you?" Ramona smoothed Ferris's tie. "Am I coming?"

"Why…" Martha hesitated. "Certainly."

"There'll be a crowd, o' course." Ferris cleared his throat. And then, in an appeal, "Lots of folks from the church."

"I won't hold that against 'em," Ramona assured him wickedly.

"It's just…" Martha recovered. "It will be very—low key."

"A housewarming is s'posed to be *warm*. Let me cater that party, I'll have your preacher bottoms up!"

"I think I'd die." Martha went pale.

"Ferris—do we have our business squared away?"

"Finished and filed." Ferris ran a nervous hand over his balding head.

"Good." Ramona smiled. "I don't want any more of those notices."

"Just make sure I get the receipts, Ramona." Ferris suddenly lowered his voice. "I can't balance the books without receipts of cash."

"That Snake." Ramona shook her head. "You cain't depend on that boy for anything. Martha—I'll expect that invitation."

"Certainly."

Ramona winked broadly to Ferris.

"If you cain't be good, be careful!"

Ferris and his wife attacked their calories somewhat less enthusiastically after Ramona's departure. Ramona searched for her next target. Next table down the line: the Bear's.

19

Ramona swayed on over.

"Hey, good-lookin'."

"Ramona. How are you?"

"Fine, Bear. And where is Laura Anne?"

"Home."

"Get done you can come home with me."

"You're gonna get me in trouble one of these days, Ramona."

"Not with your lady," the Boss disagreed. "Laura Anne *knows* what she's got! How long has it been—six years?"

"Seven," Barrett said it proudly. "Seven tomorrow."

"You should have her here."

"Taylor called in."

"He's always callin' in."

"I know."

"At some point in life, Bear, you got to know when to tell people to get fucked."

Barrett laughed. It felt good to laugh. Even alone.

Ramona smiled. "Buy you an anniversary-eve drink."

"Thank you, ma'am. But I got a mid to work after this."

"You go home, you wake up Laura Anne," Ramona advised. "Light that fire early, she'll come in here tomorrah burnin' like a barn."

Barrett rose, fighting equal claims of pride and embarrassment. "Thanks."

"Ain't but one way to thank me, honey," Ramona said as she slid her leg across his. "And you already turned me down."

Barrett paused on his way out the door. He wanted to take just a moment to see anew the place he knew so well. He wanted to see Doc and Taff and Smoot and every other local in the place seated, as they always were, with their wives in couples or foursomes beneath the slowly churning fans. He wanted to see the younger folks, the first dates, the first and second babies. It was a grand way to spend a Friday night. Or a Saturday.

Barrett found himself thinking about how Laura Anne would look tomorrow beneath one of those fans. With him. With everyone looking. A proud man with his knockout wife. And on their seventh anniversary.

He left Ramona's, looking forward to coming back.

Barrett had been gone only a short while when Ramona finished her turn around the tables. She was in the office after that for maybe half an hour, poring over a trash can full of receipts when a frail stick of a waitress tapped shyly at the door.

"What is it, Betty?

"We got a problem. It's Delton."

He was at the dart board, the Delton in question, a black man well over six feet tall in work boots and jeans. If he shaved and dressed he'd be a hunk in his mid-forties. A handsome face. Close-cropped hair. And powerful. Melon-sized arms sprouted from sleeves cut to the shoulder. He had a Bud in one hand and a dart in the other.

"Want me to get Snake?" Betty trembled at Ramona's shoulder.

"That's all right."

"I could call Bear."

"No. I'll take care of it."

A circle was already widening at the dart board as regulars moved off. A few other regulars followed Ramona from their seats as she strolled calm and composed to scoop the beer from Delton's fist.

He whirled around. She faced him almost eye to eye. "You've got a bar bill, Delton."

"You fire a man you cain't exactly expect him to give a shit about that. Now can you?"

He swiveled from solid, narrow hips back to the board. *Plunk—* the dart buried into the cork as if shot from a nail gun.

"What are you here for, Delton?" She might have been inquiring about the weather.

"Severance pay." He buried a second dart in the wall beside the board.

By now the locals knew there was a storm brewing. A couple nearby dropped some bills on their table to leave.

Ramona seemed to have all the time in the world.

"You've been paid," she told Delton.

"Call it—good faith money."

"Call it what you like." Her voice never wavered. "You don't work here anymore, Delton. We're settled. Closed out. That's all there is to it."

"I want more!"

Knives, forks, and glasses halted as if frozen all around the restaurant. Snake had pulled a two-handed baton from behind the bar. Ramona waved him off, her eyes locked the whole time on Delton's.

"Maybe you need to see me after work."

"Now!" A cord began to pulse in the black man's neck.

"After."

The pause hung just a moment, like snow on a steep tin roof. And then—

"Fine by me." He threw the darts carelessly aside.

"My place," Ramona said firmly. "Try to sober up."

"Oh, I don't know, I think I'll just stick around an'—"

"Out." Ramona stood aside. "Or I'll put something between those legs besides a drainpipe."

The cord which pulsed in Delton's neck now swelled to the size of hemp.

"My place, Delton." Ramona kept her voice low and firm. "After work."

Delton practically knocked Doc down on his rush to the door. A winter silence lingered among the diners. Ramona stepped from the dart board to face her customers.

"You know." A smile tugged innocently at a not-so-innocent mouth. "I bet if you poured that boy's brain in a thimble it'd roll around like a BB in a boxcar."

Laughter broke over the tables. Knives and forks returned to plates of snapper and pilau. Snake deposited his metal baton beneath the bar.

Ramona smiled widely. Flashed a leg. Back in business.

There was another kind of business going on in the boathouse behind Ramona's restaurant. Toothpicks were supposed to double as chits for these transactions but the four or five hundred dollars which splayed in bills beneath a green-shaded lamp reputedly rescued from a Perry whorehouse indicated that the toothpick convention had given way to the rituals of serious play.

Splinter Townsend worried a matchstick between his lips as he shuffled a badly worn deck with hands more used to tire irons and crescent wrenches. Hoyt Young's hands, softer, delicate, quivered like willows in the wind over his fan of cards. A pack of Marlboros and a Zippo lighter led to the third hand at the table; Frank Sienna offered Hoyt a poker smile.

Hoyt swallowed.

"I'll take a hit."

Splinter dealt him three cards. Hoyt slipped them one by one into his fan.

"I guess I can bump the pot for fifty," he said finally.

"Fifty?" Splinter sucked on a bottle. "Don't go broke on us now, Hoyt."

"A man never went broke showing a profit. Right, Frank?"

"I see your fifty," Sienna said, ignoring him. "And I call."

"Look who's going broke."

"I'm paying to see," Frank said patiently.

Hoyt spread his cards along the table. Jack and queen high.

Splinter whistled into his bottle. "Nice cards."

"Sure are," Hoyt agreed and reached for the bills piled on the table.

"Aren't you interested in mine?" Sienna inquired—

And dropped four kings onto the table.

"*Damn* nice cards." Splinter offered the observation sourly.

But Hoyt gave up the money easily enough. A smile and a shrug. Relaxed all around.

"How 'bout another hand?" Splinter was searching his wallet.

"Sure." Hoyt shrugged. "Be nice if we had a fourth, though."

"How about a fifth?" Ramona Walker lounged at the door.

The fifth of Wild Turkey dangled at her side. The restaurant buzzed beyond. Ramona closed the door. Quiet again.

"How's business?" Sienna lit a Marlboro.

"All pennies present and accounted for."

"We can't afford the IRS looking too close."

She planted the bottle amidst the cards.

"Haven't had a problem so far, have we?"

"No." Sienna snapped his Zippo open and shut. "Sounded for a minute out there like we might have, though."

"Who, Delton? It's all right. Doesn't affect you, Frank."

"It's affecting me right now."

"Relax." Ramona eased a half-moon of ass onto their table. "Everything's zipped up."

"Clean?" Sienna inhaled.

"As a spanked baby's fanny," she answered lightly.

"Then you're set." Splinter for the first time was ignoring his hooch. "No worries?"

"Not a worry in the world," Ramona told him breezily.

"Good." Splinter nodded. And coiled a tattooed arm about her waist. "What say we go for a ride after work?"

"Don't know how that's possible, Splinter. I don't ride. And you don't work."

Chuckles, then, from Frank and Hoyt. The python tattooed on Splinter's arm tightened around her waist.

"C'mon. We could go to Fort Meyers. Cruise the beach."

"Who's payin' for the gas?"

"My treat."

"Man's got money to burn!" Ramona winked to the others. "Party hardy! But not for Betty. Am I right, Splinter? Not a cent for a wife and kid."

"Ex-wife," Splinter countered.

"What about the boy? He an ex, too?"

"That's none of your business, Ramona."

"Betty works for me, Splinter."

"She's not gettin' nuthin."

"Well, until she does—" Ramona swiveled away easily "—neither do you."

Hoyt hooted. Something like a donkey braying onions out his nose. But Ramona was already on to new business.

"How about a cigarette, Frank?"

She beat Sienna to the Marlboros.

"Light?" she asked.

He gave her one.

"I hear the spick's causing a problem." Ramona let the smoke ease from her nostrils in luxurious coils.

"We'll work it out," Sienna told her.

"You sure?"

"Listen, doll. I'll take care of the spick. What's the deal with your nigger?"

"Nothing much." She shrugged it off.

"What's the fucking deal?" Sienna wasn't about to let it go.

"Not now." Ramona shook her head. The hair swayed rich and auburn over her shoulders. "When we're private."

"Okay…" he relented.

She legged to the door. Turned emerald eyes back to the players. A wide, easy grin.

"You boys know why Robin Hood robbed from the rich?"

No answer.

"'Cause the poor didn't have nuthin' to take."

A low, throaty laugh. A flash of green. And she was gone.

Chapter four

The home had been constructed between hurricanes sometime in the late forties. The exterior was laid in coquina rock shipped from St. Augustine. The windows were jalousied in the typical Florida fashion. A chimney, blackened over many winters with the tars of lightard and oak, rose over the roof. A local contractor had replaced the roof's original shingle with anodized metal, guaranteed, in his words, to last a lifetime.

Called a beachside home, the residence was actually situated a good forty or fifty yards off the water—though anyone could, should they desire, land opposite the thick stand of slash pine which stood between Ramona's screened-in veranda and the gulf, come directly off the beach through forty yards of pine, and arrive practically at her door.

There were three doors, actually. Out front the outermost, aluminum-framed screen door was never locked; the yellow pine monster behind it was, though. Two dead bolts were inserted below a peephole lensed by a clever brass hatch which Ramona had retrieved during one of her many snorkeling adventures. A small Buddha purchased from some curio shop smiled beneath the sixty-watt bulb which lit the locks.

There was no welcome mat.

There was a back door. Door number three. But it had not been opened in so long its lock was rusted shut. There were windows, of course, which could be broken. But who, after all, would want to break Ramona's windows?

She came home well after midnight, crunching up a gravel drive to her home of seashells and pine and glass. She popped a Bee Gees' tape out of her eight-track, gunned the T-bird's rebuilt 390 one last time, cut off the A.C. and ignition. Got out.

She fumbled for a house key on her chain and, holding the screen door open with one extremely well-turned ankle, attacked the monster front door. It opened with a pleasing *snick* and Ramona cursed as a collie puppy came tearing out, claws and all; to greet the Boss at the end of her very long day—and then to piss like a race-horse on the gravel drive.

She waited until the puppy left his haunches before getting them both inside. A large skylight over the foyer allowed a thin sliver of moon to spill fitfully inside. It wasn't until Ramona switched on the overhead lights that a person could see the vast living room which stretched beyond.

The room was finished off entirely in pecky cypress, a rare and expensive wood. The grain for this particular species of cypress was discontinuous; its surface, even planed and sanded, showed an infinite variety of craters and crevices which old-timers used to incorrectly ascribe to the workings of worms. Once a common material for finishing Florida homes, pecky cypress was now all but extinct. Ramona salvaged hers from an abandoned farmhouse which she literally stumbled across while deer hunting near Shamrock. There were a fair number of seascapes and photos all nicely framed to show off the rare walls. But not much else.

The place was virtually devoid of furniture. A single couch faced the fireplace. A wood basket held old magazines, at this season, instead of kindling. A poker stood useless in its stand. Ramona urged her collie straight past the couch and fireplace to a hallway beyond.

The hallway led to a master bedroom and adjoining bath.

She relieved herself, completed her hygiene, and showered. She took a long time in the shower but wasn't fussy about it. No complicated lotions or salves. No need to shave. And even though there was a full-length mirror built beside the valet, Ramona didn't bother to look herself over.

"Come on, puppy," she said. And went to bed.

A sliver of moon fell onto a magnificent nude. Light and darkness pooled in the curves and crevices of her legs and arms and breasts. Hips and abdomen. Ramona stretched dead to the world beneath a ceiling fan on rumpled satin sheets. The fan was silent; its paddle-sized blades cast motionless shadows over a king-sized futon which was set on a teak platform raised less than a foot above her Mexican-tiled floor. Easy enough for the puppy to climb up onto. Which he did. And whined into the pile of her hair.

"Mmmm? What is it, punkin?" She slowly roused.

The collie slobbered into her ear.

"You peed already, sugar."

Ramona pulled erect in her bed. The sheet slid down her torso to leave her bare-breasted beneath the fan. The dog whined again, pawed her exposed belly.

"Ouch! Just a minute, puppy."

The collie beelined for the door.

"Dammit."

The puppy bounced off the door once, then nosed it open and was into the hallway before his mistress, wrapped like some Greek adulteress in a satin chiton, could stumble from her bed.

It was a short dog-run down the hall to the living room. Ramona hitched up the sheet at her waist, tried a light switch. Nothing. Tried again.

"Dammit," she cursed sleepily. And then, "Just not in the house, okay, puppy? I'll be right there."

Ramona stumbled down the hall to find her living room smothered in darkness except for a puddle pooled in the moon that filtered down from the skylight over her foyer.

"Puppy?"

No answer. Ramona edged past the fireplace, past the sofa to reach the foyer and front door which waited beyond.

That's when her feet stepped into something warm and wet on the floor.

"Dammit, Snake, next time that dog pisses—!" She drew back instinctively and saw her puppy.

The collie lay beside the sofa, a little thing, almost invisible in the darkened interior.

"Puppy!"

He did not answer. Did not stir.

"Puppy—?" Two steps took Ramona to the couch. She knelt beside the animal. Touched her hand to the collar at his neck.

It was wet.

And as Ramona backed away she knew that it was not a pet's urine that stained her fingertips and feet.

It was blood.

Ramona rose slowly. Turned. Someone blocked the door. No way to tell who in the gloom and the dark. But someone of size, certainly. And someone, apparently, with a knife.

"I've got a security system," she said, following the couch back toward the hall. "Response time is five minutes or less."

No reply from the intruder. She could hear him breathing. Long, ragged breaths. As if he'd run five miles. But nothing else.

"Five minutes!!"

Ramona lunged for the hall. There was no security system. But if she could beat this bastard down the hall, she could make the bedroom. There was a phone there. *If* the line hadn't been cut. And if the phone didn't work that was just fine, because Ramona knew her shotgun would.

If she could make it.

But Ramona tripped on the satin sheet wound about her waist and when she rose screaming fury, he was there to snap a dog leash around her neck.

"You son of a—!"

The leash snapped shut. She clawed at the leash, clawed with long, red nails over her head at her assailant's calves and legs. All she got was brogans and jeans. And now the leash dug in like a garrote. Ramona's curses strangled in her throat as she was dragged, long ivory legs thrashing, back toward the couch. They reached the fireplace. He jerked her upright with one hand. Slammed a fist to her kidney with the other. She gargled briefly. Fell into a heap beside the wood basket. He let go of the leash. And when he did she drove both her feet hard into his shin.

He went down bellowing fury.

She lunged for the poker.

"Bas—! Bast—!"

Ramona came up in a crouch. That's when she recognized for the first time the man who now pulled himself erect on her sofa.

"Bastard!"

She swung the poker viciously. He ducked inside its arc.

"AHHH!!"

Ramona bent, stiffly, to see the adhesive-taped hilt whose blade buried into her abdomen.

"Oh God."

She clutched the handle with both hands. Pulled. A scream of agony. The blade wouldn't come. But the killer would. He came to her, breathing heavily. Embraced her like a lover. And jerked the blade free. He laughed when she screamed, then. A short, mirthless laugh.

And kept laughing as Ramona slid, still alive, through his arms to the floor.

Chapter five

Barrett got the call a little after six in the morning. He'd dropped by the house around midnight hoping to find Laura Anne awake. Hoping maybe to complete a small transgression between shifts. Light that fire early.

He found her on a blanket asleep between the boys' beds. Two six-year-olds slumbering beside their mother as *Wind in the Willows* narrated raspily over a cassette player patched with duct tape and Super Glue. Moley had just bailed the Toad out of one of his many misadventures. Barrett debated a moment whether to wake Laura Anne. Decided against it. They had tomorrow.

"Sweet dreams." Barrett kissed his wife goodnight.

He left the tape playing.

The Bear was in his unmarked six hours later, catching some badly needed winks himself when the radio squawked. Every cop knows what it's like to have a radio-call interrupt a few stolen seconds of sleep. Barrett's motor reflexes would often trigger the radio's mike, and his automatic pilot provide the usual, "PD-2 here, go ahead," before his brain could comprehend the first few seconds of information which passed across the line.

A few seconds did pass, therefore, before the Bear, rousing himself stiffly, had to apologize, "'Scuse me, Dispatch. Could you run that by again?"

Barrett took in the preliminary information, grunted acknowledgment. "I'll be right over.... No, it's all right. I'm sure, yeah. Arrive in ten."

The sun was just lifting its ocher lid over the pines and palmettos which bordered Ramona's graveled drive by the time Barrett pulled in. The home's coquina walls glowed pink in the early light. A host of law enforcement swarmed over the site. Deacon Beach only had fifteen full-time officers and two detectives in its entire department; there must have been a dozen of them out here now, their flashlights still leaving long, white beams in the early dawn's heavy humidity.

Barrett noted the familiar faces and gaits of the men and women poring over the house and grounds. He noted the empty gurney which was jacked up beside the EMS idling out front. A whiff of carbon monoxide was oddly stimulating. Like a whiff of smelling salts. Barrett had eased past the EMS before he saw that Doc Hardesty's station wagon was there, too. Doc had worked forensics for twenty years and had served as county coroner for almost eight more before he retired, swearing to Rawlings that he'd never for any reason investigate another suspicious death. The chief must have pulled out some kind of stop on Doc. Or maybe Doc had broken his pledge because of who lay inside.

Barrett steered his sedan carefully past the chief's cruiser, found a niche next to Hardesty's wagon. He had barely killed the ignition and tightened his tie when a klieg light exploded directly through the windshield.

"Goddammit, Stacy! Not right in the eyes!"

Stacy Kline took cover behind his Channel 7 cameraman as the Bear came heaving out of his car.

"Detective Barrett, can you give us an update?"

Kline was one of those perennially cynical white boys who only escaped death by hiding behind things which decent folks were forced to respect. Stacy hid behind his Channel 7 ID and a microphone thicker than his preternaturally pale and slender arm. Barrett waved arm and mike aside.

"I just got here. Hey—keep 'em outside the tape."

"We've heard that Ramona Walker has been murdered. Is that true?"

"Give me a minute I'll find out."

Barrett snapped the yellow crime-scene tape over his head, ducked under. "Morning, Bear." Sergeant Dick Hanson strolled over with a cup of coffee. Dick was one of the few men on the force with whom Barrett regularly socialized after work. Their friendship was something of a local buzz for several reasons, not least of which was that Dick's dad ran the Klan meetings in Taylor county. Dick himself wasn't at first happy about having a black man on "his" police force. Had events run any kind of normal course, Hanson and Raines would probably never have developed more than a wary distrust for each other. But events hadn't remained normal. Things changed the moment Dick saved Bear's life.

It had happened only a couple of years after Barrett was hired. A convenience store near Deacon Beach had been robbed, its manager shot. The suspect took off in a bright red Dodge pickup. Barrett picked up the description, made the vehicle, and was in pursuit when a deer, an ordinary 130-pound Virginia whitetail, bounded into his headlights.

Barrett hit the animal at high speed; the impact threw the car into a skid. The car hit a telephone pole and rolled over into a ditch swollen with spring rain. There was only about four feet of water in that ditch, but Barrett's car had gone wheels-up after impact. Barrett dangled in his seat belt, stunned and certain to drown.

Dick Hanson was in his own car off duty that night and saw the whole thing. He swung over to the ditch, immediately plunged into the pitch-black water, and dragged Barrett out. The experience left a bond between the Klansman's son and the black cop that grew stronger over the years.

Barrett took the coffee gratefully. "Thank you, Dick. Rawlings here?"

"Yes, he is. Got a little problem."

"A *little* one?"

Barrett followed Dick to a front door latticed with gargoyles of light and shadow. And there on the steps, trembling below Ramona's smiling Buddha, was a young boy, nine years or so of age. A double bag of newspapers spilled beside a bicycle on the drive. Barrett recognized the paramedic who was trying, unsuccessfully, to coax a cup of cocoa into the boy's hands.

Chief Rawlings emerged out of a rising sun.

"Bear. What're *you* doin' here?"

"I got the call."

Rawlings turned to Hanson. "I told you to get Taylor."

Taylor Folsom was, besides being a truant, the only other and very junior detective on the payroll.

Hanson cleared his throat, "Taylor's called in sick, Chief."

"He's got a phone."

"Couldn't reach him."

"Why would you want to reach him?" Barrett asked his Chief. "I took his shift."

"Thought today was your anniversary." Smoot almost bit it off.

"Look, Cap'n, are you doing this one yourself? 'Cause if you are, I'd be happy to get some sleep."

"No, no. You're the detective, Bear. Go to it."

Barrett nodded to the paperboy. "Say he found her?"

"Yeah." Rawlings nodded. "But that's all he's sayin'."

"Stay with me, would you, Dick?"

Barrett approached the boy. Hanson followed. The youngster huddled on the front steps, trembling like a leaf in the wind.

Barrett nodded to the paramedic at the boy's side.

"'Lo, Wanda. Parents notified?"

"We can't get a name." Wanda Folsom was Taylor's cousin. Had the best of the family gene pool, too, in Barrett's opinion.

"He hasn't been able to say much," she went on. "I don't want to push."

"No, don't force him," Barrett agreed. "Call Trauma, though.

Tell 'em we've got a minor coming in. Tell 'em to have somebody qualified from Social Services waiting."

"You—!" For the first time the boy looked up. "You're taking me to jail?!"

"No, son." Barrett slowly settled beside the boy. Placed his coffee on the steps. And then, very quietly, "Jail's the last place you're gonna be."

"She was a nice lady." Twin tracks of tears ran down the boy's face.

"Yes, she was," Barrett agreed. "Real nice."

"She always wanted the paper dry." The boy sniffed, looking now at the papers wilting in the dew. "She'd even tip me. There was a drizzle this mornin' early so I came up close. I came up and I saw—I saw the door open?"

"Mmmhmm. Good."

"And I...went in." The boy declared it as if admitting a crime.

"'Course you went in." Barrett bent so he could see the boy eye-to-eye. "You went in and you looked. Who wouldn't've? But then you did somethin' else."

"What?"

"You called us. Now that was brave."

"It was?"

"Very brave. Lots of grownups would've run like hell."

The boy trembled again. But only once. Violently. And then he cried. Long, gut-wrenching, terrified sobs. Barrett cradled the boy, rocked him back and forth. Back and forth. Doc Hardesty stepped past them both on his way out of the house. Hardesty took Rawlings aside. They conferred briefly. Rawlings looked once in Bear's direction. Briefly. Barrett noted that fact, returned his attention to the youngster in his lap.

"That's good. That's fine. Here—" He offered the boy a handkerchief. Only after the boy accepted the kerchief did Barrett reach over to retrieve his steaming styrofoam cup.

"You a sheriff or somethin'?" the youngster at his side asked cautiously.

"Detective." Barrett slurped his coffee. "My name's Barrett but folks call me Bear. Know why?"

The boy shook his head.

"'Cause most people put sugar in their coffee. But I like honey."

It got a smile, anyway. A smile through the tears.

"What about you, son?" Barrett borrowed the hankie long enough to wipe the youngster's nose. "What's your name?"

"...Jimmy. Jimmy Riggers."

"That make you James Riggers's boy? James and Mary?"

"Yes, sir."

"Well, rest easy, Jimmy. It's not your fault. Do you understand? It wasn't you did this."

Jimmy Riggers wiped a hand across his face. Barrett glanced up at Wanda.

"You'll take care of him?"

"You bet."

She led the boy to the EMS van. Helped him climb up in the driver's seat. Barrett rose stiffly to find his chief and Doc Hardesty returned to the door.

Rawlings shook his head.

"Kid shouldn't have to see something like that."

"Neither should we," Barrett replied.

And stepped inside.

It was the collie he saw first. Ramona's puppy. Stiff as a board in a black coagulation of blood.

"I remember when she got that dog," Barrett said, pulling out a ballpoint and spiral pad.

"I'm guessing it's his blood by the door. We'll verify, of course." Doc's voice was determinedly impersonal.

"Got the camera, Dick?"

A flashbulb popped in reply.

"Pretty warm in here," Barrett remarked.

"Power was cut off at the fuse box," Rawlings told him. "When we got here we noticed the lights wouldn't work. The A.C. wasn't running. Figured it was either a power outage or the fuse box. That's when Dick checked out back."

"Somebody busted a lock to get at the master switch," Hanson elaborated modestly. "We figure it was the killer."

"Could very well have been." Barrett's affirmation was only slightly qualified. "We have a time?"

"Digital clock on her vcr froze at three-thirteen a.m."

"Okay." Barrett nodded. "Good work. And where's the victim?"

"Other side of the couch," Smoot said.

It was a beautiful, well-toned leg that twisted half-hidden behind the overturned sofa. Smoot and Doc trailed Barrett around the couch to see—

"God Almighty." Dick stood with the camera hanging in his hand.

A body so vital and appealing in life was in death grotesque and obscene. A dislocated elbow twisted awkwardly as if to hide a badly bruised breast. A purple welt circled Ramona's throat. A hematoma swelled darkly over her right kidney.

"Took a lick there," Smoot grunted.

The blood came mostly from her abdomen. The gash was only about two or three inches wide. It ruptured her stomach like a badly crafted zipper. A loop of her intestine extruded from the wound.

"You all right, Bear?" Smoot asked.

"Fine," Barrett replied.

But he was not. The thing that he saw here violated and destroyed had, only hours earlier, bought him dinner, flirted with him, flattered his wife. Ramona had stood up for him, years ago, when no one else would. She had been the kind of woman all men would like to claim. But it was she who claimed them. All of them and equally. And now...

Barrett felt bile for the first time in a long time gorging his stomach. He fought the nausea, scribbling nonsense into his spiral pad to buy himself time. He had to control it. He was the Man here. He couldn't look at this thing on the floor as if it were his friend or even as if it were someone he recognized. He couldn't afford to feel anything. The only thing he could do, the only thing that would ever matter for Ramona now, was to find her killer, and to do that, Barrett had for the moment to forget that he ever knew her. If you couldn't do that you'd miss things. And there was definitely something amiss here besides the obvious. Something not quite on the level.

In fact, something was a bubble and a half off plumb.

Barrett palmed his pen and pad, laid himself eye-level with the floor. He was looking for any trace of physical evidence. Some kind of fiber. Dirt or mud. Anything. But all he could see was her hair. Her hair spread auburn and fine in the river of blood which meandered from her belly. It was as if a butterfly's wings were captured in a pool of tar. And then he saw her face shattered like a piece of pottery. But the eyes remained, even in mortis, the brightest emerald.

Barrett rose, nodding toward the blood. "Looks like somebody tried to mop up."

"Mmm," Rawlings grunted. "But whatever they used they took it with 'em."

"Okay, Doc." Barrett turned away from the body of what used to be a friend. "Tell me what you know."

"Don't *know* a lot. I'd estimate a time of death somewhere between one and four this morning. That's *this* morning, you understand."

"Somebody cut the power a little after three." Barrett nodded. "If it was the killer, that would fit."

Doc shrugged as if it didn't make a damn bit of difference to him one way or the other.

"There were many superficial wounds as you can see," Doc went on. "Perpetrator used a garrote of some kind on the victim; dog leash by the fireplace'd be a good candidate. But the larynx is not broken and other symptoms consistent with strangulation are not present. So I'm presently inclined to believe the victim died of trauma and blood loss incurred by the wound to the lower abdomen."

"Any idea how long a death like that would take?" Barrett asked.

"Hard to say 'til I get to the lab," Doc replied. "But it took a long time to bleed like that. My guess is she may have survived the knife and the garrote for quite a while."

"My God," Hanson said again. And then, "Sorry."

"It's always worse when you know 'em." Doc shrugged as if he were exempt from that influence.

Barrett felt another surge of nausea.

"Do we have a rape?" He jotted a note on his small spiral pad.

"Penetration, at least. Semen and pubic hair."

"Before or after the attack?"

"Might as well ask me before or after death. Again, 'til I get to the lab—"

"Do what you can," Barrett cut in brusquely. "Chief...?"

"Right here."

"Can we talk a second?"

Barrett guided Smoot out of earshot before he started. "We need a crime unit out here."

Chief Rawlings knew that Barrett was referring to the Mobile Crime Unit from Tallahassee. The Florida Department of Law Enforcement was created in part for poor counties who couldn't afford expensive forensics or diagnostic tools. Upon request the FDLE would send a team to sweep a homicide anywhere in the state from soup to nuts.

There was, however, a problem. Smoot Rawlings had requested the FDLE's assistance on a drug-related case the previous year. Before it was over the chief, the mayor, and a couple of Deacon's finest found themselves in FDLE handcuffs and charged with conspiring to sell heroin. The charges were later dropped and even the FDLE admitted that the State's prosecutor had built his case on an informant who was notoriously unreliable. Feelings were soothed with apologies from on high but that didn't help the folks running for office. Deacon Beach's voters righteously threw out the two exonerated council members trying to get reelected. Smoot had almost lost his appointed job himself. So it was pretty obvious that Chief Rawlings was not willingly going to invite the FDLE onto his turf.

"No." He shook his head.

"Just the mobile unit, Chief. We can keep jurisdiction over the investigation."

"We're not going to need a mobile," Rawlings declared.

There it was again. Something not quite plumb.

Barrett stared at the older man. "How the hell can you possibly know that?"

Rawlings would not look Barrett in the eye. Finally—"We run into something we absolutely cannot handle for ourselves I'll consider it. Until that time—no."

"Okay." Barrett turned from his chief to speak across the room. "Dick. Could I see you?"

Hanson placed his camera on the couch and came over.

"Yes, Bear."

"Sweep for everything. Take whoever you need. Tell 'em they'll get overtime. We need prints, samples—you've done it before."

"Roger that." Hanson was making notes.

"And when you get done here I want you to call Tallahassee. Tell 'em we'll be needing a DNA on blood and semen at least. Maybe some hair."

"Cost a damn fortune," Rawlings groused.

"Put it on MasterCard," Raines replied. "The government does. You see any signs of burglary?"

"Nope. No forced entry, either."

"You sure?" Barrett was scanning the interior.

"Front door in," Rawlings told him. "Front door out. That's how it looks."

"Fits with the dog, anyway," Barrett mused.

"Pardon?" Rawlings was frowning.

"The collie." Barrett stopped to face him. "Doc can tell you. Anybody at all came into this house that collie would've run like hell. Unless—"

"—the dog knew 'em," Hanson finished the thought.

"That's right." Barrett retrieved his coffee. "And if the killer knew the dog, chances are he knew Ramona, too."

Rawlings looked suddenly uncomfortable. Doc Hardesty cleared his throat. "That might, ah, explain the entry."

"How's that?" Barrett kept his eyes caged on Smoot.

"Doc!" Rawlings growled.

"He's got to know sometime," Hardesty said gruffly.

So. There was something amiss.

"What the fuck is goin' on here?" Barrett challenged them both. "Captain, you oughta be in bed. Doc, you look like a man just swallowed a turd. You gentlemen holding out on me? 'Cause if you are I'd just like to say it's not appreciated."

Doc Hardesty was the one to tell him.

"Delton was at Ramona's last night. After you left. Must have been around eleven. He was drunk. Something about back pay. She'd fired him, you know."

"Yes, I do know." So that was it. 'Course. That's what they'd been dancing around.

"Well, anyway, he was pretty steamed. Ramona told him to meet her here. After work. 'Course, Delton would know about the spare key."

"A *spare key?*" Barrett wondered what else he hadn't been told.

"That's right." Doc pointed out the door. "It's always in that little statue by the door."

"How the hell do *you* know about the key, Doc?"

"I drove Ramona home one night. She'd been drinking. But I already knew where she kept it. Snake knows. Delton, too. God knows how many others."

"How can you be sure Delton knew about the key?"

"'Cause he had to walk the dog."

"The collie?" Barrett was racing ahead now. Connecting the dots.

"That's right." Doc took a deep breath. "See, Ramona always sent somebody from the restaurant every Friday to let out the dog. Snake does it now. Before him, it was Delton."

"Makes sense." Barrett jotted a note.

"I'm sorry, Bear." This from Smoot.

"Why? You didn't kill her. Did you, Chief?"

Rawlings didn't reply. Barrett turned to Dick Hanson. "You'd better pick him up."

"You don't have to rush, Bear," Rawlings offered solicitously.

"I'm not rushing," Barrett replied flatly.

"Just 'cause Delton had a few words with Ramona doesn't mean he was here."

"Either way we've got to check it out. He many have been the last person, almost last anyway, to see her alive."

"All right." Smoot moved to intercept Barrett's exit for the door. "But let me handle the interrogation."

Barrett stopped dead in his tracks.

"Let's just pause a goddamn minute. Do I look like I need help, Chief?"

"No. It's just—"

"Just what?"

"Come on, Barrett," Doc intervened. "Delton's your brother."

Barrett nodded woodenly. "Delton Raines is my brother. Yes. That's a fact."

He nodded to the corpse on the floor.

"That's another fact."

The Bear pushed past his chief. Sergeant Hanson followed him out the door.

Stacy Kline and his microphone were waiting. "Detective, is it true that Delton Raines is a prime suspect in this investigation? Detective Raines—?"

"We have no suspect at the present time." Barrett had to turn sideways to keep from jostling the camera thrust into his face.

"Happy anniversary, Bear," Kline tossed out.

Barrett kept moving. The button had been pushed and he knew he had to get out of there. He couldn't risk a reply, couldn't even risk a look at the bleach-white, stick-thin reporter who grinned from the cover of his camera and microphone.

Hanson was there to cut off pursuit as the Bear headed for his car.

"He'll be at the mill," Barrett tossed over his shoulder. "Or hung over."

"You all right, Bear?"

"Take some backup."

Chapter six

Barrett took about an hour going into the station. He decided not to call Laura Anne. Too early for that. With luck Delton would have an incontrovertible alibi. He may have spent the night in the drunk tank at Perry. Or shacked up all night with one of his girl-friends, or perhaps even his ex. But if there wasn't something of that nature to take Delton off the scene of the crime—

"Well, shit," Bear announced to the air around him. "Here we go again."

A dull knife was turning in Bear's own gut and he knew from where it came. Something always came up with Delton. Drugs, fights, whores. Just exactly the kind of image that Barrett wanted to expunge for himself, his family, and, yes, even for his race.

Couldn't think about that now, though. Barrett snapped out his spiral pad. You had to take things one at a time. He radioed Dispatch, got a roster started for off-duty personnel, and made assignments for the investigation. He left a message with Doc asking for some specific tests related to serotonin levels in Ramona's—the victim's—blood. Doc would know why Barrett wanted those tests and probably would do them whether told to or not. Barrett wasn't really worried about Doc's lab work; it was just his way of telling Doc that he wasn't going to let anything slide on this investigation, just because his big brother might be its focus.

Then Barrett got on the car phone and called the *Deacon Beach Herald*. Bear knew he wouldn't get a break from Kline and Co., but Pauline Traiwick had a reputation for being bluntly honest and fair. She had run the paper for years. Everyone read it. Bear ran down the events for Pauline, concluding with the fact that one possible witness would be questioned immediately in connection with the case.

"This possible have a name?" Pauline asked.

"It's Delton."

"Oh, God, not *your* Delton?"

"He's not mine, Pauline. I didn't take him to keep."

"No, no. Of course not. My God, though. Hasn't that boy caused you troubles enough?"

"I can't comment on that, Pauline."

"Lord." She clucked like a hen. "Is there any kind of physical evidence that links Delton to the house?"

"Not at present. Absolutely not," Barrett replied. "But we still have some lab work to do about which, Pauline, I wish you wouldn't speculate."

"Have I before?"

Barrett immediately wanted to bite his tongue. "No."

"It's all right, Bear," Pauline assured him. "I hope nothing does come back. I hope for the best. For your sake."

"For the record: I will follow every scrap of evidence. Every idea or lead. Wherever it goes."

There was a short silence before she spoke again. "She was a really popular woman, Barrett."

"Yes, she was."

"A lot of folks aren't going to like how she died."

"I don't like it, either, Pauline."

"I know. I know."

Barrett ended with a few noncommittal remarks and then signed off. Pauline's conversation brought memories of Delton's many transgressions vividly to mind. Some of the things that got his brother in trouble were almost funny. An overgrown boy making mischief. Like the time Delton "borrowed" Deacon Beach's fire truck. People laughed about that one for weeks. Talked about it after church. At the grocery store. Delton loved that. He loved the limelight.

There were other, more serious things, though, which were not a matter of mischief. Delton had never served time for those darker accomplishments. Had never been convicted for the things that were not, to anyone's mind but his own, funny.

But Barrett couldn't afford to think about that now. He could not think of Ramona Walker as his friend in the course of this investigation. And he could not afford to think of Delton Raines as his brother.

A few minutes later, Barrett parked his sedan in an unreserved slot beside Deacon Beach's Municipal Police Department. The Department was housed in a modest complex which wilted on a sunbaked corner that looked as though it had been scraped level with a butter knife. A razor-wired Viking fence corralled the station house itself, the sally port, police vehicles, towaways, and Rawlings's coveted custom-made airboat. An ordinary chain link fence surrounded the station's maintenance sheds, gas pumps, and never-used basketball court.

The station house had a central A.C. stacked in sheet-metaled symmetry atop its flat-topped roof. The front entrance was recessed into a cinder-block exterior. A cut-out bleach bottle displayed a brilliant bouquet of hydrangeas.

That's all the landscaping there was.

Barrett pushed through glass doors to enter Municipal HQ. A pair of soft drink machines hummed to one side of the desk sergeant's waist-high counter. The old-fashioned machine dropped Coca-Cola in six-ounce, sea green bottles. The more modern machine offered a variety of soda in cans. Cases of Pepsi and Mountain Dew and Dr. Pepper were stacked beside the single metal door that segregated the front desk from the mostly open cubicles beyond. A comfortably paunched veteran manned the formica counter out front; "Roach" MacGuire displayed a Pepsi can as if it were the Hope Diamond.

"This time I got it right."

MacGuire tapped the can. A pair of Florida roaches fell out, their feelers and crawlers stiff as cardboard.

"Stuff I use now," MacGuire was beaming, "it don't just kill 'em. It sticks to the healthier ones and interrupts their breeding cycle."

"Sounds like a good plan." Barrett perused the sign-in log.

"'Good,' hell, it's brilliant! Female only mates once, y'know. For life." MacGuire pronounced the fact with reverence. "So, see, if I can get the bitch early, why, I've cut off her an' all her offspring with just one kill."

"You're a sick man, Roach."

Barrett fished his pockets for quarters for the machine.

"You take your basic cornstarch and boric acid, that's not good enough," MacGuire insisted. "I mean, sure it gets on their feelers, and sure they take it back to the nest, but *this* little concoction—!" MacGuire's eyes grew large. "We're talking casualties in the billions."

"Hell of a crusade." Barrett dropped fifty cents.

"We don't do something, they're gonna take over the planet."

"They'd probably manage it better than we do." Barrett selected a bottled Coke. "H'lo, Blondie."

Blondie was a transient who regularly scoured the soft drink area for aluminum cans and bottles which he carted almost six miles outside of town to the recycling plant.

"'Lo, Bear."

"Those new shoes?"

"New used. Yup."

"Where'd you get 'em?"

"G'rage sale. First Baptist."

Barrett turned back to MacGuire.

"Has Sergeant Hanson brought Delton in?"

"Yeah, he did."

"Any problems?"

"Naw. Fact he was cracking jokes the whole time. But then, you know Delton."

"Yeah." Barrett swigged his Coke. "Where'd Dick put him?"

"Interrogation."

"The hell. Who with?"

"Taylor."

"Taylor—? Whose idea was that?"

"His."

Barrett turned for the metal door.

"What about my trap?" MacGuire called after him.

"Build one catches bad guys, Roach, you'll make a fortune."

The desk sergeant pressed a button to release an electromagnetic lock. Barrett went through on the buzzer.

Blondie stayed as he always did—behind.

Delton Raines, forty-two years old, lounged in one of two folding chairs placed on opposite sides of a table bolted with hurricane braces to a cement floor. A grille protected the window in the single door behind him. Had he spread his long and powerful arms, the elder Raines could almost have touched the walls on either side.

A detective barely out of his twenties sat in rapt attention in the small room's other chair.

Delton deposited ashes from his cigarette into a tray which lay beside the much younger man's untouched pen and pad. The black man was fresh from work, filthy in jeans and a sweat-stained cut-off shirt. Taylor Folsom was red-haired and clean cut in a pair of pleated slacks and a polo shirt. The young man displayed a badge from his belt. Delton displayed a pair of sunglasses from his.

"Pity to the world," Delton took a drag on his cigarette, "losing titties like that. You ever seen Ramona's tits, Taylor?"

"Ahm. I can't say."

"Could if you'd seen 'em. An' I bet you wondered, too—plenty of times. What's it *like* to be inside of that? Hmm? Inside Ramona Walker! Tell me you ain't thought about that."

"Delton, maybe we should wait for Barrett."

"Why? Am I under arrest?"

"No."

"Don't you want to know about Ramona?"

"Why, yeah. Sure."

"Then you got your man!" Delton leaned back with a broad wink. "We used to meet Friday nights, y'know. B'fore work...?"

"Work. Right." Taylor fumbled for his pen.

"She'd get me a hard-on, you know? And then wad up this little silk handkerchief. Little silk one?"

"Silk." Taylor took it down.

"Jam it up my ass." Delton hunched over the table.

"Delton—"

"God's truth! Up my ass. One poke at a time 'til I was just *about* to come and then—"

Taylor leaned forward to hear.

"She'd pop that puppy outen my butt—*God!* You never felt anything half that good in your *life.*"

"No," Taylor said regretfully. "I guess not."

"She was mag-damn-nificent," Delton proclaimed with authority.

"She was. Yes." Barrett stepped in. "But now she's dead."

"Morning, Bear." Taylor scrambled to his feet. "I was just—*we* were just—"

"Killing time." Delton smiled.

"Is that all you killed?" Barrett standing over his older brother.

"What kind of question is that?"

"The first one," Barrett replied. "Go get some coffee, Taylor."

"Don't you need—?"

"Coffee. We'll talk later."

Taylor gathered his pad and pen and stalked out of the room. Barrett shoved the door with the heel of his shoe. He took a swig of his Coke. Placed the bottle onto the table.

"Not smart of you, Delton. Playing the stud."

"Little romance never hurt nobody."

"This isn't about romance," Barrett said. "It's about murder."

Delton shrugged and dropped his cigarette into Barrett's bottle. It hissed shortly.

"I never killed nobody."

"That's a start. Now, I'm going to ask you some questions,

Delton. You'd best answer straight: Where were you last night at approximately eleven o'clock?"

"At the restaurant." Delton was suddenly irritable. "Ever'body knows that."

"You there to see Ramona?"

"Sure."

"You weren't exactly happy with her."

"Hell, I was drunk."

"You were supposed to meet her later, weren't you?"

"Was I?" Delton swirled the cigarette around in the bottom of Barrett's bottle.

"After work." Barrett remained patient. "Her place."

"She said somethin'. I can't remember."

"I want to know where you were, Delton. After the restaurant. Were you in her house? Her bed?"

"I was in my truck," Delton finally replied.

"Your truck." Barrett shook his head wearily.

"Driving around." Delton nodded.

"'Driving—' What kind of crap is that, Delton?"

"Don't play big brother with *me*, Bear!"

Barrett leaned forward, his face a near-profile of the man's who sat across the table.

"God made you my brother, Delton. And he made you oldest. I can't help that. But the State of Florida has made me a sworn officer of the law. You understand? And it's the law talking to you now.

"You're a suspect, Delton. You've got a history of substance abuse. Violence. A count of assault. One count of assault with a deadly weapon—"

"Sentence suspended."

"—a half-dozen domestic calls."

"That was Corrie. You know that." The cord at Delton's neck began to bulge.

"You beat her." Barrett straightened up.

"She never pressed charges."

"She divorced you," Barrett countered.

"That's not against the law," Delton snarled.

"No," Barrett agreed. "But murder is."

"I want a lawyer."

"Why?" Barrett inquired innocently. "You're not under arrest."

"Then I'll just *leave*." Delton kicked back his chair.

"Think you can piss on me?" Barrett planted himself between his brother and the door. "Try."

Barrett stepped as if to go past his brother, then kicked back hard into the meat of Delton's calf.

The larger man slammed onto the bolted table with a howl of rage. And came up with the Coke bottle.

Barrett's .38 snapped free of its holster.

"Do it, son of a bitch." The Bear trained the revolver on Delton's heart. *"Give me a reason!"*

The cord at Delton's neck throbbed thick as a rope. Barrett took a two-handed grip on his Smith & Wesson.

"Drop the bottle."

Delton bared his teeth. They were feral, those teeth, trapped inside blood-red gums.

"Drop the goddamn bottle, Delton."

Delton stared a moment up the handgun's small, snubbed nose. He let the bottle slip through his fingers. It broke when it hit the floor.

"You think you can run roughshod over everybody gets in your way, *but not me*, Delton!" Barrett was trembling now.

"I didn't kill her, Barrett."

A couple of long ticks would have passed on any clock before Barrett lowered his weapon.

"Were you in her pants?"

"What? You think the field hand's done got in the big house?"

"Were you?" Barrett asked again.

"No."

"Think about it."

"I said, No."

"Sit down."

Delton righted his chair. Took a seat. Barrett holstered his .38.

"All right. We'll start over. Right from the top. And Delton—"

"What?"

"For once in your life, try not to bullshit me."

Chapter seven

Laura Anne had just gotten home from the store and had started supper when Pauline Traiwick called asking if Barrett was home. Pauline always called Bear at work.

"Has he been hurt?" Laura Anne felt a surge of panic.

"No, Barrett's fine," Pauline assured her.

"Then—is there something else?"

"You haven't talked to Barrett today, Laura Anne?"

"No."

There was a short pause before Pauline came back. "Well. I guess you're better off hearing it from me than Channel 7."

So Laura Anne labored now, woodenly, deboning breasts of chicken for the evening meal. She'd gotten a special on the breasts at the Winn-Dixie. The greens and sweet corn had come from her own garden, as would the tomatoes and lettuce which Laura Anne would later toss for the family's salad.

Laura Anne dropped her deboned chicken into a cast-iron skillet. An exhaust fan labored to suck the stove's heat up its hood. But it was miserably hot. Laura Anne never liked to run the air-conditioning low enough to cool the kitchen. It wasn't that she liked to sweat. It just cost too much. And so now she adjusted the perch of a small oscillating fan which whined across her cotton halter top in a steady buzz. A sheen of perspiration lay on her arms and belly. The late afternoon sun played off her skin. She glowed like a bronze statue.

It was normally a nice time of the day for Laura Anne. A time for her home and family. She took a lot of pride in her home. Her house. She had a notion of how she wanted to appear in public, how she wanted her family to appear, and the home was a visible sign, for Laura Anne, of discipline and decorum.

It was a Jim Walter Home. Jim Walter used to sell prefabricated two-and three-bedroom structures at a third of the cost a custom-built would run. This home had originally been a two-bedder with one very small bath. That was all Barrett and Laura Anne could afford when they first married and now that they could do better, they didn't want to. Barrett had taken some time off when the boys were young to add a bedroom, a Florida room, and a larger bath out back. And a carport.

The house lay a little farther off the road than most. No signs of the suburb here. No sidewalks or curbs. Just a blacktop street, pines, Spanish moss, and mailboxes. A couple of burglaries had panicked a few neighbors into putting up privacy fences, which threatened to destroy whatever charm the rustic, gulf-side neighborhood might once have had. Laura Anne hated fences. And she only barely tolerated the rusted-out convertible which was propped beneath a tarp in their carport.

It was a 1969 Malibu Super Sport. Convertible. Cherry-red inside and out. The coupe hitched a three-ninety-six gas hog to a four-in-the-floor. Bear's first car. He had planned to keep it on the driveway.

"No way." Laura Anne put her foot down hard. "You think I'm going to move in here, have us looking like we don't know how to live with all these people?"

She meant white people. Aside from the Raines family there were no other blacks in this part of town. That's when Barrett built the carport, poured a concrete floor, and moved the Malibu to the very back where it now oxidized beneath its blue tarpaulin. "You can hardly see it," Barrett told Laura Anne proudly at the conclusion of his labor.

"Tow it to the junkyard you couldn't see it at all," Laura Anne replied. But she let him keep it. Every man's got to hang onto some part of being a boy and that Super Sport, Laura Anne knew, was as close to boyhood as Bear would ever get.

Nice thing about the carport was that it sat very deep in an oversized lot. There was an extra forty feet of backyard, which gave Barrett a place to hide his car, and Laura a place to put her garden.

They had lima beans, black-eyed peas, tomatoes, turnips, sweet corn—

"And you worried about us lookin' country." Bear had shaken his head.

Laura also planted some shrubs, to frame the house. Some shore juniper and ligustrum. Azaleas. And she planted two oaks which now commanded the respect of every squirrel in the neighborhood.

Laura Anne could see a squirrel, now, through her kitchen window. The kitchen originally had no windows. It was Laura Anne's idea to lengthen her cooking area so that it protruded into the addition which extended across what used to be the back side of the house. There was a nice, large window, now, over a new sink and dishwasher. A sit-down bar segregated the kitchen from the Florida room without sealing it off.

"I don't want to be cut off from things," she had told Barrett. "I want to see what's happening."

The phone rang again. Laura grabbed it quickly. "Bear?"

"Miz Raines, this is Stacy Kline. Channel 7 News?"

Laura Anne went stiff.

"I, ahm, don't have any information for you, Mr. Kline."

"How do you feel about the arrest, Miz Raines? You *do* know that your husband picked up Delton Raines earlier today in connection with—"

"Mr. Kline, I'm cooking supper."

"We just wanted a reaction, that's all. Something from the suspect's sister-in-law."

Laura Anne banged the phone onto its cradle. Felt instant

regret—what if she'd offended the reporter? Would it be a problem for her? For Bear?

Most of all Laura Anne worried about the boys. What would happen to them once this thing got started? On the bus? At school? It was hard enough being the black sons of a black detective. They didn't need an uncle in jail for murder.

Especially for murdering a white woman.

"Mama." Laura Anne's elder twin resharpened a pencil already honed to a dart. "I can't find the carrot in the picture. I got the shovel and the catcher's mitt, see? It's in the lily pad! But there's not no carrot."

"Not *any* carrot," Laura Anne corrected him firmly. "And I'll bet if you stick to it you'll find it."

Tyndall was born within two minutes of his fraternal twin, but frequently behaved as if he were two years younger. They were definitely not alike, Ben and Tyndall. Separate looks. Distinct personalities. Their mother always sat the boys at the bar beside the kitchen for homework. That way if they had a question she was there to answer or, more often, make *them* answer.

There were rules for homework. Every assignment required its own kind of preparation. Take arithmetic, for instance. Laura Anne had very specific instructions about how the boys were to prepare for *that*. Ben and Tyndall were required to bring two kinds of paper for their elementary mathematics. The "good" paper was clean and ruled and bought new. The "scratch" came from computer runouts.

"You work your problems on the back side of the scratch," their mother drilled her boys. "Then when we've checked your answers, you copy it nice and neat to the good paper."

"I still don't see *any* carrot," Tyndall complained of his present labor.

"Take a break, Tyndall. Do something else and come back to it."

"Mama! Cain't you just help me?"

"Tyndall, the whole idea behind homework is to do the work yourself."

Tyndall turned to his twin.

"Ben, where's your worksheet?"

"Benjamin, you hush." Laura Anne raised an eyebrow for Tyndall's benefit. "Ben's not supposed to be doing your homework, young man."

"Wish we had Miz Hart," Tyndall sighed heavily.

"Think Miss Hart'd do your homework?"

"Nope. But she sure is pretty."

"That's always a help, isn't it?" Laura Anne turned over a breast in the skillet.

"Miz Perkins is ossified," Tyndall said of his own teacher.

"She's what?"

"Like one of those animals you see in rocks," Tyndall declared.

"That's fossilized," Ben corrected.

Ben favored his mother. Slender. Quick. Graceful as a gazelle. Tyndall was like Barrett. All elbows and knees.

"Fossilized, why thank you, Ben. And Tyndall," Laura Anne returned to her firstborn, "Miss Perkins is not a fossil."

"She's old," Tyndall insisted. "She's used up."

"'Used up'?! Tyndall Raines, where did you get that language?!"

"School bus," Ben supplied the answer. "Carey Butler."

Laura Anne planted a hand on her very fine hip.

"Your mama's getting old, too. Every day. Am I used up? Hmm? You tired of me?"

"Careful what you say, boys. Or be damned for life!"

Daddy! the boys exploded in chorus from their stools. Next thing Barrett knew, he had twin anchors around his neck.

"How's it goin', hon?" He tried to kiss her through a barricade of boys.

"Supper'll be ready," she offered coolly.

"You heard?" he asked, the boys still hanging on.

"Pauline called. And Stacy. It's all right. We'll wait 'til after supper."

The dishwasher had reached its dry cycle by the time Barrett cleaned the pots and soft-scrubbed the surfaces. He was looking forward to the fresh pot of coffee Laura Anne had brewed. A jar of homemade honey stood ready beside his battered plastic mug.

Laura Anne was already sipping her coffee over a large, glossy-paged book. It took Barrett a moment to recognize her high school annual.

"Ancient history," the Bear warned his wife.

"It's not ancient if it keeps coming back," she replied.

"That goddamn Delton."

"I know."

Delton had been a problem for Laura Anne and Barrett from the day they married. It was especially hard for Laura Anne. She knew that in her small southern and hometown community families were judged as much by appearance as by substance. And Laura Anne truly believed that appearance had something to do with substance. "You can't be disciplined on the inside," Laura Anne would tell her high-schoolers, "unless you're disciplined on the outside first."

What she preached at school she practiced at home. Laura Anne taught discipline, contrary to popular culture, from the out-side in. The boys worked beside their mother and father to clean the house, tend the lawn, and weed the garden. Laura Anne made sure that Ben and Tyndall were clean. Conservatively dressed. No rap. No caps. No hot-item jackets or running shoes. All for discipline. And what started on the outside took root on the inside. Laura Anne was her own best model. She was never late, always responsible, a prodigious laborer at school, on committees, at church.

But lawns and gardens and committees never claimed Deacon Beach's attention as did Delton Raines. It was Delton who brought Deacon Beach High School for the first and only time to within just one game of the State "A" championship. It was Delton who broke tackles and hearts with equal celerity. Taff Calhoun used to say with admiration that "Delton Raines could fight and fuck better shit-faced than a white man could sober. And still have enough piss by mornin' to raise the foam up about his knees."

Taff's paean was offered the evening before Delton broke Calhoun's arm with a tire iron.

Christ Himself couldn't compete. Laura Anne had more than once risen well dressed and well prepared for Sunday choir only to have conversation turn to Saturday and Delton Raines. Shined shoes couldn't outshine football cleats, even if long retired. A clean blazer or dress wasn't as interesting as a letterman's jacket. Discipline couldn't compete on Sunday morning with a stolen fire truck, or a fist fight, or some fling with somebody's wife.

It was as if the community participated vicariously in all of Delton's outrages. As if, unlike Christ, he lived so that others might sin through him. Only a black man could offer this kind of salvation, of course. White men simply weren't capable. And so long as Delton confined his outrages to people of his own color, or the occasional white trash like Taff, his sins would not only be forgiven, they'd be enshrined.

Every time that Laura Anne got wind of Delton's newest exploit she would feel exposed. She would know that Barrett's reputation, and hers, were somehow compromised by this powerful and uncaring kinsman. And when she'd hear snickers at church, at a ball game, or at the grocery, Laura Anne would also hear that word "nigger" some-place deep down in her deepest self, and she'd be furious about it.

But she couldn't be furious with Delton. Getting angry with Delton didn't do any good. He loved anger. He fed on it. And so Laura Anne would find herself blaming her husband—as if Bear was responsible for his brother's filthy jeans and always-exposed belly button. As if Barrett was to blame for his brother's sloth and crudity and violence. When that happened Laura Anne knew that she was giving in to Delton. That she had lost control. Lost discipline. And it was this which she resented most of all. Barrett knew the anger on his wife's face. The frustration.

"I don't know what to do." He shook his head. "Just about the time I think he's straightened up, off he goes and gets mixed up in this business."

"He'll never straighten up," Laura Anne stated flatly. "What do you want *me* to do about it, Laura Anne?" Laura Anne turned another page angrily. "I just wish he'd move. Go somewhere else."

"Hell, if he moved he'd lose his audience."

"Everybody's watching, that's for sure. Stacy Kline called here."

"For me?"

"For *me*. Wanted a reaction from 'the suspect's sister in-law.' Delton's sister-in-law! Just how I want to be known."

"I'll talk to Kline." Barrett offered it like an apology.

"What about talking to Delton?"

"Did that already."

"You think he killed her?" Laura Anne asked quietly.

"Says he didn't."

"Do you think he's telling the truth?"

"Never has before," Barrett answered.

"I guess we ought to hope he is now," Laura Anne replied, and smoothed a page in her yearbook.

"What you got there?" Barrett turned the book to see.

A single photograph filled the page. A farmer's tractor pulled a high school float past the photographer's flash. It was a Trojan horse which rose from the tractor's skirted trailer, a Trojan horse fashioned from lumber and chicken wire. And tissue dyed with food coloring.

A phalanx of boys marched below. High school boys, all of them, the Deacon High Trojans donned shoulder pads and shorts to escort their crafty gift.

And atop the horse, frozen in the photograph—

—stood their queen. She rode a good twenty feet above the armored escort. A cascade of black hair fell in braided locks over a high bust. An ice-blue gown clasped at each shoulder clung damply to a virgin's figure. Her skin was dark gold and firm. Two lesser royalty froze in the frame below, princesses pale and wan, their fragile arms extended to the masses who shouted adulation unseen or unfocused behind sawhorses and pickup trucks. The princesses smiled to the crowd. But not their queen. She remained aloof, eyes forward, as if fixed on some distant and lofty goal.

It was Laura Anne, of course. "Homecoming Queen," the caption read. "Deacon High. 1983."

"What brought this up?" Barrett smiled.

"You heard Tyndall. About Miss Perkins."

"I heard."

"They work the poor woman to death. Thirty, sometimes forty children in a class. Do that to *me* for thirty years I'll be ossified, too."

"We all get older, Laura Anne."

"Yes." She sighed. "But men can get away with it. Men get distinguished. Women get ossified."

"You don't look too ossified to me."

"Wouldn't hurt for you to show me, Bear. Every now and then."

Her top pulled up as she turned to him. Her breasts swelled full and firm, above a damp, still slender waist.

"A woman needs to be shown," she challenged him.

"Well, I work. You work."

"I *have* to work." She pulled away.

"I know that, Laura Anne. Goddammit, don't you think I know?"

"I just don't want to wind up like Miss Perkins. That's all."

"Why don't we go outside? Neck in the convertible?"

"You mean the wreck."

"We could put the top down."

"You mean pull the tarp off. I don't see why you keep that old car." But she was smiling now.

"I'm gonna fix her up," Bear told her. "You wait and see."

"You've been saying that forever." She met his kiss.

They made love. It had been—Christ, it might have been weeks. She was warm and damp and ready. Barrett could feel himself about to explode, like a teenager. She eased him off.

"Hold it! Just a little!"

He held as long as he could. He held until they both were about to burst. And then they did burst. They exploded for the first time in a long time together and then she worked her magic again. Barrett was certain he couldn't. But there she started and he did. They did.

Later on she stretched with nothing but a sheet over her butt. Acres of that firm, gold skin and Barrett beside her, a bear indeed, slabs of muscle loose on a thick frame.

"Homecoming…" Laura Anne tongued him gently behind the ear. "Who gave me my crown? D'you remember?"

He didn't. Laura Anne's breasts skimmed still taut over his chest as she retrieved the yearbook. She plopped the annual open, paged to another photo.

"Here." She pointed and he looked.

It was not a good picture. Grainy. Bleached out. The queen had left her Trojan horse to stand on a raised dais set midway between bleachers packed to capacity. Eager faces looked up fuzzily from the chalked field below. And who was that at Laura Anne's side—that woman frozen in a flash of light?

The face was overexposed, but you could see that this had been a tall woman who placed the crown on Laura Anne's head. Well boned. Her hair fell rich and long to a waist small as a girl's. A dancer's legs—

Barrett breathed in sharply.

"Yes." His wife nodded simply. "It was Ramona."

Chapter eight

Almost three weeks had passed since Ramona was murdered, and Barrett was still numb. Bear perched motionless on a tattered rollaround at his government-issue desk. Cops' desks are almost never distinguished pieces of furniture. They can, however, provide a tableau for odd juxtapositions. Bear's worktable, for instance, horseshoed on three sides by portable wall dividers, displayed a portrait of Laura Anne and the boys, a candid snap of Ben and Tyndall on a fishing trip, and a vase of forget-me-nots opposite a cork wall littered with $8^1/_2$-by-11-inch glossies of stabbings, rapes, and murders.

Ramona was spread across the cork now. A particularly hideous and frightening collection of parts. Barrett found himself riveted on her breasts, her legs, the gash in her abdomen. Photographs seemed to freeze things in time in a way that film, or even writing, could not. Barrett wondered if there might be in himself some deep perversion, something to account for the fact that a dead image of her leg or breast conjured in his mind's eye another image, alive and vibrant, of Ramona swaying toward him in the restaurant, or laughing in her Thunderbird, the wind whipping her skirt high on legs now captured in time, stiff and inert. Roland Reed was at a photo now, circling the dog leash with his truly antique fountain pen.

"You find any prints on the fuse box?"

Barrett didn't reply.

"Barrett?" Roland tapped his pen on the desk. "Barrett, you with us?"

Barrett adjusted a photograph on his desk. Roland Reed, aka Fountain Pen, was now an assistant state attorney prosecuting cases in the seven largely rural counties which constituted Florida's Third Judicial Circuit. Years back he had been the fair-haired son of Deacon Beach High School. The Golden Boy. Most Likely to Succeed. But Barrett had been there when Roland was young and drunk and driving. He'd been only a couple of cars back when Roland swerved off a blacktop road to clip a corn-haired little girl on her bicycle. With a dozen others Barrett saw Roland leave the scene, spinning tires and throwing gravel onto a lump of flesh and gingham.

That incident would have gotten anybody else charged with a felony and thrown in jail. Not Master Reed. Roland's place on the Beach was too well protected, his daddy too well connected. They paid off some dayworker a one-time settlement for the legs his daughter would never use and entered young Reed in a defensive driving course. Son of a bitch's insurance probably didn't even go up. That was Roland's notion of justice as a youth and here he was twenty years later telling everybody that justice, after all, was all that anyone sought with regard to Ramona Walker's horrible murder.

That's what Roland said. The truth was, he was here to make damn sure that the evidence Barrett collected would send his brother to the electric chair.

He looked pretty confident that it would.

A couple of other people did look ill at ease, though. Taylor Folsom was fiddling with the badge on his belt. Doc Hardesty hid behind the stacks of reports, bags of evidence, and cups of coffee which littered Barrett's desk.

"You all right, Bear?" Doc Hardesty peered over the desk. "Need a break?"

"No, I'm fine." Barrett shoved himself erect in his chair. "Where were we—DNA?"

"Fuse box first," Roland said impatiently.

"No prints," Barrett said.

"Doors and windows?"

"Lifted a ton of stuff off the door." Barrett checked his notes. "But no match to Delton."

"He could have worn gloves," Roland pointed out.

"Yes, he could," Barrett agreed amiably.

"How about the DNA?" Roland turned to Doc. "Anything there?"

"Right." Doc produced a folder. "Got the report from Tallahassee. Preliminary results indicate that the semen and hair collected from the victim are identical. One subject involved. We also have a tentative match."

"It's Delton's." Roland tapped his pen in a drum solo on Barrett's desk. "You know it is."

"Take a couple more weeks to lock it in," Doc told the prosecutor, "but, yes, it's gonna be Delton's. Motility of the semen indicates that intercourse took place at or near the time of death."

"What's the window on that?" Roland asked.

"Hour and a half or so. One side or the other."

Taylor spoke up. "Then couldn't Delton've had sex with her someplace besides the house? The murder could've taken place after?"

"It's possible, yes," Barrett grunted. "But then there's this."

Bear fished a Zip-locked bag from the pile on his desk.

A pair of badly charred workboots were tagged inside.

"Dick Hanson had his eye out," Barrett explained. "Found these in a trash barrel at the sawmill."

"They're Delton's, I gather." Roland made a note.

"Yeah. They're burned. But we still got traces off the sole. It's blood, all right. Ramona's."

Barrett squeezed honey from a bear-shaped container into his coffee.

"There you are, Roland. What do you think?"

"I can have him on trial in a month." Reed pocketed his pen.

"You have enough to do the job?" Barrett stirred his honey in.

"Between what you have here and what I have outside I do." Barrett stopped stirring.

"Not sure I follow you."

"People are crying for blood, Bear. Ramona was well liked. And it doesn't help Delton that she was white."

"Or that Delton's black." Barrett eyed the State's attorney.

"C'mon, Bear. The jury's gonna be influenced by racial considerations no matter what I do. You know that."

"That's pretty damned cynical," Doc spoke up.

"That's a damn fact and we all know it," Roland retorted. "It's got nothing to do with *me*. Plus, even if Delton was white as snow, he's got a history of violence, he's got convictions—"

"None of which are admissible," Barrett pointed out. "Judge Blackmond won't allow it."

Fountain Pen Reed's collar seemed a tad whiter around his neck than usual.

"This defendant won't need an introduction," Reed said with some portion of venom. "There won't be a juror sitting hasn't heard a story about Delton Raines at one time or another. And most of 'em aren't pretty."

"You can't convict a man for his reputation," Barrett said.

"Not by itself. But we're gonna have DNA; that's pretty damning. We've got motive. And the shoes—! Hard to explain away blood on the bottom of your brogans."

The state's attorney leaned forward. "What do *you* think, Barrett?"

"About what?"

"Could your brother have killed this woman?"

"Right now I'd have to say he's our best suspect," Bear replied.

"Doesn't answer my question," Roland pressed. "What about it, Bear? You think Delton's capable of something like *this*?"

The inquisitor jabbed his pen at the bits and pieces on Barrett's corkboard. Taylor Folsom looked suddenly as though he wished he were anyplace else. Doc Hardesty found refuge in a manila folder.

"I'll tell you straight." Barrett turned to face the prosecutor. "I think the son of a bitch is capable of just about anything."

There was a collective exhalation then, as if everyone had held their breath in their lungs and let go all at once.

Roland leaned onto the corkboard. "Well. Do we arrest this man or don't we?"

"Give me five minutes with the chief." Barrett was already out of his chair. "I'll be ready to go." Barrett left Roland and the others inside his cubicle. Smoot's office was directly across a similar arrangement of cubicles and open desks. As Barrett wended his way through his coworkers' workstations and desks he began to realize that for the second time in as many days he was missing something.

Exactly what the hell was it? Barrett took a quick inventory. The uniforms were all studiously at their desks, for one thing. No bullshitting. No salacious jokes. No sharing the morning tacos which Dick had lately begun to bring from some new Mexican place. Not one man or woman looked up from their suddenly medieval dedication to smile at Bear or even meet his eye. Usually a trip across that landscape of familiar faces would be accompanied by gentle ribbing and pleasantries. A grin or a curse.

But today—nothing.

Barrett spotted Lois Laughton at the Xerox machine.

"Better get those hydrangeas some water, Lois," Barrett boomed with a friendly smile. "Damn things're gonna dry up."

"Sure thing, Bear." Lois smiled weakly.

Just yesterday Lois had jumped his ass for drowning her hydrangeas.

That's when Barrett knew for a fact that everybody else knew something which he did not.

Didn't take long to change that. Smoot Rawlings hit Bear with it almost before the detective could step inside the only private office at Deacon Beach's Municipal HQ.

"Look, Bear, I don't want you on the case."

Boom. So there it was.

"Excuse me?" Barrett could feel a cold knot tightening in his stomach.

"We'll find somebody else," Rawlings said as if reassuring him.

"Who?" Barrett challenged Smoot quietly. "You? When's the last time you worked a homicide, Chief?"

"You don't have to remind me."

"That leaves Taylor. He'll be ready in about another forty years."

"He might manage. I could assign some people."

"You could call the FDLE."

"No, I can't." Smoot's red neck got redder. "And you know why."

"Fair enough." Bear crossed his arms. "Maybe we should check our resources. What's our caseload, anyhow?"

A Marlite board behind Smoot's desk was crisscrossed with magically marked assignments.

"How many burglaries we have outstanding, Chief? Assaults? Rapes? Narcotics? Hell, there are two drug-related deaths up there we haven't even interviewed the witnesses."

"That's not the point."

"What is the point?" Bear knew damn well what the point was, of course, but he was going to make Smoot spell it out.

Rawlings took his time.

"I may only have two detectives, Barrett. But you've only got one brother."

Well. At least it was out in the open.

"Delton and I are not buddies," Bear told his chief.

"I'm not sure that makes a difference."

"What d'you mean?" Barrett's pulse began to pick up. Easy, now, he told himself. Discipline.

"I have to worry about perceptions, Bear," Smoot was saying. "Small town like this—people might feel like, well, just because Delton's your brother maybe you won't push so hard. You won't look as close as you might with somebody else."

Barrett inhaled a barrel of air. Exhaled slowly.

"You're worried about that, are you, Chief?"

"You know what they say—blood's thicker than water."

"And coon blood, why, that's thicker than any. Is that it, Smoot?"

"Now wait a minute, I didn't say that. I didn't say anything *like* that and you *know it!*"

"You don't have to say it to be thinking it," Barrett retorted. "'Perceptions!' Who the hell are you kidding?"

No reply to that one. Barrett knew there wouldn't be. He closed the gap between them by a step.

"Smoot, I am a detective. A damn good detective. You might not have known that when I came into this job but you sure as hell know it now.

"If you don't think I can be professional on this case then you can't trust me on any case. Any time. Any place."

"Don't do this, Bear!"

"Either trust me," Barrett went on, "or take my badge."

"Settle down, now. Just settle down."

Barrett slammed his badge onto Rawlings's desk.

"*Trust* me. Or *take* it."

"I don't want to lose you, Bear." Rawlings suddenly looked very tired. "You know that."

"Good." Barrett reclaimed his shield. "I'm on my way."

"I want you to know you've got my sympathy," Rawlings roused himself to say.

"I don't need your sympathy, Chief—"

Barrett paused at the door.

"I need your trust."

They took Dick Hanson's cruiser out to the mill. Barrett drove. Dick took time along the way to chamber some Number Ones into the squad car's resident twelve-gauge. Then he armed a second shotgun.

"Just in case." Hanson turned, embarrassed, to Barrett.

"It's gonna be all right, Dick," Bear reassured his sergeant. "He's been arrested before."

It was almost noon by the time they pulled up to Red Walker's sawmill. Barrett opened his door. The heat and din of the place hammered him like a blast furnace, reminding Bear that his maternal grandfather had worked himself to death at a mill like this. On a day like this.

It was a busy morning. Log trucks pulled up like Jurassic beasts dragging giant, pine tails in tow. The logs were cut in the forest and skidded to the trucks for loading onto what Barrett always imagined to be a Tinkertoy trailer. Once loaded, a truck's longest log would be tagged with a red handkerchief, a warning for motorists unused to judging such lengths. Not everyone took the warning seriously. Barrett had seen more than one car run up under the rear of a trailerload of logs.

There wasn't much you could do, then, but find something to bury.

Once to the mill, the logs had to be safely off-loaded from their trailers. Barrett liked to watch Taff Calhoun at that job. Taff ran the loader with a sense of aesthetics. The loader was a giant, steel mouth whose articulated jaws could pluck a pair of twenty-foot logs from their trailer as if they were soda straws. Lots of folks would just drag the logs off by twos or threes, pulling other logs off in a tangled mess. Not Taff. Barrett watched now as Calhoun finessed a pair of twenty-footers into the loader's jaws and extracted them from their tangled heap with the same dexterity a serious child might give to a game of Pick-up Sticks.

Once they were off the truck, Taff lowered his giant twin sticks onto a pair of parallel rails called "ways," fashioned from actual railroad rails left years earlier when Boatwright Lumber Company ran its own trains through the middle of the yard.

Those were the years when Barrett's grandfather sawyered at the mill. Barrett was always reminded, when he came out here, of his grandfather, was always reminded of the stories his papa, on the porch of a sharecropper shack, would tell of how things used to be. The mill in those days was a town unto itself, a vertically integrated industrial complex which proudly boasted of its ice makers and band saws and electric generators right along with its "colored" accomodations. Why, they had themselves a clinic right there at the mill. They had a school. They even had a company commissary to which every black worker was perpetually indebted.

They had other things, too. Whorehouses in Cross City and bars and fights. Terrible accidents with Clyde skidders and saws and snakebites. The white workers in those days got paid good money in hard cash. Barrett's grandfather, paid lower wages to begin with, only saw half of his lowered wage in real money. The other half of his already-depressed remainder came in scrip which was redeemable only at the company-owned store.

It was a way to keep the niggers from drinking away all their pay, Barrett's grandfather used to say, as if obligated to defend the company where he worked for thirty-three years.

The way Papa said it you'd think the rules didn't apply to himself. You'd think the other rules—the separate bathrooms, separate water buckets, separate doctors and schools and churches—were for some other black man.

But the rules did apply to Barrett's grandpa, just as they had applied, sometimes not as obviously, to his father.

Randall Grant Raines worked up from driver to foreman at the mill from 1952 until his own death in 1976. The Boatwrights were long gone by 1952; Red Walker had started his business on the ruins of that grander operation. By the time Barrett's father picked up the peavy and cant hook there wasn't any scrip to spend, or company store to buy from. More important, there also wasn't any original timber left to cut.

The area around Deacon Beach used to be famous for a particular kind of timber native to the region. Tidewater cypress came to be as fashionable for builders in the thirties and forties as the better-known hardwoods from forests in the north. Long-leaf yellow pine provided a second major source of timber. The Boatwrights made a fortune cutting cypress and pine from the swamps and lowlands of Taylor and Dixie County. But there was no incentive to reforest in those years and the cypress, some of them five or six centuries old, were cut down to the last tree. The original-growth pine were gone shortly thereafter. By the early forties there was nothing left. In one three-month period, Red would tell anyone who'd listen, the old-timers pushed out twenty-two *million* board feet of lumber onto a railroad which ran quite literally through the middle of the mill's yard. Red wouldn't do a tenth that much business in three years. It was a mark of how much the region had declined that Red's one-saw operation was even now one of its larger employers.

Here he came.

Barrett was brought back to the present as Mr. Walker stumped unhappily over to the squad car.

"Mornin', Red."

"Bear. Sorry about all this mess."

"Not your fault. Where's he working?"

"Circle saw."

"Dick—"

"Right here," Hanson replied.

"Let's go get him."

Barrett knew the way. He tried not to think about arresting his brother. He tried to tell himself that this was just another incarceration, like any of hundreds he'd done in the past. He tried not to think about what Delton might do, or *not* do. "You're the law, here," Barrett kept reminding himself. "People have to see you call the shots."

Barrett led Red and Dick past the loader and ways, past strong, hard men who bucked the logs from the ways to a moving sled where a single worker with a mallet dogged down the log for Delton Raines.

Delton ran the saw. It was a circle saw. The blade was six feet in diameter. Its replaceable teeth were fashioned from tungsten-carbide. Red had a Farmall tractor rigged to power the saw. The tractor's transmission was long frozen shut, but the engine still worked, and so did the power take-off. Red used the Farmall's P.T.O. to turn his circular blade. The saw's chassis remained stationary, carefully calibrated directly below the sawyer's perch. Another jerry-rigged tractor would power the capstan which pulled each log cut by cut past the saw's spinning blade.

The blade was howling now, a deafening, banshee howl. Chips

of wood and sawdust sprayed beneath a hellishly hot sun as Delton pulled a twenty-foot log on its first pass through the six-foot saw. Delton would square off the log first. Then he'd cut planks in standard widths from the log's entire length. It took a great deal of skill to pull a piece of timber straight as a string through a circle of screaming steel teeth. It took a steady hand and a good judge of timber. Barrett knew that Red hadn't wanted to have to hire Delton. But he wasn't going to get anyone better. And he sure as hell wasn't going to get anyone cheaper.

Delton ran Red's saw from what looked like a tree house of angle iron and scrap metal that was hoisted above the jerry-rigged power plant. Barrett had to pass by a dozen or more workers, black and white, to reach Delton's perch. One by one they froze as they saw his shotgun escort.

Delton seemed to pay no attention at all. Barrett was sure Delton had seen him, was sure his brother could see him now, with Dick in tow, even as he seemed to see only the log which howled past his circular blade.

Bear noticed suddenly that his mouth was dry. And just as suddenly he was glad for the mill's deafening racket. He was glad for the heat and the chips which flew from Delton's banshee blade. He was glad for the sawdust and the resin and the stench of the place. Otherwise, surely, Dick and Red and everyone else would see his fear, would hear his heart pounding like a bass drum in his chest.

Barrett was afraid that Delton would resist arrest. Short of shooting the son of a bitch Barrett didn't know that he'd be able to do anything about it. Barrett had some respect for his own size and strength. He was not a small man. In fact, at a hundred ninety or so honest pounds and with his shorter height, the Bear was more than most men would want to engage one-on-one.

But Barrett knew that Delton, even though five years older, was also five years harder. Morning walks and abdominal crunches might give you a good heart and a flat belly. But it didn't keep you in the same kind of shape that pulpwooding did. Delton was harder.

He was also five years meaner. Barrett had reviewed Delton's sheet just that morning. Lots of savage behavior there, coded into cop talk. A dozen arrests in the last four years. Barrett had made one of those arrests himself. Or, more accurately, he had tried to.

It had been one of many weekends when Smoot found himself short of uniforms and so the detectives had been called to fill in. Midway through his shift Barrett got tagged by Dispatch to investigate a domestic beef. It was an unfamiliar address, a house trailer propped on blocks in what folks still called nigger-town. When Barrett arrived, though, he recognized Corrie Raines's beat-up Toyota. Corrie had only divorced Delton the previous week.

Barrett hoped against hope he wouldn't find Delton inside.

But he did. Delton had beaten Corrie with his fists until he broke a rib. Two children were screaming in the trailer's cramped interior. When Delton saw his younger brother he lowered his head, just like a tailback, and charged.

Barrett hadn't come in with his weapon ready. Mistake Numbah One. He had no backup. All he had was a baton, which he swung with all his might. The stick glanced off the big man's back just as Delton caught Barrett numbers high and drove the Bear, sans baton, *through* the trailer's screen door and onto the Toyota outside.

There's no kind of hurt quite like the hurt that comes when you take a shot to that nervous intersection just below the sternum. Barrett had taken Delton's blow right in his solar plexus. He couldn't breathe and he couldn't black out. All he could do was hurt. When the hurting abated Bear noticed Corrie's little girls. They were holding hands outside. Crying.

Barrett dragged himself into the trailer to check on Corrie. She was seated at the trailer's kitchen drinking coffee. No concern for her children. None for Barrett. Not even a phone call to 911. Just a teaspoon of instant Folger's beneath a hot water tap.

Barrett radioed out the code to bring Delton in. But when his brother was booked, Corrie not only refused to bring charges for her own assault, she declared loudly that Barrett had provoked Delton to self-defense.

The charges were dropped. That had been almost three years

ago and yet Barrett still wondered—what if Delton had carried a gun that night? Would he have used it? Would Barrett have used *his*?

Could he kill his brother?

Barrett could feel his heart pounding now, faster and faster. Slow it down, Barrett told himself. Slow it all down.

Delton was pulling back his log for another cut. Leisurely. Unconcerned. Just as if cops with shotguns came regularly to admire his labor.

Barrett displayed his badge.

"DELTON, I NEED TO SEE—"

The blade kicked in screaming to cut off Barrett's command. Delton was smiling from his iron tree house. Yes. He knew Barrett was there. And so did everyone else.

Every son of a bitch who worked at the mill—drivers, loaders, stackers—was watching. And every son of a bitch watching knew what Barrett was there to do. They had seen him try to call his brother down from his high throne and they had seen Delton refuse.

The blade howled like a hyena.

What would Barrett do now?

"Dick—"

Barrett turned to Hanson. Handed the sergeant his revolver.

"WHAT THE HELL?!"

"JUST BACK ME UP."

And then, with everyone watching, Barrett hoisted himself up onto Delton's log. Perhaps ten of the log's twenty feet had pulled past Delton's tungsten-toothed blade.

That left ten feet to go.

Barrett rode the log as it edged inch by inch toward Delton's screaming circle of teeth.

The blade hit a knot. Barrett stumbled—

—and caught himself on a hand. He was back up, now. Erect and riding the log. Sawdust sprayed into Barrett's face and lodged in his hair. Chips of pine ricocheted off his arms and trunk. But he didn't move. He didn't budge as he rode the log straight toward Delton's saw.

"BEAR?!" Dick tried to shout above the din.

Three feet away, now. Two.

"Oh, Jesus!" Dick chambered a round into his shotgun.

Barrett could stand inside the six-foot circle of steel which screamed now in his face. It was a blur of steel. A blizzard of steel.

Barrett rode the log.

Dick slapped his shotgun to his shoulder.

Delton cut the engine which turned the take-off which powered the saw.

The mill was suddenly quiet.

Barrett stood covered with sawdust. He had not moved. Had not even twitched.

"Mornin', Bear." Delton grinned as though it were all in good fun.

"Delton, you need to get off that thing."

"Oh? Why's that?"

Barrett pocketed his badge with careful discipline.

"'Cause you're under arrest."

Chapter nine

Stacy Kline's EMG van was waiting for Bear at the police compound's rear gate. Two other news crews, the ABC and NBC affiliates, were waiting, too. Roach was there with a couple of uniforms to keep the reporters outside the Viking fence. Delton would not be taken out of the squad car until the cruiser was inside the sally port and the port's heavy doors rolled shut. The sally port was not much more than a garage contiguous with the area inside the station house where Delton would be mugged and printed and booked. It was an important garage, however, because its doors, once closed, prevented a suspect from having anywhere to run. Except inside.

Barrett expected Delton to mouth off on the way in, but he didn't. Never said a word. Even the Miranda had only been confirmed with a nod. Barrett made sure Dick had his elder brother inside the station before he stepped out front to deal with the media.

The reporters didn't like being forced to scramble from out back, where the pictures were sexy, to the bleached-out hydrangea at the station's street entrance. But Barrett wanted to avoid as much sensationalism as possible. Lacking any kind of briefing room, the station's front entrance presented the least exciting image he could imagine.

Channel 7's Kline led the pack.

"Detective Barrett, Stacy Kline."

Once more Barrett found that reed-thin arm holding a microphone in his face.

"What the hell, Stacy," Barrett drawled conversationally. "You're acting like we never met."

"Is it true your brother has been arrested for the murder of Ramona Walker?" Stacy asked as if they never had.

"He has, yes." Barrett faced a rival newsman's camera.

"Who'll be in charge of the case?" Kline shouted over the other competing microphones.

"I handle the homicides, Stacy. You know that."

"But surely this is different." Another reporter got the question in first.

"You mean because my brother's involved."

"Exactly."

Barrett decided to play this one cards up.

"Why don't we stop the song and dance, ladies and gentlemen? You can have this: For the record. Delton Raines will get the same consideration that any other citizen gets under the law. No more. No less."

"Doesn't sound as though you're very sympathetic," Kline barked.

"Sympathy's got nothing to do with it." Barrett suddenly felt the sudden drop in blood sugar that frequently follows a rush of adrenaline. He needed to get out of this heat.

"But you arrested your brother!" Stacy proclaimed that self-evident fact as if it were an outrage.

"I enforce the law," Barrett replied evenly. "That's my job. That's my duty."

"What about your duty to your family?" Kline demanded as Barrett pushed past the cameras.

"Detective? Detective!"

It was getting really hot.

There were other calls to his back but Barrett ignored them all as he took refuge in the Deacon Beach jail.

The small interrogation room was even smaller this time around. Roland Reed took one side with Barrett. Delton slouched at the bolted-down table with his attorney. Barrett knew Thurman Shaw when he was still cropping sand-lugs in the tobacco fields of Lafayette County. Thurman had gone to Madison's junior college, finished up at FSU, and then had gone directly into law school. He shingled with a couple of personal-injury types in Taylor County. He loved controversy. He loved attention. And Thurman could already tell from the news vans outside that this case would generate *lots* of attention.

"Bet the bastard can see himself on *Hard Copy* right now," Barrett thought to himself.

And on cue Thurman jabbed an indignant finger at Roland Reed.

"I won't be bullied, Roland! You can*not* make my client plead for a crime he did *not* commit!"

"Look, Thurman." Reed played with his pen. "Your client claims he didn't have sex with the victim. Claims he hadn't even been by the house. We know that's a lie. We know he was there and we know why.

"We know your client was drunk," the prosecutor continued. "And we also know that Delton is prone to violence. This is Florida, gentlemen. We fry first-degree killers here. And we do *not* use the sunshine."

"That's out of line," Thurman retorted with some genuine heat.

"Plead manslaughter." Reed shrugged.

"But I didn't kill her!" Delton's interjection startled Barrett, not for its content, which would have been expected, but for its tone. There was no swaggering stud here. This was the voice of a frightened man. A man fighting for his life.

"My God, Barrett, tell 'em!"

Delton was turning to him, now.

"I couldn't of killed her. You *know* that! I couldn't kill anybody!"

"You lied to me, Delton," Barrett said coldly.

"'Course I did!" Delton raised his awful arms in supplication. "I knew damn well if I tol' you I was over there you'd haul me in. But I didn't kill her. Honest to God, I did not!"

Barrett found himself actually harboring a shred of hope that his brother, somehow, was telling the truth.

Roland was under no such strain.

"Tell me something, Delton." Reed capped his pen. "When you screwed Ramona, was that before you killed her? Or after?"

"Don't dignify that with an answer, Delton," Thurman intervened.

But Barrett wasn't sure his brother had even heard the question. Delton was staring at some spot, some very small spot in the table before him. It was as if, suddenly, Delton was not even in the room.

Barrett had seen that look before. He remembered once when Delton had been called to the principal's office. A white boy name of Sands killed a cat and put it in the girls' bathroom. Then he told the principal Delton had done it.

Now, Delton *had* done lots of things when he was in school. Petty theft. Property damage. Fights. But Barrett knew Delton had nothing to do with that cat.

He wouldn't defend himself, though. Didn't even offer a denial. It was the oddest thing: Here was this boy already as big as a man who wouldn't back down from anyone. But when confronted with something he had not done, Barrett remembered, Delton had simply fixed his eyes on a spot, as if looking for some distant island, as the principal dealt him a dozen licks with the paddle.

Of course, it wasn't long after that that Delton got Rickie Sands on the school bus and beat the living shit out of him.

"Delton." Barrett lowered his head level with his brother's. "Just run through it again for us. Just the big pieces."

Delton ran a hand over his boulder skull.

"I went over there. I go in. All set for a shoutin' match. She owed me money. But she comes right out, 'Let's let bygones be bygones, Delton.' That's exactly what she said. And then she said, 'Let's have a drink.'"

"And of course you went along." Roland rolled his eyes.

"Wouldn't you?" Delton replied simply.

"Not that difficult to believe, is it, Roland?" Thurman Shaw turned in his chair. "The woman wasn't exactly stingy with her favors."

"But your client admits he was there," Roland retorted.

"I was there. Sure. We went to bed. I left."

Barrett knew damn well that everyone would like to know what went on in that bed. He was a little surprised when no one asked. Maybe Ramona's death had brought out some genuine decency in them. Maybe, even in death, she was the woman you wanted to talk *to* and not about.

"Okay, so you went to bed with her." Barrett decided it was time for him to step in. "You left the house, but then you went *back?*"

"Uh huh."

"Why, Delton?" Roland took it up. "You'd gotten laid. Gotten your trophy. Why go back?"

"'Cause we hadn't talked about the money," Delton answered. "I mean, I didn't *expect* her to be hot to trot. Once I saw she was, well—you don't stop something like that to talk. And once things got clickin'…"

Delton stalled. Thurman's turn to step in.

"What my client is saying is that once one of the most beautiful and provocative women any of us has ever seen invited my client to have sex, it was amour and not moola which preoccupied his admittedly inebriated mind. Is that hard for you to understand, Roland?"

"Not at all. In fact it *explains* why he came back. It was about the back pay, wasn't it, Delton?"

Roland for the first time left the wall.

"She suckered you, didn't she? Big Bad Delton comes over to claim his cash. She gives you a little nookie and sends you home!"

Reed rapped his pen sharply on the table.

"How far down the road did you get before you realized you'd been screwed twice, Delton?"

"It weren't like that!"

"You did come back, didn't you?"

"Well. Yeah."

"And you wanted your money, didn't you, Delton?"

"Well, sure I did!"

"But she wouldn't give it to you so you killed her."

"*No!*"

Thurman put a restraining hand on his client's shoulder.

"I came back, she was *dead*." Delton was breathing heavily. "She was dead when I got there!"

There was a shocked silence. Barrett found himself wondering if at least some of what he was hearing could be true. Finally he turned to his brother.

"Question, Delton."

"What?"

"Why'd you burn your shoes? The brogans—why'd you burn them?"

"They had blood," Delton replied as if that explanation ought to suffice. "They was blood all over the place. First I thought it was just the dog. But then I looked over the couch…"

Barrett nodded.

"It was…" Delton fumbled for words. "Terrible. I felt sick. It wasn't just the shoes. I burnt my shirt, pants—ever'thing!"

"I wish you'd called us." Barrett shook his head.

Delton strangled the laugh that leapt to his throat.

"Why, for God's sake?! Would you of believed me? Do you believe me *now*?!"

Barrett paused. Could he believe his brother? Did he want to? Did anyone?

"That's not the important question." Roland might have been reading his thoughts. "Whether Bear believes you. Whether I believe you. Makes no difference, does it, Delton? The important question is: Will a jury of men and women—locals, Delton. People who know you—will *they* believe you?"

"I'm stopping this right here." Thurman was rising from his chair.

"No," Delton objected softly.

But his attorney was already snapping his briefcase shut.

"You have a case, Roland?" Thurman said briskly. "You make it."

"No!" Delton placed his hand like a paw on his attorney's arm. "No trial, dammit. Not for me! Not in this town!"

Delton appealed to Roland Reed.

"I didn't kill her. But I might have an idea who. Or at least—why."

Barrett felt his heart leap, but he controlled it. This might not be anything after all. Probably wasn't. Just the desperate talk of a man facing a lynch mob.

"Go ahead," Barrett told his brother.

Delton's chest lifted with a lungful of air.

"Ramona was pushing a lot more out that restaurant than shrimp and lobsters."

"Oh, Christ, here it comes," Roland groaned. "Now you're going to tell us that Ramona Walker was a drug runner."

"Not drugs." Delton shook his head. "It was guns."

He turned to Barrett.

"Assault rifles. Kalishnikovs. Uzis. Just like TV."

"What a crock." Reed dismissed it flatly.

Thurman wasn't much happier about this new line.

"Delton," he said. "Maybe we should—"

Barrett cut Shaw off. "How do you know Ramona was running guns?"

"Heard her talking about it one night," Delton answered directly. "Her and Snake. Something about a Mexican. Buyer or somethin'. They figured to make a pile."

"A pile of shit," Roland said heatedly. "I'm surprised you didn't jump in yourself, Delton. Get rich right along with 'em."

"I tried to." Delton shrugged.

And for the first time people were paying attention.

"How?" Barrett asked.

"Blackmail," Delton replied.

Barrett jotted a note in his pad. Just another interview. Just like any other.

Thurman Shaw cleared his throat.

"Delton, as your attorney, I have to advise, strongly, against this."

"If I don't they're gon' nail me for murder."

He turned to Barrett.

"I got two payments from her. Cash. Twenty-five hundred each. Sure as hell weren't back pay."

"And you expected more?" Barrett made the note.

"I was s'posed to get more. She cut me off, though. Cut me off cold."

"Why?"

"I was a dumbshit. Played my hand too soon. Once she figured out I didn't know very much, couldn't of really proved anything, she tol' me to fuck off."

Delton waited for a reaction in the room. Nothing from Roland. Nothing from Thurman, not even a blink. He came back to his brother.

Nothing there, either.

"My God, Bear!" Delton was pleading. "If you don' believe me, who will?"

The session broke up shortly afterward. Thurman left to start paperwork for his client's bail. Barrett had Roach take Delton back to his cell. Then he and Roland went across to Chief Rawlings's office for a private debate.

Roland threw up his hands in disgust.

"Even if, *if!* everything Delton told us is true, what's it got to do with Ramona's murder? Other than give Delton a better reason to kill her?"

Barrett squeezed some honey into his coffee.

"Guess that'd be my job to find out."

"I can't believe we're even talking about this. Gun runners!"

"You said it'd take a month to go to trial," Barrett reminded him. "Why not let me follow up? What've we got to lose?"

"A *conviction!*" Roland exploded. "You'll be running around hell's half acre looking for the Man from Mexico when you *ought* to be looking for evidence of Ramona's murderer. Witnesses. A weapon—anything!"

"He's got a point, Bear." Smoot was probably more than an umpire for this discussion. Barrett knew that. He also knew better than to push too soon for Smoot's support. He might need it a whole lot more later on.

"I very much doubt that Ramona was running guns or anything else," Barrett soft-shoed. "But I do think a month oughta give us plenty of time to check Delton's story, that's all. Put it to rest."

"Let me tell you something." Roland pointed his pen at Barrett as though it were a pistol. "If I had any doubts at all that Delton Raines murdered Ramona Walker, *this* little tale obliterated 'em. Why do you think he invented this cock and bull anyway, Bear?! 'Cause he's scared! He's scared we'll nail him for what he did to Ramona and he'll do anything, *anything*, to throw us off track!"

Smoot regarded Barrett thoughtfully.

"What about it, Bear? Roland could be right."

"Maybe he is," Barrett shrugged. "Probably he is. But that's no reason not to check it out."

"How are you gonna check out a story like that?" Roland inquired archly.

"Well," Barrett said thoughtfully, "I expect I'll start by taking myself a little drive."

Chapter ten

I t was past five by the time Barrett started out of town. Deacon Beach really wasn't organized into anything like grids or blocks. The single sidewalk and curb which ribboned around the station house gave way quickly to blacktop streets that ran level with bahaya grass on either side. Fenced-in frame houses or beach houses or an occasional condo latched onto the blacktop like beads on a carelessly tossed necklace. Once you were past the necklace it was nothing but county roads and soft sandy loam that might lead out into nowhere.

Nowhere was pretty much where this particular road was taking Barrett now. He didn't mind, though. In fact, Barrett would take almost any excuse to drive into the lowlands which surrounded Deacon Beach. There was a wilderness out here filled with squirrels and deer and foxes and gophers and quail. Alligators, of course. An inventory of seagoing birds. Panther or two. Just about everything. Barrett could see a flight of egrets, now, spilling across the road ahead like a gaggle of eager schoolchildren. Their wings flashed a brilliant white against a sky gone indigo with the approach of a thunderstorm.

Barrett could hear distant static break over the FM station he'd tuned in. He tuned daily at this time to the university station at Tallahassee for Noah Adams and the National Public Radio news.

There were the usual depressing updates today about deficits and health care and yet another horror in Africa. But then things went on to a spirited debate between a Florida congressman and a California professor about the influence of the religious right on the Republican party. Barrett happened to think that the Republicans had grabbed themselves a tiger by the tail on this one. The party had been ecstatic during the Reagan years to get the Pat Robertson vote. Everyone on the right wanted to court Jerry Falwell and the Moral Majority. No one cared in those years about the tactics which Pat and Jerry and the rest used on those demon Democrats. But now, guess what? God's army was targeting fellow Republicans, well-respected officeholders who until now had been valued for their moderation in both ideology and politics.

"Nothing a zealot hates worse than somebody in the middle," Barrett mused aloud. He was thinking of Deacon Beach's home-grown zealot. Ferris Boatwright had come back from Dallas and the Southern Baptist Convention bragging about how "they" were going to shut down Texas's Baylor University and Senator Hutchinson in the same year.

Wouldn't that be one hell of an accomplishment?

Barrett was a good ten or fifteen minutes out of town, now. The county road stretched straight as a string before him, a wall of green on either side rising to a sky now threatening rain. There was a mailbox off to one side. You could see a small half-moon of rut worn away where the mailman daily swung off the hard road to make his appointed round.

Barrett swung off to make his.

*   *   *

Just as Bear remembered it, the house trailer rusted in an isolated stand of cypress and scrub oak. There was no window unit to cool the trailer. Nothing like central air. At least there was some shade. No need for that either at present. A gust of too-cool air came with the thunder that rumbled low against a sky turned black. Two unkempt black children, both girls, played nearby at a tire swing hung from a tree. A clothesline ran from the tree to a corner of the trailer. A haggard mother greeted Barrett and served him tea at the potting table outside the house.

They sat without speaking. Barrett accepted a refill, noting that Corrie Raines's glass remained untouched.

She sat there in cut-off Levis, her breasts spent and sagging beneath a faded denim top. Barrett was thinking that Corrie Raines had probably looked good a couple of years back in a halter and jeans. Back when that sturdy frame carried muscle instead of fat. But not now. He started his second glass of tea.

"Corrie, the only way I can help Delton is if you give me something to do it with."

"Oh, you'a big help, Barrett."

Corrie's mouth opened to smile, but then she closed it, embarrassed about her two missing front teeth. Barrett knew she didn't have the money to fix that little problem. In fact, she hadn't had the money to fix those teeth for the three years since Delton had knocked them out.

"Big help," she went on, closemouthed. "Always have been. When I usta get beat on, you were a big help, then. And when Delton was out of work you and Laurie Anne, why, y'all just bent over backwards helpin'."

"That's not fair, Corrie." Barrett still remembered the sight of her drinking coffee beside the phone.

"Guess we're just not good enough," she said breezily. "Wrong side of the tracks."

Somehow he'd managed to tell himself this wouldn't be like family.

"You know there's bad blood between Delton and me," Barrett admitted. "But that's got nothing to do with you or the children."

"Hell it don't. Look around, Bear! You see a Cadillac? A dryer? Clothes for the kids? It has *ever'thing* to do! With them *and* with me!"

There was no mistaking the hatred in that voice. She tossed her untouched tea to the sand.

"He loved me. I know he did."

She hitched up her halter.

"He could love me still."

"He'll pick up any woman has the time," Barrett said coldly.

"Any man will," she replied. "If he's got the chance. 'Cept you, huh, Bear? You never were much with the women, were you?"

Barrett put his own tea aside.

Corrie smiled then, unashamed. Ran her tongue through the space left by her missing teeth.

"Now, Delton—the women always come to *him*! Like bees to a blossom. You can't stand that, can you?"

She had let the halter drop over a swelling shoulder.

"Got nothing to do with it, Corrie." Barrett could feel himself blushing.

"What a goddamn liar you are!" she spit out. "You've always been jealous of Delton. Always! He whipped you in ever'thing that matters, hasn't he, Bear? Well, hasn't he?!"

"Easy does it, Corrie." Barrett's legs felt heavy as he rose from the table.

"But Barrett's done got him a badge!"

She hooked her thumbs in the loops of her Levis. Aping his posture. His manners. His movement.

"Yassuh, that Bear's done got him a *shiny* new badge! An' he hates gettin' his black ass whupped! Yes, he do! So what's he do with that badge, huh? You tell me, Bear!"

He couldn't say. He didn't even want to believe he could think it.

She cackled in his face.

"Time to turn the tables—am I right, Bear? You couldn't whip Delton's ass face-to-face. So you put his ass in jail. Hah! Some brother!"

Barrett grabbed her hands and held them in a vise. He could see his fists close around her bones.

Tighter. Tighter!

The knuckles popped cheerfully. Like small firecrackers.

Tears sprang into her eyes. But she kept smiling. A groan broke through those shattered teeth but she smiled, still.

He wondered if he could break her hands.

"Tell…me…somethin', Bear," she asked through clenched teeth. "Did you ever…get a piece…of anything…that Delton didn't…get first?"

He wanted to hit her. He wanted to wipe that idiot grin off that demented face. Give her a few more places to stick that tongue.

"Do it!" she urged him. "Show some…balls!"

And Barrett was going to. He was going to hit her with his fist when he remembered the girls. Two girls. Four and five. Whimpering from their swing.

Slowly, slowly—he let their mother go.

She just stood there, cradling her own hands.

"I may not be the best family, Corrie." Barrett was heaving like a distance runner. "But I'm the only brother Delton's got. If you wanta help him then by God you'd better help me 'cause there's not another soul'd rub two dimes together to save his sorry ass! And that's a fact."

Tears ran suddenly in rivers down her cheeks. She wiped them away furiously. And then—

"Why don't you come on in. I'll make us some more tea."

The girls were propped on pillows watching *Sesame Street* by the time Corrie strained enough boiled water through her used Lipton bags to make another, very weak pitcher of tea.

The trailer was not well kept inside. The girls' things (Corrie never called her children by name, only "the girls") were sorted by rough category, shoes and socks, shirts and underwear, into brightly colored plastic milk crates. They slept on a pallet beside the TV, which Barrett suspected was their near-constant nanny.

There was some Kool-Aid in the cupboard, Bear noticed. Some over-sugared cereal. Not much else. No produce. No fresh vegetables. It had begun to rain. Solitary, heavy drops. Barrett couldn't help glancing out the window to the verdant earth outside. Laura Anne would have a garden there.

Corrie rinsed out their glasses for the newly strained tea. "Thank you." Barrett accepted his tea, embarrassed suddenly by her bruised hand. He, an officer of the law, had done that.

It made Barrett wonder what else he was capable of doing. Jesus! He felt a pang of guilt and fear. Was he no better than Delton? Was there some seed in them both that—? Barrett shook it off. No. Don't blame anyone else. Don't blame any*thing* else. Just pick it up. Start over.

"Thank you, Corrie." He accepted sugar, this time.

She smiled through her shattered teeth. "You welcome."

Barrett turned to a fresh page in his spiral pad.

"Did Delton ever say anything about Ramona's business? I mean, when he was working for her?"

"Said she made money out the ass. Which I took literal."

"Delton see any of it?"

"Not 'til right at the end. He brought a wad home, then. Made more in those two months than he did in a year workin' off and on at the mill."

More than in a year—?

"How much money we talking about?" Barrett kept his voice casual.

"Nearly five thousand," she responded without hesitation. "And he 'spected to git more."

"How you know that?"

"We were talking 'bout gettin' us a house." She sat a little straighter in her aluminum-legged chair.

A house? Delton had money for a house?

"Damn." Barrett allowed a smile of his own. "Where were you thinking about buying?"

"Little two-bedroom over near the high school. It's still there. And now some teacher has it. She don't even have kids!"

Barrett listened carefully. It was important anytime you were asking questions to listen as closely for what was left unsaid as what was said openly. Corrie finished this last as if being single and childless, the teacher did not deserve the house on Cinnamon. As if, except for that single, selfish, white woman, Corrie would now be living in the lap of luxury with cable TV and air-conditioning, a leather sofa and lots of hot water.

"You think Ramona screwed you out of that house, don't you, Corrie?"

Corrie's lip curled to bare purple gums.

"Ramona fired him. Fired Delton just when things was goin' good. Just up and—let him go. He came home I knew something was funny. He *had* been real...Well. Real excited for a while."

"Excited?"

"Something at work." Corrie shrugged. Pouting. "He wouldn't tell me. I thought he was gonna move up. You know, like to bartender or somethin'. And then she ups and fires him."

Corrie took a sip of her twice-strained tea.

"There went my house."

So—Delton *had* acquired some extra money. Barrett was relieved to find verification, any verification, for any portion of his brother's story. Five thousand dollars, Corrie had said. Just as Delton claimed. But that didn't mean the money had come from blackmailing Ramona. Where else, Barrett wondered, might Delton have possibly acquired that kind of cash?

Could be drugs. Anyone who'd use drugs would sell them. But Barrett didn't think Delton pocketed five grand in two months by selling drugs. To sell five grand of anything you first had to have money to buy it and Barrett absolutely knew that no druggie anywhere would extend merchandise to Delton Raines on credit.

Where else, then? If it wasn't blackmail, where else might Delton have lucked into some money?

Barrett glanced out the window. The pines rose like sawteeth against a gray wall of rain.

"Delton ever play poker?" he asked abruptly.

"Sometimes," Corrie affirmed. "She was the poker player. Bitch. She'd go back there. Hike up those legs. No wonder those boys couldn't hold they cards. Hell, they had they hands in they pants."

"Any chance Delton could've got that cash at cards?"

Corrie hooted laughter. "You should be the one tellin' me! Did Delton ever win a hand in his life?"

No. He hadn't. Barrett had almost forgotten. Coming into his room after school one day he found his cash-kitty broken open. All the coins stolen. And he saw Delton the next day spilling dimes and nickels and quarters behind the gym.

No luck at cards. Still—

"I don't suppose Delton ever mentioned anybody else at those games? Snake Adders, for instance?"

"Not Snake." Corrie shook her head back and forth. "That man's still got the first penny he ever made. Now Splinter usta spread it around some."

"Splinter Townsend?"

Barrett had some memory of a child-support case which involved Splinter. He was a bony, red-necked mechanic. Mostly unemployed. Always had a toothpick or matchstick in his mouth.

"Splinter likes the cards, huh?"

"Mmmhmm. And they like him." Corrie leaned forward. "There's a cabin-cruiser down at Esther's Marina he owns free and clear. And it wasn't on no bank note, neither."

"Hell of a player." Barrett was jotting notes.

"But not Delton." Corrie returned to the earlier subject. "Naw. He never had any luck."

Barrett stopped writing.

"You'd take him back, wouldn't you, Corrie?"

She waved her arm like a wand about the trailer.

"Here's my castle. I got two kids. I get four sixty-five an hour at the dry cleaner's. If he'll put bread on my table, Delton can have my bed any time."

Barrett didn't doubt for a moment that he could.

"Thanks for the tea." He closed his spiral pad.

"Ever'body's all upset, ain't they? About Ramona."

"She had a lot of friends," Barrett said.

"Not me."

For the first time Corrie looked him straight in the eye.

"It was Ramona came between me and Delton."

Was there something else here? Something else he hadn't seen?

"She run him off from me," Delton's ex declared.

"Now, Corrie." Barrett watched her closely. "You don't know that. You don't know that Ramona had anything to do with you and Delton."

"Hell I don't."

And for just a moment Barrett could see that hate come back into her eyes. Corrie didn't seem to care that he saw.

"Delton was fine 'til he started with her. Got him a taste o' that white meat. Bitch. I'm glad she's dead."

She looked Barrett straight in the eye.

"Wish to God I'd done it myself."

Chapter eleven

Frank Sienna was well into his final approach onto a strip which clung to the Old River like a dirty Band-Aid when the birds burst like flak into his windscreen.

Only minutes before Frank had been nose-heavy at a thousand feet and 2400 normally aspirated RPM with no certain idea whether he'd even be able to find the dirt runway whose coordinates only that morning had been marked on his chart.

Frank liked to fly, liked a challenge, and liked the primitive terrain which lay shrouded in mists below. There was a lot of history down there. The Old River, for instance, had served in the tenth century as a major artery for the most advanced civilization in the Americas. Nothing advanced down there, now, though. Kiskadees. Tapirs. The best of the lumber was already cut, the hardwoods and pine, cedar and rosewood. You could still make out where the British had stripped the jungle for mahogany. That activity peaked out in the late nineteenth, early twentieth century, back when the place was still known as British Honduras.

There were still plantations, of a sort, which thrived mistily below. But the owners of these concerns were not interested in agriculture. Their well-kept estates and guarded peripheries appeared only briefly through the jungle canopy. Fleetingly. Ethereally. Like dollhouses peeping damply through a swath of cotton.

Frank rolled in some trim to relieve the back pressure he had felt since his descent to a thousand feet. The nose came up just fine. If there had been a horizon to see, Frank had no doubt the Cessna would be on it wings-level and solid as a bird dog.

This Cessna 172 belonged to Frank's supplier. The supplier couldn't be reached in the rainy season except by air. It was a purposeful exile and Frank didn't mind. It gave him some free hours in the left seat. And, of course, the challenge.

"I can have someone bring you in." Armstead had smiled politely. "You can try it yourself, of course, but it won't be easy to find and I can't offer you the courtesy of any radioed communication."

He was British, was Armstead. A British expatriate in a land of Kekchis and black Caribs and a half-dozen other mixed and mingled gene pools. He was very blond, was Mr. Armstead. Very polite. He got his Uzis from a dealer in Nigeria. The ammunition he got in lots of five and ten million from Korea. Which Korea didn't much matter.

"Just have the plane ready," Frank told him. "And half a million rounds."

Frank smoothed the sectional which he had spread over the copilot's empty seat and checked a projected position against the Garman GPS he'd packed for the trip. Two clicks more downwind and he could turn on base knowing that his satellite-based navigator was accurate to a matter of meters.

But there was no instrument landing system on the unimproved runway which Frank had added to his chart.

You had to be able to see the strip to land on it, and once you committed your aircraft to its descent you only had four minutes or so to acquire a visual reference. After that, physics being what it was, you'd be plowing at seventy or eighty miles an hour into an ancient and unforgiving soil.

Frank knew there was a runway down there somewhere, but at a thousand feet he couldn't see it. Overcast was the way a pilot might describe the usual flight conditions in Belize at this time of year. Overcast with limited visibility. And today was considerably worse than usual. Frank pulled back the power to 1800 RPM, and as he banked thirty degrees onto a base leg he toggled in half-flaps and rolled in more trim for a gentle slope to seven hundred feet of altitude.

From here on in it was instinct. How long should he stay on base, that imaginary corridor in the air which stood at right angles to the end of a runway he could not see, before he turned ninety degrees again to establish his final approach?

Frank kept a mental stopwatch. Six seconds. Eight. He banked once more. Thirty degrees of bank and descending on a line which, if he timed it perfectly, would be at right angles to his base leg and aligned perfectly upwind on a runway which—dammit!—he still could not see.

Clouds of mist and moisture drifted past the windscreen. Four hundred feet. Three hundred. Power's fine. Flaps—go full. Airspeed—indicating seventy-five miles an hour. His aircraft could actually approach more slowly than that, but Frank wanted the extra airspeed in case he had to go around and at the very instant when he passed two hundred feet without a visual and thought he would in fact be forced to pull back into the cotton sky, there it was—

It materialized out of the mist, an iron-red fairway gouged narrowly between walls of jungle green. Instinctively Frank adjusted his glide slope to the mental picture he'd honed a thousand times. A little hot. His right hand eased the throttle back another notch.

That's when the birds burst like flak from the end of the runway.

Frank had done this hundreds of times, landed a Cessna on an unfamiliar field. But no matter how many times you did it there was always something that could bite you in the ass. He took a bird in the prop. Just a flash of white and then *bam!*—a sheet of blood on the windscreen and the whole plane started shaking. Shaking like hell with a violent, violent yaw to the right.

Frank hit the left rudder and pulled the throttle back to the rings. Mixture back full. No engine now. Nothing but a twisted piece of metal out front and a windshield covered in blood and guts. Little more rudder. Aileron.

And put that nose down, down! Keep that airspeed! Frank was flying blind and without power, easing fifteen hundred pounds of aluminum and fuel and flesh to the earth at seventy or so miles an hour hampered by what in lighter moments might be described as a feathered prop.

Twenty feet, ten. Frank made his flare looking out the side for a reference.

He touched down without a chirp. Both feet gently on top of the rudders. He braked moderately and straight ahead. Shut down the radios, other electrics, master switch. Set the brake.

Frank had gathered his grip and logbook and was looking for the plastic cap that protected the pitot tube when Armstead appeared on his strut with an Uzi submachine gun.

"I could have had my man bring you in." The Brit was smiling.

"Got my rounds?"

"Naturally."

Frank found the pitot cap. "Been your man I'd be dead," he said.

And climbed out of the cockpit.

Chapter twelve

Ben rifled Tyndall a perfectly spiraled snurfball in a fourth-quarter drive down the fruit juice aisle. Laura Anne trailed her children, a bemused spectator, as the boys set up their first downs and fifty-yard lines on the Del Monte pineapple and Hi-C displays. A touchdown now waited mere tiles away. A pyramid of jarred peaches marked the goal line. Mounds of melons piled up like Penn State linebackers to provide an imagined defense. A new play was hatched beside their mother's cart. Another pass. The spongy ball skipped off Tyndall's first-grade fingers.

"Interference!" The youngster aped an adult ballplayer's outrage.

"You just missed it." Ben managed to convey resignation and disgust at the same time.

"*You* threw b'fore I was ready!" Tyndall scrambled back down the aisle.

"Boys, settle down," Laura Anne cautioned, but the boys were off.

Tyndall snatched up the snurfball. Ben ran for his make-believe life.

"Tyndall!" Laura Anne called out.

Down the aisle they went. Shrieking like two little Indians. Except of course they were not Indians. Ben and Tyndall were just children. Black children. And with their mother they were the only people of color in the store.

Tyndall was almost on top of Ben now, almost ready for an open-field tackle when Ferris and Martha Boatwright blundered like twin hippos around the corner.

"*Boys!*" Laura Anne cringed as Ben and Tyndall bounced off the Boatwrights' cart.

Ferris and Martha looked along after the two youngsters. Just stood in the aisle looking. Laura Anne brought up the rear—

"Morning, Ferris. Martha. My, you're looking well!"

Not a word in reply. Ferris and his wife remained beside their shopping cart as if they didn't know the boys who had just gamboled by. As if they had never seen Laura Anne or gone to church with her or sat at the same table with her. As if she was not native to their region.

Laura Anne forced a smile to her face. The boys were in another aisle now. She'd just go settle them down.

That was when Betty Townsend appeared at her side.

Betty looked awful. A waitress's polyester uniform hung on her rail-thin figure like socks on a rooster. A single basket dangled from a bony wrist. Laura Anne nodded recognition to Splinter Townsend's wife.

"Betty. How you doin'?"

"Oh. All right." She wrung nervous, dishwater hands together. "Could be better, I s'pose."

"You're working hard, I know." Laura Anne tried to avoid the Boatwrights' hostile inspection.

"I just hope they don't fire me." Betty's voice almost broke.

"Fire you? Who's gonna fire you?" Laura Anne left the safety of her cart. "Who's 'they'?"

"Whoever takes over the rest'runt now that—well. Now that Ramona's gone."

"You don't know who's taking over?" Laura Anne clucked compassion. "Not even a manager?"

"Nobody seems to know anything."

A different edge came to Betty's voice. A hard, accusatory edge. "Somebody said she didn't even have a will. Who could blame her? She was still young."

"Yes, she was," Laura Anne agreed.

"And she was my friend!" Betty rushed on. "She took care of me when—when Splinter wouldn't!"

"I know. I'm sorry, Betty."

Laura Anne tried to retreat. But there were Martha and Ferris. Immobile. Massive.

"Tell you what—" Betty took a rigid step into Laura Anne's face. "And you can tell Barrett for me!"

"Betty!"

"You tell him! The man who killed Ramona Walker—whoever he is! He oughta die hard. You hear me? He oughta—he oughta—!"

Betty Townsend burst into tears, her single basket dangling from an emaciated wrist like a corsage.

A circle of customers had accumulated by now. Local folks. Neighbors. All converging around Laura Anne and Betty, pulled over by Betty's cries. Barrett's wife thought they were congregating to help.

"Here, Betty." Laura Anne moved to comfort the woman. "Come on, now. There's nobody gonna take your job."

Laura Anne reached out to take Betty's hand.

She slapped it away.

"I don't need pity!"

"Betty, I—"

Laura Anne turned embarrassed to find herself surrounded by white faces. All locals. All familiar. Neighbors.

And not one was looking at Betty. They were all looking at her.

Laura Anne placed a hand on her cart. Tried to ease it back. She was blocked. There were carts before her. The Boatwrights were behind. A couple more to the side.

And Betty screaming at her from the floor.

"You just tell Barrett, brother or no! If Delton Raines killed

Ramona Walker he should *hang*—you hear me? He should hang and burn in *hell!*"

"I have to go now, Betty."

"You tell Barrett!"

"I have to go," Laura Anne repeated quietly. "Boys?"

Nowhere in sight.

"Boys, we need to go." Laura Anne announced her intentions with another gentle effort to free her cart.

But she was trapped in a cordon of men and women with hostile faces—people who used to be familiar. Laura Anne felt shame rush irrationally and irrefutably to her own face.

"May I leave? Please?"

There was a kind of smirk, then, from the gathered circle. Some kind of satisfaction. But no one moved until—

"Touchdown!"

Ben and Tyndall danced at the aisle's end. High voiced. Innocent.

"Ben!" Laura Anne called out. *"Ben and Tyndall! Over here!"*

The boys caromed through the gathered locals like a pair of bowling balls, split Martha and Ferris like a pair of pins.

Laura Anne shoved her cart into the breach.

"Time to go, boys."

She was past them, then. Past the contemptible, stony gazes. Past the sudden, unexpected hate. The embarrassment. The shame.

Laura Anne was just about past it all when Tyndall's sneakered foot snagged a single jar of peaches from its pyramid. The jar fell forever. Burst like a grenade on the floor. And then the whole pyramid followed. Peaches and broken glass and syrup exploded all over the Winn-Dixie's polished tile. All across the aisle.

There would be no retreat now. Laura Anne returned to the malignant stares of persons whom until this moment she would have regarded as neighbors and friends.

Ben and Tyndall had abandoned worksheets and arithmetic for *The A-Team* by the time Barrett pulled his squad car nose-to-nose with the tarped-over Malibu. Machine-gun slugs ripped in rerun through the bad guys. Mr. T took a grenade with barely a flinch. Laura Anne was snapping string beans at the kitchen counter.

Bear gathered the remote control from the couch.

"Daddy! It's almost over!"

The protest came in chorus.

"It sure is," Barrett acknowledged cheerfully, killing the tube and dropping heavily into the sofa.

He turned then to the lady snapping beans in the kitchen.

"Why're you letting the boys watch this?"

"Just wasn't paying attention."

"Laura Anne, it doesn't do any good to have rules about TV unless—"

"Unless I enforce them, is that it? Well, what about you, Bear? Why don't you enforce the rules awhile?"

He cradled the remote in the palm of his hand.

"What's wrong, Laura Anne?"

"Tell you later."

Her fingers flew at her work.

Barrett jabbed the remote again. The television came back to life on a different channel. A good-looking, badly dressed anchor-woman droned Channel 7's latest.

"...Local citizens were glad to hear, today, that an arrest has been made in connection with the murder of Ramona Walker."

The boys perked up with the familiar name.

"Change the channel," Laura Anne said.

"They're gonna hear it anyway. Rather they heard it with us."

Barrett had made a careful cocoon around his sons. So far as Ben and Tyndall knew, Delton was sinless in the world. The elder brother's recent history was never discussed. His earlier exploits were sufficiently remote as to be rarely encountered; the boys were infants, after all, when Delton was raising hell and other things at Florida State.

History was dangerous. Barrett worked hard to keep his sons' minds set on the future. For Ben and Tyndall, finishing college was not presented as an option for advancement but a requirement for life. Blissfully ignorant of Delton's college past and completely insulated from his criminal present, the boys regarded Uncle Delton with uncritical admiration and affection. And Delton, on those rare occasions which brought him in contact with the boys, was a perfect and ever-playful elder brother. An untarnished hero. Until this.

The TV anchor stared straight into her prompter.

"Delton Raines has been charged with the brutal murder and possible rape of the local businesswoman—"

"Uncle Delton?" Ben made the connection before Tyndall.

"Charged, son. Not convicted."

"One intriguing aspect of this case is that the investigating officer, Detective Barrett Raines, is the accused man's younger brother—"

"Daddy?!"

Tyndall this time.

"Just listen for now, son."

"Our man on the scene, Stacy Kline, asked Detective Raines how the detective could remain objective while investigating his only brother. The detective was quick to reply—"

"Look, Mama! Daddy's on the TV!"

And there he was. Turned quite deliberately away from Channel 7's camera.

"Delton Raines will get the same consideration as any other citizen under the law. No more. No less."

The anchor's white face replaced the cop's black one onscreen.

"No more. No less. That would seem, in this case, a difficult standard to uphold. Chief of Police Smoot Rawlings has nevertheless expressed complete—"

The television went blank with a ping. Barrett Raines turned his attention to his children.

"Are you putting Uncle Delton in jail, Daddy?"

That was Ben. Little Ben. Always seeing the heart of the problem.

"When there's cause to make an arrest I have to make it, son. No matter who it is."

"But he didn't do anything," Tyndall protested. And then—"Did he?"

"If he didn't he doesn't have anything to worry about." Barrett repeated the cliché mechanically. And then, trying to sound more convincing, "That's why we have trials, son. That's why we have judges and juries."

"But do they…?"

The question died in the air.

"Yes, Ben?"

"Do they ever make mistakes?"

Laura Anne pulled an ivory-handled brush through hair silky straight and black as ebony. It was Laura Anne's one concession to vanity, her hair. And normally this would be a peaceful time for her and for Bear. He was in the shower now. You could see the steam roll out and fog the mirror above their single sink. He would come out, towel off. Dress for work. Sometimes Bear would sit beside her, take that brush, pull it through her hair…and then, sometimes, on to other things.

Not tonight.

"What happened today, honey? What's wrong?"

Barrett settled in beside her, ignoring the brush.

She glanced at the holster he had slung at his shoulder. The weapon. Then at the vest he'd left in the closet.

"I wish you weren't on this case."

"No choice," he replied.

"There's always a choice, Bear."

She turned to him, high and yellow and firm. Barrett stroked her cheek gently.

"Hell, he might not even be guilty. He might get off."

"If he does, they'll say it's because you covered up." Laura Anne withdrew. "And if he's convicted, they'll say you wanted it. They'll say you played the hangman."

Barrett remembered Corrie's vitriol. Laura Anne turned once more to the mirror and her hair.

"There is one other alternative, though, isn't there?"

"What?" She paused.

"Somebody else might have done it," Bear replied simply. "I might find out who."

"Delton makes another mess. You clean it up. Is that it?"

"Always has been."

"You've done enough."

"Not according to Corrie," he grunted, massaging his hand.

"She's made her bed." Laurie was suddenly cold. "Let her lie in it."

Barrett raised his face to the one in the mirror.

"Sorry," Laura Anne's voice quavered. "That sounded mean."

"Something else goin' on here, Laura Anne? Anything I ought to know?"

"Something's always going on!"

She finally put down the damn brush.

"And it's always Delton. Whoring! Drinking! Beating his wife! We have a family. We try to be decent. And none of it counts!"

"Sure it does."

He tried to pull her close. She shrugged free.

"You. Me. The children! We're all the Raines Bunch. Same blood, right? Same as Delton!"

"Laura Anne—"

"And if the blood's bad, what the hell—nothing you can do about it—everything else is bad, too!"

"That's not true," Barrett objected. "You know that's not true."

Barrett wrapped his arms around her middle. So firm in there. So warm.

"This'll pass, honey," he promised her. "It'll be over and when it is I'm going to claim my overtime and sick leave, every day of my vacation—"

"And we'll go off?"

She burrowed into his chest.

"Just you and me and the boys," he assured her. "No bad guys. And no Delton Raines."

Barrett held her face to his own. They kissed slowly. It lingered. Finally—

"I'll be back."

"Take your vest."

"I'll be back."

Barrett left his wife and his vest in the bedroom. Laura Anne switched off the light at her vanity.

Something else to worry about.

Chapter thirteen

A pair of ice cubes chased each other in a whirlpool of bourbon. Snake Adders trained his blue eye and his brown one carefully on the swirling fluid before, satisfied of its potency, he downed it in a gulp.

Barrett Raines had his spiral pad opened beside the Jack Daniel's Black which, Bear noticed, Snake seemed a long way toward killing.

The bottle tipped now toward him.

"Sure you won't?"

"Not on the job, Snake."

"Never shied away b'fore."

"Let's say I'm being extra cautious." Barrett eased the bottle away.

"We finished here?" Snake asked.

Barrett had been at the bar, questioning Snake pretty gently, for less than ten minutes.

"Almost done," Barrett reassured Snake with a smile. "Now about this dog—"

Snake stiffened suddenly.

"What dog?"

"Come on," Barrett eased him on genially. "Ramona's dog. The collie. Seems you had a little extra responsibility?"

Snake reminded Barrett, squirming as he was on his bar stool, of some of the nightcrawlers Barrett had seen writhing on a cane pole's hook.

"Snake?" Barrett tapped his pen on the bar. "What about this job with the dog?"

"Ramona'd usually eat at home. But not Fridays. Friday was her big night. She liked to be here, you know, for the customers and all."

"What time would she be at the restaurant?"

"Three or so," Snake replied. "And then she'd stay," he added quickly. "'Til we closed out the register."

"So somebody had to go back to her place." Barrett pretended to jot a note. "Let the dog out. That it?"

"That's about it." Snake finished his drink.

"And that was your job—walking that dog," Barrett went on.

"My job now," Snake said. "When Delton was here, it was his."

"Chickenshit job," Barrett commented drily.

"So's yours," Snake flared. "I don't see you complainin'."

Barrett thought for a moment Snake was going to let his hostility out into the open. But then the white man retreated into his empty glass.

"How'd you get in the house, Snake?"

"Spare key," the bartender replied. "She kept one by the door."

"Mmmhmm. I guess Delton would've known about that."

"He'd of had to, wouldn't he? To get in."

Barrett rewarded the sarcasm with a gentle smile. "Anybody else getting in?"

"Hell, I don't know. It wasn't a fort if that's what you mean."

"You don't get along with Delton, do you, Snake?"

"You don't either."

"Let's stick with you, Snake." Barrett dropped his smile. "What about it? You got a hard-on for Delton or don't you?"

He pulled back the bottle Barrett had put away.

"Let's just say I don't get along with assholes and Delton's a grade-A asshole."

Definitely in the open now.

"Don't hold back." Barrett penned a note.

"Ask anybody."

Snake was tired of the old cat and mouse. He was going to open up. Yep. More bourbon in the tumbler.

"Delton. Shit." Snake dragged a hand across his mouth. "Shoulda fired him the first week."

"Why's that?"

"Hell, he'd show up late. He'd let the kegs go dry. Skim cash off the register."

"You're sure about that? About the register?" Barrett inquired crisply.

"Why he got fired," Snake said, as if that were the most common knowledge in the world. And then amended, "One reason among others, anyway."

Barrett decided to let that last go for the moment.

"Why do you s'pose Ramona ever hired Delton to begin with?"

"You'd have to ask her." Snake smirked.

"I can't." Barrett's reply seemed to remind Snake that Ramona was dead.

The bartender tossed back another Black Label.

"Ramona was a sexy woman. Delton's a stud. You might not like the sunnuva bitch but you do have to give 'im that. I think she liked havin' the bastard around."

"You think she took him to bed?"

"None of my business."

"Ramona ever take you to bed, Snake?"

"None of your business." But he flushed.

"It is now," Barrett replied.

By now the ice had melted in Snake's empty tumbler. Barrett snapped his notepad shut.

"One other thing."

"Make it quick," Snake grated.

"Who handles the cash?"

"Whatta you mean?" Snake came back slowly.

He knows what I mean, Barrett thought. He knows exactly.

"The cash, Snake. From the restaurant. Who counts it? Reconciles the register? Keeps receipts?"

"That'd be me," Snake answered sullenly. "Well—Ramona'd help now and then. But it's my job."

"Must be quite a bit of cash goes through a place like this." Barrett surveyed the empty tables which spread around them. "Lots of seafood. Booze."

"She did all right," Snake replied cautiously.

"Uh huh," Barrett agreed. Pocketed his spiral pad.

And without preamble turned for the door.

"Delton did it, Bear!" Adders called to his back. "He killed her."

"Man's innocent until proved guilty, Snake. You know that."

Barrett stiff-armed the door with his left hand and didn't break stride until he hit the street.

Chapter fourteen

Splinter Townsend wormed a toothpick back and forth over a pair of aces that went unnoticed. Frank Sienna popped his Zippo open, then shut. Open and shut. Open and shut. Hoyt's young hands quivered as always like willows in the wind. The poker table's lampshade sliced Snake Adders's face into hemispheres of light and shadow. His blue eye sparkled in the back room.

"He's askin' about the money. The receipts!"

"He's just barking." Sienna snapped his lighter shut.

"Doesn't sound like a bark to me." Hoyt's voice wavered almost as badly as his hands.

"Could be the man's just doing his job," Frank replied tiredly. "Ever think of that—any of you? A woman's killed. A cop's got his brother on the grill. Doesn't it make sense Barrett's gonna turn over some rocks?"

"I just wish it wasn't Delton in jail."

"He's a fucking jungle bunny. That's all."

"He was more than that to Ramona."

"Bullshit," Frank retorted.

"She was taking him to bed."

"She'd take a fuckin' horse to bed."

"Naw, but it was more than that." Snake shivered.

"Snake, you got something to say, say it."

Adders pulled a card nervously off the deck.

"Ramona was having some kind of problem with Delton."

"What, you mean the buck couldn't get it up?" Splinter hooted laughter.

"Shut up," Frank said.

The laughter gargled just a moment in Splinter's throat before it died.

"What kind of problem?" Sienna turned poker-faced to Snake.

"She said it was back pay." Snake shrugged his shoulders.

"Any reason to think it wasn't?"

"I'm...not sure."

"Not sure!" Hoyt's voice rose in panic. "You were *there*, for God's sake! You keep the receipts!"

"Shut up, Hoyt."

Hoyt fell instantly silent. So did the others. Frank took time to light a Marlboro.

"Now, listen up. We've got a buyer can make us rich. He pays cash. He wants guns and more important he appears to want them on an ongoing basis. But we have a package to deliver first. No biggie. Just some ammo. Half a million rounds. The spick gets his bullets—we get our bucks. Okay? Plus the chance for God knows how much more down the line. We are not gonna piss that opportunity away because we panicked."

Frank paused. Splinter cleared his throat.

"What do you want us to do?"

"I'll need the boat over the weekend," Sienna replied.

"She's ready." Splinter nodded.

Frank shrugged. "Then get outta here. Go home. Low profile, gentlemen. We do not want to draw attention to ourselves."

Ramona's players rose to leave. Sienna aimed his cigarette at her bartender—

"Snake. Wait up a minute, would you?"

Hoyt Young and Splinter Townsend ducked out the door.
Sienna crushed a Marlboro pack in his fist.

"How much we got in the kitty?"

"Fifty thousand," Snake replied. "More or less."

"I'll need twenty-five to cover the ammo. Prob'ly five more to
cover shipping. Armstead's gonna boat it across. How're the receipts
looking?"

"Closed out for the month."

"Good. Get me thirty grand. Everything else: cash, guns—I
want cleared out. Tonight."

"Tonight?" Snake seemed taken aback.

"I didn't stutter," Sienna said irritably.

But Snake didn't respond. Not right away. And he didn't leave.
Instead he took a seat across the folded cards from Frank Sienna.

"If everything's all right, how come I'm covering our tracks?"

"Just covering our bets." Sienna remained deadpan.

"It's Delton, isn't it? There is something."

"Don't go soft on me, Snake."

"Nobody's soft!" Snake burst out angrily.

"I don't know any more about Delton than you," Frank
reassured him calmly. "Bring me the thirty. Everything else—out.
Tonight."

Snake left the chips to Frank. Sienna waited for the door to
close. Waited for Snake's footsteps to recede in the empty restaurant beyond before he bent to the floor and fished a phone in by
its line.

He tapped in a number, barely got the receiver to his ear—

"It's Frank. Caught you working?...No, I'm down at Ramona's. Barrett Raines was by.... Raines, yeah.... No, he's gone, now.
Gave Snake a real once-over, though. Sounded real interested in the
money.... The restaurant, right.... Nothing specific, no. One question for you: Are we covered? Good. Let's keep it that way. What?...
Clean, right. As a spanked baby's fanny."

Barrett had left his wife warm in bed to begin a midnight shift. A
pink glow on the horizon told the detective it was almost over. He

was tired. He hadn't been able to sleep before his night's work and he knew he'd probably have to go in for at least part of the day's. He'd parked the cruiser with a view of the water and now rolled down the windows hoping to clear the cobwebs behind his burning eyes.

It was nice out. The previous day's storm had washed some of the oppressive humidity from the air. There was a pleasant breeze coming off the Gulf. There were still stars in the predawn, bright and shining overhead.

Kind of night a man ought to've been in bed, Barrett reflected.

He rolled up the windows and fired up the Crown Vic. A minute or two later Barrett pulled through Ocean and Chavis at one of the town's few traffic lights, stayed on Ocean for about a mile, took a right on SeaWay, and there, open to the bay, dark and lonely against the water, was Ramona's restaurant.

Local businessmen were falling over each other trying to buy out the business. There were even investors coming in from Jacksonville and St. Augustine. Ferris and Martha Boatwright protested that ownership should remain local and had themselves made loud offers to acquire the place, commenting as they did so that, since they were Baptist, the restaurant under their management would naturally cease to serve anything like beer, wine, or liquor.

There weren't too many folks rooting for the Boatwrights' success.

Ramona had years before made Doc Hardesty executor of her estate. Doc just told Snake to keep the place running until things could be sorted out. The restaurant itself was not connected to Ramona's murder by anything other than Delton's accusation. Nevertheless, Barrett had obtained a warrant and searched the premises. Nothing turned up that looked anything like a gun. And Ferris reported that the books were in order.

So there wasn't any particular reason Barrett should be out here at six in the morning at all. Nothing, except perhaps the urge to stay near the water. Or perhaps there was some instinct working deeply suggesting that things at Ramona's were not as they seemed.

The place brought back memories, Barrett thought to himself as he played his cruiser's spot over the exterior of the building. Nothing going on this early, though. Everything shut down. Barrett played the spot back once more, almost playfully as he reversed the car to leave.

But something stopped him.

Was that a light?

Barrett directed the spotlight through the dining area's large windows. Gargoyles took shape in the shadows inside. Nothing else.

And yet, just now, as he was backing up, Barrett thought he had seen just a fleeting pencil of illumination. Just a small beam of light lancing through the main dining area. Could just be his own spotlight, maybe. Refracted somehow in the restaurant's interior.

He stopped the car, released the Velcro which secured his flashlight to the dash, and thumbed the radio's push-to-talk.

"PD-2 to Deacon Beach Police."

"Dispatch here, Bear."

That would be Roach. Roach was very casual with radio protocol. And prone to be casual with just about everything else.

"Roger, Dispatch, be informed I am 10–20 outside the Walker restaurant. Thought I'd just do a little walk-around."

"Roger that, Bear."

"Requesting radio check."

Barrett turned down the volume on his cruiser's radio. Barrett carried, as did every officer on patrol, a radio rigged at the belt which ran a mike clipped at the epaulet of his windbreaker. The belt radio wasn't intended to reach the station; its signal was picked up by the cruiser's radio, boosted, and repeated. With this system an officer with a light, five-watt radio could stay in contact with his Dispatch miles distant.

Barrett triggered the mike on the lifeline at his shoulder.

"Check one, two, over."

"That's a 10–26, Bear. Good hunting."

Barrett left his cruiser. The flashlight left a feeble pearl pool which rippled over the sand that bordered the restaurant. Barrett decided to check the back first. Back where the dining area faced out to the water.

He followed the north perimeter of the restaurant, soft sand already pouring into his socks, and as he turned the corner to reach the west and rear perimeter of the restaurant Barrett saw Snake Adder's van.

It was hidden behind the restaurant, on the beach, beneath the windows that looked over the bay. Unmistakable murals sprawled the length of the vehicle. A psychedelic sunset blossomed out of a bikini blond's belly button. Seashells and other ocean creatures of various kinds swam in brilliant and unnatural shades of red and turquoise.

The thing was, if Snake had just parked out front and kept on the lights Barrett wouldn't have been the least curious. Snake worked here, after all. And it would be reasonable, especially since Ramona's death, to see Snake working at odd hours. He could be repairing some equipment. Or more likely trying to reconcile the cash register—everyone knew how bad Snake was at *that*.

"But why the hell's he parked back here?" Barrett wondered.

And why the hell hadn't he switched on the lights?

Barrett triggered the mike on his shoulder.

"PD-2 to Deacon Beach Police."

"Come in, Bear."

"Got a possible Signal-15 here, Roach. Do you copy?"

"10–4, that's a Signal-15 possible."

"Send me backup. I'm going in."

Ramona's bar was an island in the middle of the dining area. A high counter enclosed the bar on four sides so that Snake Adders was completely concealed inside. Even so, Snake had seen Bear's spotlight play over the wine glasses hanging from their crystal stems like butchered pullets overhead. He was on the floor at that moment, juggling a flashlight and a corkscrew from his Swiss Army knife. For a few, heart-stopping moments Snake ceased his labor. But then there was nothing. Nothing but darkness.

Just some headlights, Snake told himself. Just somebody toolin' along the beach.

He went back to work. A square of plywood around three feet by three feet was set into the floor. Snake had already pulled back the beer-soaked carpet which concealed the plywood panel. The object of his labor was hidden in a cavity beneath. Snake used his corkscrew to get a purchase on a fingerhole drilled into the panel. Then he yanked the plywood cover free.

There was a recess beneath the floor perhaps three feet by three feet square and another three or so deep. Inside that hidden keep Snake's narrow beam found a floor safe. Nothing fancy. Just an American Security vault fireproofed with concrete. Snake trained the flashlight on a combination lock. Spun the dial.

Barrett made his approach through the kitchen. The dining area's sea-facing windows were set much too high to allow Barrett a peek inside and even if they had been lower he'd have been loath to risk it. Too easy to be silhouetted in those large plate-glass windows. So Barrett chose the kitchen.

He had already pulled his weapon from its holster. A pain in the ass, now, to manipulate the revolver, the flashlight, and the enormous ring of keys which Bear had taken from his belt. Barrett had keys for several residences and most businesses along the Beach. Most folks wanted him to have easy access in case of an emergency. Ramona had given Barrett a key to her restaurant long ago.

Not her home, though. It was Delton who'd rated a key to her residence.

Time to shake that off.

He unlocked the door and tucked his light into his armpit, reclipped the keys to his belt. Then he pulled his revolver's hammer back two clicks to single-action. And eased into the kitchen that used to be Ramona's.

Snake was almost finished. Only a couple of sacks left. He lifted them carefully out of the floor safe and uncovered as he did so one last deposit.

An Uzi assault rifle nestled clipped and armed in the bottom of the vault. Snake retrieved the weapon. Retrieved a half-dozen or so clips of ammunition. All he had to do now was replace the panel and carpet. He'd be outta there.

Barrett swung his flashlight left and right around the kitchen. It was deserted. Nothing but ovens and cutting tables and refrigerators like obelisks. Three huge grills stood silent as nuns beneath their sheet-metal hoods. A long cutting table ran down the center of the kitchen. A variety of cookery hung from a rack overhead, bread pans and broilers and ladles and sieves. There were knives, too, neatly racked; their blades gleamed long and silver in the fitful moon that spilled through vacant windows.

Barrett stepped quickly to the door which separated the kitchen from the restaurant's interior. It was a steward's door. A gravity hinge allowed free passage from the kitchen to the diners beyond. A large porthole set at eye level in the door was designed to prevent collisions between waiters and waitresses running in and out. Through that round window Barrett scanned the dining room.

Looked empty as a grave. Linens draped like shrouds over the tables. Chairs were upended on top. The bar rose almost dead center amidst the ghosts of absent diners. Its crystal snifters and chalices and jiggers either hung or were stacked above.

The place had died with Ramona, Barrett realized. Not even her ghost could make it come alive.

The Bear switched off his flashlight. He was just about to leave when something caught his eye.

It was the lobster tank. The lobster tank sat atop the bar. Ramona kept a light on in the tank. So much the better to display the wares therein. There was no light on in the tank now. Barrett could barely make out the shifting shadows of the lobsters stirring lazily inside. But he could see something else, something wavering intermittently on the glass face of the aquarium itself. Some sort of illuminant, perhaps?

No. It was a rainbow. A rainbow traced its arc fitfully over the shifting shadows of crustaceans that stirred in the seawater atop the bar.

It took a luminator of some kind to spark a rainbow. For a moment Barrett thought it was the sun's work, newly rising, which cast the rainbow. But a glance out the window told him that the sun was still hidden below the horizon. Okay. So if it wasn't the sun…?

And then Barrett knew from where the light came.

Bear stuffed his own flashlight into the small of his back. He took a two-handed grip on his .38. Inhaled deeply. Let it out.

Stepped inside.

The kitchen door squeaked on its falling hinge.

Barrett stopped. No reaction.

So far, so good.

He took a couple of careful steps toward the bar. Cocked the hammer to single-action.

"All right." Barrett kept his voice low-keyed but firm. "Deacon Beach Police. I know you're behind the bar. Come up, slowly. And show me your—"

Snake came up, all right. And showed Barrett the muzzle-flash of an Uzi submachine gun.

The restaurant exploded in a medley of light and sound. The sound was what would paralyze you; people who hadn't been under fire found it hard to appreciate how the sound of a shell or a weapon could be *felt* as well as heard, how it made the skin crawl at the nape of your neck, made the skin ripple.

Barrett managed to get off a single round before he dove for cover. He rolled right as Snake came charging past, emptying his clip on the run.

Barrett returned fire almost blindly. His revolver kicked short, sharp explosions of thunder into the steady detonations which ripped from Snake's Uzi.

The lobster tank shattered with a stray round. Fifty gallons of salt water spilled lobsters onto the floor, their claws still bound with rubber bands.

Barrett kicked over a table as he scrambled for cover.

He had only had one round left in the cylinder.

But Snake wasn't interested. He fired one more burst as he broke through the steward's door, then tore out back through the kitchen.

Barrett grabbed the mike on his shoulder as he scrambled to follow.

"PD-2 to Deacon, officer under fire! I am 10–31 on Snake Adders. Suspect will be driving a customized '88 Chevy van. Get out a B.O.L.O."

Roach came back in a burst of static.

"Dispatch, 10–4 to your request on Snake. Backup on the way. Direct your traffic, Bear."

Barrett was fumbling cartridges into his .38 as he edged out back. By the time he was armed and at the rear door Snake was spinning sand from under his van. A short burst from the Uzi drove Bear briefly back inside. And then Snake's tires gained traction. He roared for the blacktop, strafing Barrett's cruiser as he went.

The Uzi sliced ribbons of metal and glass from Bear's car. Not a window was left in the entire vehicle. A second, sloppier burst ripped holes through the hood.

Then Snake was gone. Barrett scrambled to his car. Was there anything left?

He still had tires. Did he have an engine? A radiator? Oil? No way to know if the thing would even run except to—

Barrett stumbled into his cruiser. And then hesitated.

Should he wait for backup?

Snake's van hit the street like a scalded ape.

Barrett turned the key just once. The Crown Victoria roared to life.

"Fuck it," Barrett thought to himself. And then, for the radio—

"PD-2 *in pursuit. South on Ocean.*"

Seconds later Bear was fishtailing after Snake's van, juggling the seat belt, the radio, and breaking out the twelve-gauge from its clamp on the dash. His face stung suddenly with shards of glass blown from the spidered remains of his windshield.

Just don't take one in the eye.

"*All units*, I've got the van. Turning north on Oldtown Road. Roach, I think he's gone for the bridge. Any chance of a block, 10–4?"

"Block the bridge, 10–4. I'll get 'em down there, Bear."

"Use *extreme caution*." Barrett finally broke his shotgun free from its restraint. "Repeat—*extreme caution*. Subject has a fully automatic assault rifle."

Any high-speed chase is dangerous. Barrett had already nearly missed death chasing something no more dangerous than an inebriated teenager.

He was hitting over eighty miles an hour, now, on a blacktop road, the glare of a rising sun in his face, chasing a desperate man with a goddamn machine gun.

"Pedal to the metal," Barrett muttered.

The cruiser leapt forward like a stallion, siren screaming, to place Barrett's vehicle and Snake's side by side.

Snake was wild-eyed at the wheel. Staring straight into Barrett's leveled shotgun.

"*Pull over!*" Barrett mouthed over the wind.

And for a moment he thought Snake might do just that.

But then another vehicle rolled in what seemed slow motion onto the road.

It was Taff Calhoun. Taff was there, taking his half of the road out of its middle in a battered Dodge pickup. He nosed at maybe twenty miles an hour head-on toward the van and cruiser barreling down at over eighty ahead.

Sirens and horns and headlights.

Taff froze at the wheel.

Snake didn't even touch his brake. Neither did Bear.

The van missed Taff on one side. Bear missed him on the other. Bear could see a cane pole bouncing like a loose titty over the tailgate. In later years Taff would say that if he'd been carrying another coat of paint he'd've been carryin' that pole through the Pearly Gates.

Barrett gunned his cruiser again to close with Snake's van. To force him off the road.

That's when he hit the oil. Just a patch of oil from some pulp-wooder, probably, sitting there a deadly pool on the blacktop. Slicker than snot on a doorknob.

Barrett hit the slick at eighty-five. The car went sideways with Barrett's stomach. And then went spinning down the narrow road. Spinning like a top.

Counter-steer! Counter-steer!

Barrett came out of two complete three-sixties still running seventy miles an hour.

Snake's van had regained the lead fifty yards ahead.

Barrett jammed his foot to the floor again.

Oldtown Bridge lay ahead, a narrow two-lane strip which ran a mile and a half and straight as a ruler on a railroad bed thirty feet above the sandbars and cypress knees which thrust like rhinoceros tusks from Withlacoochie Creek.

Barrett could see a pair of headlights flashing at the bridge's far end. That would be the roadblock, two cruisers set like sawhorses directly in Snake's path. Bear could see lights tumbling from the pods on their roofs. And he knew there would be officers settled on their hoods. Officers with rifles and shotguns.

Nowhere to go now, buddy. Barrett grinned furiously as he dropped back a hair from Adders's psychedelic ass.

Snake didn't even slow down. He hit the bridge somewhere between eighty and ninety miles an hour hurtling at the wedge of cruisers that blocked the road ahead.

Barrett could barely hear his radio for the wind which screamed through the cruiser's cockpit.

"Be advised we have a block on the bridge, Bear."

"*We got him!*" Barrett acknowledged as he slid his cruiser to a halt.

Snake hurtled on down the bridge. Hell-bent for election.

Barrett could see the officers leveling their weapons.

But then a blue-gray cloud of smoke enveloped the van. The vehicle skidded with the squall of locked brakes.

It took Barrett a second to realize what was happening.

"Oh, shit," he said aloud. "He's coming back."

Snake whipped the van into a sliding U-turn not twenty yards from the waiting roadblock.

And then came hauling ass back down the bridge.

Straight back for Barrett Raines.

And this time there was something a little different.

Barrett could see it—the short, ugly muzzle which rested on the strut of Snake's side mirror.

Bear triggered his radio.

"Son of a bitch is coming back west on the bridge!"

The van built speed. Faster...faster!

"He's coming—fuck it." Barrett threw down his radio and stomped his accelerator through the floor.

Two vehicles on the bridge, now. Head-on.

Faster—faster! Barrett could see smoke pouring through the slug holes which ventilated his hood. The radio squawked.

"Bear, what are you doing? Bear—?!"

Barrett slammed the shotgun onto the dashboard of his cruiser, shoved the barrel straight out of what used to be the windshield. Straight into the wind at eighty-five miles an hour.

Ninety.

Barrett Raines and Snake Adders hurtled toward each other like medieval knights, their iron steeds braced for collision at a hundred and eighty miles an hour.

Barrett drove with his left hand. Clipped off the shotgun's safety with his right.

Snake's muzzle flashed. Slugs ripped past Barrett's face. Into the dash. The seat. The headliner.

The Bear shoved his shotgun further over the dashboard. Onto his hood. Burning oil and coolant streamed in a cloud over the nicely blued barrel.

The Ford's engine skipped one beat, then another.

"Stay with me, sugar." Barrett fingered the twelve-gauge's trigger with his free hand. That's when he remembered Ramona's joke. The one about the teenaged lovers—?

Don't you think you oughta use *two* hands, boy?

"NAW, *SUH!*"

Barrett screamed like a madman into the wind.

"I NEEDS *ONE* TO DRIVE!"

They passed so close Barrett could see Snake's eyes, the one wild blue and the one brown, staring wide from a face not recently shaved.

Snake sprayed his Uzi again into Barrett's cruiser. A long, long burst shredded the cockpit. Plastic and steel burst like shrapnel all around.

Barrett fired just once.

The shotgun exploded like a cannon off the cruiser's hood. Snake's windshield ruptured along with his face and everything else.

Barrett flashed by the van untouched.

Snake left the bridge at ninety miles an hour to fall with his bikini blond forever onto the cypress knees that rose like sabers thirty feet below. The explosion that followed rocked the bridge. The cruiser's engine died.

Barrett slipped the transmission to neutral and coasted unscathed into a rising sun.

Chapter fifteen

First light brought a small army to Oldtown Bridge. Half the Deacon Beach population came out with Channel 7 to see the carnage, and the other half came out to work on it. Medics and firemen and divers and police labored for an hour trying to recover Snake's body from the van.

They got most of him.

Turned out that the explosion came after the van impacted the creek's bed. The van plunged into shallow water on the driver's side. Doc's autopsy would later show that among other trauma Snake had taken a cypress knee through the liver as cleanly as if he had been gored by a bull. Or a rhino. Snake's head was found still with its mismatched irises but singularly dispossessed of its body. The skull was bagged separately, tossed in with the other remains like a bowling ball thrown into an outsized athletic bag.

"I hope the fire didn't kill him." Barrett was in the middle of the shakes. Trembling worse than Hoyt Young's famously nervous hands. He was leaning for support on Dick Hanson's cruiser, nursing a cup of coffee.

"Got him with the shotgun, didn't you? To the head? I doubt he felt a thing."

Dick offered the comfort and Barrett appreciated it though they both knew that without a postmortem there was no way they could be sure. Dick had been one of the officers blocking the bridge. Hanson brought Bear the coffee from his own thermos. Barrett had scrounged some honey from the glove compartment of his cruiser; a nine-millimeter slug had cut right through the plastic bear's rotund tummy.

Barrett turned the bottle over and over in his hands.

Taylor Folsom arrived, lungs laboring from the short incline which led down to the activity below the bridge.

"Well, I'll be damned," Barrett observed silently. "He's at work."

"Found this." Taylor waved a wad of bills from a water-soaked bag.

"He must have thrown it out when he made that turn on the bridge."

"More likely came out on impact," Barrett observed. "How much is it?"

"Fifteen, twenty thousand at least."

"That's a lot of lobster." Hanson whistled.

"Assuming it came from lobster." Barrett gulped his coffee without tasting it.

"Whatchyou mean?" Taylor asked.

"You see the weapon he was using?" Barrett directed the question to Dick.

"You mean this?" Dick pulled an Uzi from inside the cruiser. "One of the first things we retrieved," he explained shortly.

Barrett took the weapon in his hands. He was surprised how heavy the Uzi was. TV and movie violence would lead you to believe these things were as light as toys but the implement Barrett now hefted in his not insubstantial hands must have weighed close to nine pounds. Not much lighter, really, than the woodstocked M-1 the marines had for ages used as hand-me-downs from World War Two.

But that's where the similarity ended. The Uzi was a true submachine gun. Straight blowback. Fired from an open bolt. An excellent weapon, its reliability, accuracy, and rate of fire made the Uzi a continuing favorite among arms dealers.

Uziel Gal had designed and manufactured the Uzi for the Israeli military in 1951. Since that time the weapon had been licensed for production in countries as far apart in geography and resources as West Germany and Haiti. The Uzi could be purchased illegally almost anywhere. Americans typically got them from middlemen in Nigeria, or more recently Mexico, but Barrett knew that arms dealers could set up shop almost anywhere.

Even in Florida.

He folded his hand around the weapon's pistol grip. Tapped the trigger gently.

"What's the tape?" Dick inquired, pointing to a band of adhesive wrapped around the rifle's pistol grip.

"Depresses the grip safety," Barrett replied. "There's a second safety on the side over here. Works the same as most any weapon. But the designer wanted a spring-loaded safety in the Uzi's grip, too, so that if you let go of the weapon, say, or drop it, the thing won't accidentally discharge. Some Rambo wannabees don't like the safety in the grip, so they'll tape over the depressor."

Bear handed the weapon back to Dick.

"Very popular weapon. 'Specially for gun runners."

"Or burglars," Taylor countered. "Or drug pushers. Or practically anybody else. We aren't jumping to conclusions now, are we, Bear?"

Barrett regarded the much junior man.

"Just checking possibilities."

But Dick Hanson was onto a possibility of his own.

"You think…?" he began.

"What is it, Dick?"

"Well." Hanson hesitated a second before taking the plunge. "Maybe it was Snake Adders killed Ramona. He had her key. He knew her habits. Hell, you caught him stealing her money. Maybe Snake did her."

Snake's corpse rolled by, then, its various parts homogenized beneath a body bag slick with dew.

It was a possibility. It was a real possibility.

Barrett tasted his coffee for the first time.

"I want the restaurant closed down," he said with sudden energy. "Sweep for everything."

"We're stretched pretty thin this morning," Taylor protested.

"Stretch some more," Barrett replied. "And get hold of Ferris Boatwright. Tell him I want another look at those books. Cash in. Cash out. Let's see if Snake was living on a barkeep's pay."

"Sounds like somebody's fishin'." Taylor shook his head.

"Taylor, are you running this investigation?"

Barrett's voice, normally mild, came out a bark.

"I asked you a question, Taylor."

It wasn't much nicer the second time than it was the first.

"I just don't know what you're lookin' for," the younger man answered, pale and tight.

"We're looking for a reason," Barrett told him. "A motivation."

He nodded to the body being gurneyed away.

"Anything that'll tie that bastard to Ramona's murder."

Chapter sixteen

Barrett received a curious mixture of compassion and distance as he entered the station house. Everyone knew what had happened on the bridge, of course. Some of the younger officers actually offered the Bear high-fives as he passed by, which was not, in truth, appropriate. Any sane officer involved in a shootout resulting in death needed some time, not to celebrate, but to grieve. You could doll that word up, of course. Call it decompression, or reflection, time to oneself. But the fact was, even experienced officers facing justifiable circumstances did not like taking a human life.

Not that Bear's comrades regarded Snake as a nice guy. Snake Adders wasn't the kind of person about whose health locals regularly inquired. But he was not actively disliked, either. More important, Snake was not anonymous. He wasn't a transient. He wasn't a drug dealer from some other county who'd come in to exploit the locals. Snake was himself a local. His death, even if deserved, would come as a shock to the people of Deacon Beach.

And so the officers who greeted Barrett on his return from Oldtown Bridge could be divided into those who offered high-fives and those who felt they should isolate him. They might smile briefly when encountering Barrett at the Coke machine or Xerox, they might offer some clichéd consolation or pleasantry. But then they would break off contact and busy themselves with some pressing task.

Their mouths greeted Barrett. But not their eyes.

Barrett knew there were some second-guessers here. There always were. Fortunately the circumstances of the morning's events were straightforward. Snake sealed his fate the moment he opened fire on an officer of the law. But tension at the station remained and Barrett could feel it. Could sense the ambivalence around him.

Take Chief Rawlings's reaction, for instance: "Clean shoot." Smoot boomed the verdict before Barrett had even reached his desk. The chief's pronouncement seemed, to Barrett, intended more for the other officer's consumption than for his own solace.

"Thanks, Chief."

"Thanks, hell, that was some piece of work." But then Rawlings added, "Too bad you had to total the damn cruiser."

As if, somehow, the Bear was at fault. Barrett wondered if what he felt then was some small part of what a rape victim felt when the crime was somehow turned around to be made her fault.

Snake Adders was an asshole. He became a felon. But he was also a local. And, yes, there it was—he was white.

"Take the day off," Smoot advised Barrett with all the kindness in the world.

"I need to get a warrant first."

"Snake's place? You don't need a warrant for that."

"I was thinking about a boat," Barrett said.

"What—Snake had himself a boat?"

"No. But Splinter Townsend does."

"Splinter Townsend?" Smoot frowned. "What the hell's Splinter got to do with Snake? What the hell's he got to do with anything, for that matter?"

Barrett hesitated. He couldn't answer that question. That was why he wanted a look at the man's boat.

Smoot leaned back in his chair. "Are you trying to connect what happened out there this morning to Ramona's murder?"

"There are some pieces that fit," Barrett said woodenly.

"What you mean is, they fit what your brother told you in that cell of his."

"Snake *did* use an Uzi, Chief. There *was* cash hidden under the floor."

"One gun don't make a gun ring. It's only common sense in a place that busy to have a safe for your cash. And you still haven't told me how Splinter Townsend ties in to *any* of this!"

"Let me run it past Judge Blackmond."

"What? You gonna just walk in and say, 'Judge, I'd like to go on Splinter's boat.' You got to have some kind of justification!"

"I know that. I do."

"Well, what have you got?"

Barrett hesitated. A search warrant was not as simple a thing to acquire as folks typically believed. You had to have some reasonable basis to believe that a specified item was involved in a specific criminal activity before you could gain permission to beat about some citizen's premises. What was reasonable or specific enough to suit the law depended a lot on the interpretation by the judge whose permission you sought. Or your boss.

"Off the top I guess I'd point to a suspicious circumstance." Barrett's opener sounded weak even to himself. "Thirty thousand dollars' worth of boat? Where'd Splinter get that kind of money?"

"Maybe he ran some good dogs," Smoot replied. "Maybe he drew some good cards. Just maybe he got a loan—who gives a shit? Doesn't give you cause for a search warrant."

"If I can prove Splinter had a criminal association with Snake—" Barrett began.

Smoot cut him short. "You don't get a warrant with an 'if.' That's final, Bear."

"Fair enough. But I've got a feeling about this thing, Chief. I just don't think Snake was acting on his own."

"Sure he was. Look. You caught a man robbing a restaurant. He panicked. That's all there is to it."

Bear nodded. "Maybe." Barrett was moving before Smoot

could reply. He needed to know more about the money in that restaurant. He needed to know more about the gun that was recovered. He needed to know more about Snake and Splinter and the other men who played poker in Ramona's back room. There were questions, now, which, contrary to Rawlings's assessment, begged to be answered. Snake Adders wouldn't be answering anything anymore.

Barrett hoped to hell that his brother could.

Delton was out of his cot before the cell door slid back in its steel-gray tracks.

"Mornin', Bear." Delton flashed his younger brother a brave smile.

A knife dug into Barrett's heart. Easy now. You can't do this if you're too close.

"Heard you been busy," Delton was saying.

"Busy enough," Barrett admitted.

"Well? You find anything?"

"Some cash," Barrett nodded.

He didn't want to tell Delton too much. But it was hard not telling him anything.

"He looks small in here," Barrett thought. "Smaller than when we put him in, anyway."

And scared. Looking for any encouragement. Any shred of hope.

"We did find a weapon. An Uzi."

Delton lit up like a lamp. "That enough to get me out of jail?"

"No." Bear shook his head.

Delton worked to keep up a smile.

Another knife twitched in Barrett's heart.

"How 'bout bail? Say, Bear—any chance I can get bailed outta here?"

"That's up to Judge Blackmond," Barrett said quietly. "I'll be seeing him at eleven this morning. But I have to tell you—I doubt it."

Delton ran a hand over his scalp.

"Just like me," Barrett thought.

"They're gonna convict my ass. Aren't they, Bear? They're gonna say I did it."

"Saying's not enough, Delton. We have to—they have to prove it."

"What're my chances?"

Barrett found himself wishing there was something he could say that would reassure his brother.

"You're not off the hook." Barrett gauged his answer in his brother's eyes. "Not by a long shot."

"My chances, Bear."

"If you went to trial today I'd say slim to none."

Delton folded up onto his cot. Barrett rose to leave, but stopped.

No. I can't leave him like this.

"How about a smoke?" Barrett offered abruptly.

Delton's head came slowly up.

"Yeah. Sure."

Barrett tapped a pair of Camels from its pack. Took out a book of matches. Delton took the book, lit a cigarette for himself. One for Barrett.

And choked back a laugh.

"What?" Barrett didn't know whether to be insulted or surprised. "What? What is it?"

"Me lightin' you a cigarette. Cain't remember the last time I did that!"

"I can," Barrett replied.

It was the last time Delton had jumped his ass. He'd just blown his scholarship to FSU, had Delton. Barrett was barely a freshman. Their parents were both away at work when Delton came home broke and looking for cash. But this time Barrett fought for the coins in his coffee can.

Delton slapped Bear all over the bedroom until he gave the money up. And on the way out, as Barrett lay there bleeding and ashamed, Delton had given his kid brother a cigarette from their father's pack. And had lit it.

Barrett leaned over now, and snuffed out Delton's match.

The smile left his brother's face.

"Guess I wasn't a particular good big brother."

Barrett felt something else coming up from inside. Starting low. Working up.

"Y'know, the thing about big brothers, Delton—they're supposed to look out for you."

"Why, sure."

"They're supposed to take care of you. Keep you out of trouble. Aren't they, Delton? They give you their shoes and they give you their jackets and jeans and *Playboy* magazines. They play by the rules so when it comes your time to get the car you don't have to work so hard. 'Cause Mama and Daddy, why—they already had one son do it. And he never caused them any worry. Any pain.

"You take an older brother—he's supposed to fight the good fight, isn't he, Delton? So that the younger one maybe can find his way a little easier. That's the way it's supposed to be, only that's not the way it was, Delton. Not with you and me."

Neither of them said anything. Nothing for a long time. Finally, Delton stirred from his cot.

"We get past this, Bear, maybe I can turn it around."

Barrett found he couldn't answer. Instead he hauled himself wearily to his feet.

"Where you headed?" Delton asked.

And it was Barrett's turn to laugh.

"I used to ask you that. Do you remember? Every time you hit that screen door, 'Where you headed, Delton?' And do you remember what you'd say?"

"'Hell, if I don't change.'" Delton nodded.

"And I'd always laugh."

But Barrett wasn't laughing now.

"You never took me serious," Delton accused him weakly.

Barrett nodded gravely. "That was a mistake."

Dick Hanson offered to run Barrett over to Judge Blackmond's office. The judge had his office in Taylor County's courthouse. It was he who would most likely preside over any trial which might proceed from

Barrett's investigation. And it was Judge Blackmond to whom Delton's lawyer, Thurman Shaw, had applied for bail.

It was twenty miles to the courthouse. But Barrett was a lot more concerned about the twenty feet or so separating the station house from the street. A sullen gauntlet of protesters stretched from the station's front door to the squad car Dick had waiting at the curb. Men and women whom Barrett had known all his life were carrying signs on cardboard or sheets:

WE WANT JUSTICE!

FIND RAMONA'S KILLER!

And most alarmingly—

HANG DELTON RAINES!!

It was the nearest thing to a mob Barrett had ever seen.

He pushed past a cardboard gallows.

"Hang Delton Raines!" a solitary, strident voice called out. And then others followed.

"Hang him! Hang him!"

The crowd began to close in. Barrett had begun to wonder if he was in trouble when a microphone was shoved into his face.

"What do you think about this demonstration, Officer Raines?"

Stacy Kline was there. And for once Barrett was glad he was.

"I'd say people are angry and ought to be," Barrett replied loudly enough so that the demonstrators could hear.

"That doesn't mean—I repeat, *that does not mean*—that we're going convict *suspects* on the sidewalk."

"Was the shooting this morning related—"

"We have received new evidence which we believe bears on the case." Barrett gave Stacy the prepared answer before he could finish his question.

"Is Snake Adders connected with Ramona Walker's murder? Was he a suspect?"

"That's all I can tell you for now, Stacy. We've already got one man prejudged out here." Barrett met his neighbors eye-to-eye. "I wouldn't want to make it two."

Then Barrett walked quietly, calmly, right through the midst of the gathered protesters. Through the gauntlet. To the car.

Barrett Raines was thinking that there was a lot more than a fancy office and a frost of white hair to distinguish Judge Alfred Carey Blackmond from other citizens of the region. The judge was one of the few folks in Taylor County who had accomplished things of note beyond its lines. He was a graduate of Yale law school. He had served in a minor capacity in the Ford administration and two terms as a state legislator before settling down for what he thought would be retirement.

That was thirteen years ago. He had occupied this second-story office ever since. Barrett always liked this office, perched in the Old Courthouse, that original structure built shortly after the Civil War. There were newer and centrally cooled offices which had been added on to the original architecture but the judge wouldn't move. Barrett could understand why. This older, more spacious set of chambers carried a calm which you just knew had outlasted many storms. And the view was unbeatable. Through the judge's airy, lead-paned windows you could see Perry's town square, see the shops and people. You could even see the Emporium where, years ago, Barrett had bought his first pair of shoes.

It was like a set for *Our Town* but what was playing out here now was more appropriate for Eugene O'Neill's characters than for Thornton Wilder's. That distinction would not be lost on Judge Blackmond. The judge loved the county in which he had spent his youth but he had no illusions about the people who, each term, brought him to office. "If they knew what I thought about anything they'd ride me out of town on a rail," the judge once confided to Barrett.

But fortunately for them both, folks didn't find out. And didn't care to find out. A couple of trials early in the judge's first term sent three men to Florida's death row. Their fate earned the judge the reputation of being "hard on crime." That was enough to relieve the good citizens of Taylor County of any doubts concerning their homegrown's Eastern education, or any further curiosity regarding what His Honor might think about anything.

The result of that confidence and lack of curiosity was that the judge had since run unopposed and seemed to be headed without opposition for yet another term. He was disciplined, stern, and fair.

He would almost certainly, Barrett reflected, be the only unprejudiced man at Delton's trial.

It was Judge Blackmond to whom Delton's attorney applied seeking bail. The state's attorney, determined to prosecute Delton for premeditated murder, was now doing his best to convince Judge Blackmond that Barrett's brother ought to be kept in the calaboose. Roland Reed was at his most obnoxious, preening himself in his suit, jabbing rhetorical points in the air with his goddamn pen. And there was Thurman Shaw, almost as irritating and ineffectual, pleading Delton's interests as Roland was pleading the State's.

"The bottom line is—" Thurman spread his arms wide, "—my client is cooperating!"

"Bull."

Roland's reply. So much for the subtlety of the state.

"He's incriminating himself, for God's sake! And he's doing it to give *you* evidence!"

"What he's giving me are accusations." Reed sniffed. "Ramona Walker selling guns? Delton wanting to be her *partner*?!"

"He wanted her cash, Roland. That's all."

"Blackmail. Extortion. What's the difference? All you've done is provided yet another reason why he killed her!"

"Gentlemen, gentlemen." Judge Blackmond cut off Thurman's riposte.

The adversaries fell silent.

"We're not here to try the case," Blackmond admonished the counsellors. "We are here to set terms for bail."

The judge turned to Barrett.

"These gentlemen have made their positions immanently clear. But I've heard very little from the man who presumably knows Delton best."

"Not sure I'm the most objective source, Your Honor."

"Nevertheless, you believe that Delton Raines is a reasonable risk for bail?"

Barrett felt all the eyes in the room on him.

"Delton's no saint," he said finally. "That's for sure. But, as Roland himself points out, everything Delton's volunteered so far has made him a more likely candidate for murder. That's a funny kind of strategy for a man planning to run."

The judge leaned back, swiveled his highback chair to survey the street below. Even here, in Perry, there was a thin line of Deacon Beach protesters who carried signs urging the Hanging Judge to, once more, protect his community.

"I must tell you that I am not inclined to grant bail without some exceptional provisions." The judge frowned. "Ms. Walker's homicide has stirred this community in a way I haven't seen for years. There is a cauldron of hate out there. Race-hate. It can turn neighbors into lynchers."

"I understand, Your Honor." Barrett nodded. "We'd have to arrange some sort of recognizance."

"My thoughts exactly," Judge Blackmond affirmed. "But I wonder if you will agree to the arrangement I have in mind?"

Chapter seventeen

*H*ave *Delton?* HERE? Barrett, have you lost your mind?!"

It was safe to say that Laura Anne would have been more blunt in her evaluation of Judge Blackmond's arrangement than Barrett had felt possible for himself to be.

"It's the only way the judge will grant bail, Laura Anne. Just a few weeks."

"Weeks?! Let the judge keep him!"

"He's not the judge's responsibility," Barrett said woodenly.

"Well, he's not yours! He's not mine! My God, Bear, *we* didn't kill that woman."

"Got news for you. Delton didn't either."

That stopped her. Laura Anne lowered a basket of tomatoes to the carport's concrete floor.

"What did you say?"

"I don't think Delton killed Ramona Walker," Barrett repeated.

"Roland's telling everybody it's open and shut."

"Right now, he's right," Barrett agreed. "But Delton didn't kill her."

"How do you know that?" Laura Anne challenged him.

"I can't prove it," Barrett admitted. "But Snake Adders would never steal from Ramona. The cash in that vault—I think it came from somewhere else."

"You have any idea where?"

"Delton does."

"And you believe him?" Laura Anne was shaking her head.

"Yes, I do," Barrett answered simply.

Laura Anne hefted the tomatoes to a shapely hip and turned for the door.

"I know what Delton is, Laura Anne." Barrett spoke to her back. "I don't have any illusions about that. But he is, after all, my brother. He's in trouble. And this time—"

"Yes?"

"This time he might just be telling the truth."

Chief of Police Smoot Rawlings joined Dick Hanson and Barrett to lead interference through a cordon of locals and media converged on Deacon Beach's Municipal HQ. Delton Raines followed their blocks like a halfback.

Stacy Kline blitzed.

"Captain Rawlings! Is it true Delton Raines has been released on bail?"

"You see him," Rawlings rasped.

"Is there any kind of special treatment involved here?"

"Man has the right to apply for bail, Stacy." Barrett tried to take some of the heat for his boss.

"And under your recognizance, Detective? In your house? Is that the man's right, too?"

Barrett swung a newly purchased squad car beneath his carport, bumper to bumper with the decrepit Malibu.

Delton hadn't said much on the way home. Barrett hadn't, either.

They were barely out of the car when the back door banged open and two deliriously delighted young boys attacked in chorus.

"Unca' Delton!"

"Hello, peckerwoods!"

Ben and Tyndall practically bowled their giant uncle over. Delton laughed under their assault. Booming, baritone laughter.

Barrett felt a smile on his own face. He couldn't help it. You had to smile seeing something like that.

"God A'mighty, you boys have grown!"

Delton scooped them up like puppies. A boy on each arm.

"We're gonna have fun, Uncle Delton," Ben said sweetly.

Barrett felt a twinge in his heart.

"Come on in, boys. Delton, Laura Anne'll have supper."

Barrett was setting the kitchen table in the midst of a very uneasy veneer of civility. Laura Anne scooped shrimp from a vat of boiling grease onto a paper towel spread beside the stove on a drainboard. Delton was standing nearby. Trying to look helpful. Trying to stay out of the way.

Laura Anne transferred the shrimp to a colander.

"Sure smells good," the elder brother said enthusiastically.

"I'm doing this for Barrett," she said without a glance in Delton's direction. "Not for you, Delton."

It was a very silent table. Delton dipped shrimp into a homemade tartar of mayonnaise, catsup, and lemon juice. Laura Anne chewed a salad like cud in stony silence. Barrett had managed to clear his throat a couple of times only to come up short of anything to say. Finally—

"Uncle Delton?"

It was little Ben who broke the ice.

"Yes, peckerwood."

"His name is Ben," Laura Anne sniped. "Or Benjamin."

"But Mama, I like *peckerwood!*"

"That's not your name."

"Laura Anne." Barrett used his most diplomatic I-don't-mean-to-intrude voice to intervene—

And came up short once again for words.

Fortunately, Benjamin was not deterred.

"Uncle Delton is it true you killed that woman?"

"Benjamin Raines," Laura Anne exploded.

"Boy's just bein' honest," Delton responded so softly you had to work to hear him.

"Ben. Tyndall." Laura Anne folded her napkin rigidly into her lap. "I want you to take your things to the sink. Get ready for bed."

"Oh, Mama!" Tyndall pouted.

"Tyndall, you heard your mother. You, too, Ben."

Tyndall grabbed his plate and stalked off toward the kitchen. Ben followed. But he stopped, on the way, at his uncle's side.

"You'll stay with us. Won't you, Uncle Delton?"

"A few days. Sure."

"And you'll play with us?"

"You betcha I will."

The first-grader hesitated just a moment. As if making up his mind. And then, quickly, Ben rose on tiptoes to kiss his uncle Delton on the cheek.

"Night-night, Unca' Delton."

"You, too, little man. Sleep like an angel."

"That's what Daddy always says!" Ben pronounced delightedly.

The boys left the field, then, to their elders. Time for Delton to clear his throat.

"Ben's the brains of the two, is he?"

"And quieter, normally." Barrett nodded. "Tyndall's more— physical."

"Just like you and me. Huh, Bear?!"

"No," Laura Anne said. "Definitely not 'just like.'"

"I'm sorry, I just meant..." Delton stumbled. "They're sweet boys."

"Yes, they are."

Laura Anne rose from her seat with that and left the table.

"Come on," Barrett said finally. "I'll show you your room. It's Tyndall's—he'll double up with Ben."

Light from the hallway spilled into the small bedroom.

"Hate running Tyndall out." Delton had to duck his head to enter.

"There's a double-bunk in Ben's room," Barrett said. "We did that knowing we'd have, well—guests."

"Easier havin' guests sometimes than family. Huh, Bear?"

Barrett didn't reply. What he did do was kneel down beside Tyndall's bed, reach far beneath—

"What you doin', man?"

And pull out a suitcase. A Florida State pennant was glued over the suitcase's cardboard exterior.

"I'll be damn." Delton smiled slowly.

Barrett opened the luggage. A litter of pennants and faded newspaper clippings inside. Photographs. Barrett switched on a lamp beside Tyndall's bed, rummaged out a black-and-white framed in plastic. Handed it to his brother.

There was Delton. A tall, proud, smiling young black man with the helmet and pads of a Florida State Seminole. And standing next to Delton, hand raised to be placed on a Bunyanesque shoulder, was Bobby Bowden.

"He said you were the fastest big man he'd ever coached," Barrett recalled.

"He went out on a limb for me." Delton extended a hand for the picture.

"Yes, he did."

"An' I let him down."

Barrett didn't second that verdict. Instead he nodded to the memorabilia stashed in the cardboard case.

"Mama kept it all. She died when you were—gone somewhere. Anyway, she told me to save everything. Keep it for you."

"Nice of you, Bear."

"Nice of her," Barrett said a little coldly.

Delton placed the photograph carefully on a nightstand beside the bed.

"Y'know, Bear, I 'preciate what you've done for me. This place is a hell of a lot better than a jail cell. And I'm glad to breathe free air. But seems like ever' time I turn around it's either you or Laura Anne remindin' me what a piece of shit I am."

"Couple of days ago Laura Anne had to practically fight her way out of the grocery store. Just because of you."

"Bastards." Delton sifted a ream of newspaper clippings through his hands. "Time was I could drop in on any swinging dick in this town. Black or white. Set down for supper."

"That was before you started drinking, fighting, and fucking everything that walked."

"Everybody raises a little hell."

"I don't," Barrett said bluntly. "Laura Anne doesn't. We want to count for something in this community. Do you understand that, Delton? We want to do what's right."

"Shitload easier to do what's right when you got a decent job," Delton replied sullenly. "When you got a roof over your head."

"Nobody gave it to me," Barrett answered with heat.

An argument seemed well joined. Delton straightened to his full height. Almost a head taller than his younger brother. But then Delton seemed visibly to shrink.

"You got the brains, Bear. What have I got?"

"What you've always wanted, Delton."

"And what's that?"

"Attention," Barrett replied. "The limelight. Everybody wants it, don't they? Even if it's at the edges. Mama and Daddy were bad as the rest. Delton gets drunk, gets into a fight, maybe gets some little girl pregnant, that was all right—long as he kept scoring touchdowns. See how it was, Delton? 'Cause when you got attention, they got attention, too.

"You break a tackle, Daddy wasn't just another nigger at the mill. No, suh. He was Somebody—Delton Raines's father! And Mama— why, every Friday you ran between the goalposts, that Saturday she was Queen for a Day."

"Didn't hurt 'em any," Delton said.

"It hurt you. It hurt me. And now it's hurting us."

Barrett gathered up his brother's cheaply framed claim to glory.

"I was valedictorian of my class. You ever know that?"

"Why—sure." Delton nodded vigorously.

Another lie. Barrett let it pass.

"The first black ever, *ever* at that high school to get those kind of grades. I was so proud! And then graduation comes along. Big deal in a little town. The principal sits up there and says to the whole wide world: Barrett Randall Raines has the best marks of anybody in his class. So finally—it's my time for some attention. My little time in the light. Daddy was dead by then. But Mama was there. Aunts and uncles and cousins. Everybody.

"But you got drunk that night, Delton. Stole the sheriff's car and totaled it. Down by the Oldtown Bridge. Next day that's all people talked about. Delton, Delton, Delton."

Barrett put the photo back onto Tyndall's nightstand.

"I might as well have finished dead last."

Delton swallowed hard. "I'm sorry."

"So'm I. 'Night, Delton."

Barrett killed the lights on his way out.

Chapter eighteen

A match scratched to life in the abandoned building rotting beside the bay. Perry Como smiled down with Doris Day over the single table which survived beneath the diner's bullet-starred roof. Frank struck his Zippo's flint next to a Coleman wick. Kerosene came to life, blue and dull, to flicker like heat lightning on the horizon of "the spick's" handsome Latin face.

He was dressed impeccably as usual, was Hernando, in a white linen suit. And he waited patiently as usual for his more poorly dressed companion to speak.

Frank didn't keep him waiting long.

"I need you to kill Delton Raines."

Hernando leaned back in his backless chair.

"Is this revenge?" he said at last. "Because if this is a matter of vengeance it should remain private."

"It's business," Frank responded shortly. And then explaining, "Delton may have something on us. That's 'us,' Hernando. You and me. And if he does have something God knows how much of it he's told the police."

"How much can he know?" Hernando inquired.

Sienna shrugged.

"Ramona was going to tell me. That's the night she got herself killed."

"Where can I find this man?"

"Staying with his brother. Problem is, his brother's the town cop."

"Then we have to move quickly."

"That's a roger. A suggestion: Take the bastard alive. That way it looks like he jumped bail. That way, too, we can work with him awhile. Find out if he's spilled anything to the cops."

"I will want payment for ensuring your safety."

"*Our* safety, my friend. And naturally I'll pay. Nobody does something for nothing."

A bright, clear sun cast a shadow just now edging from the pines past Laura Anne's sweet corn. Barrett could see the garden easily from the kitchen.

He was squeezing honey from a fresh decanter into a mug of coffee. A tattered yearbook was propped on the toaster.

"You're gonna burn the house down, Barrett."

Laura Anne reserved his given name for either humor or direct orders. She looked nice. A light cotton blouse and a brightly dyed skirt. Narrow waist and firm belly. Long, bronze legs.

"Ready for school?"

"I'm worried about the boys," she replied.

"They seem to be coping pretty well so far," Bear observed drily.

Peals of laughter came drifting in from outside as if to confirm Barrett's diagnosis.

He walked with Laura Anne to their sliding-glass door.

There they were, Ben and Tyndall, swinging from a tire Delton had suspended from a tree limb. Delton was with the boys. Clowning with the peckerwoods. Back and forth the boys laughed from their jerry-rigged swing. Back and forth. Delton would catch the tire if it began to gyrate too wildly, gently propel the boys with one pie-sized hand into another long, long arc beneath the tree.

"Doesn't look a man would kill anybody, does he?"

"Can't judge a book by its cover," Laura Anne replied.

"Speaking of which." Barrett took it up. "Lookee here."

He displayed the yearbook. A grainy snapshot caught a powerful, young teenager donning a welder's mask. The sleeves on his madras shirt were cut to the shoulders.

"Is that Delton?"

"Sure is." Barrett sipped his coffee. "School shop. If Mr. Suggs said fix a fender, Delton'd build a slingshot. Or a pipe bomb. Anything. He was a regular terrorist."

"Some things never change," Laura Anne quipped.

Barrett looked toward the sliding door, to the tree, the boys, and the man beyond.

"I think he's trying. Don't you?"

"I'd love to think so, Barrett. Honestly. For your sake I would."

She turned to leave.

"Here's your purse." Barrett lifted it from the counter, pulling Laura Anne to himself as he did so.

Their lips met. She yielded to him briefly. Yielded even more—

And then went stiff as a board.

There was Delton at the sliding door.

"Oh, I'm sorry."

"It's all right." She shoved Barrett away angrily. "Just on my way to work."

"I'll drop the boys by school," Barrett covered lamely.

"Make sure they're not late." Laura Anne took her keys off the ring by the carport door. And then, to Delton, "They've got all the attention now they can stand."

* * *

The boys were doubly excited this morning, first for riding in the squad car to school, and secondly for having their uncle in the back seat.

Ben and Tyndall grilled Delton about his arrest as if their father had not even been involved. They swapped questions about handcuffs, about jail cells, about the food.

"Gag a maggot." Delton grinned.

On and on until finally Barrett intervened with a stern admonition for the boys to respect their uncle's privacy and to say nothing—nothing!—to anyone at school regarding Uncle Delton's case.

They dropped the boys off at a playground shaded with pine trees and matted with straw.

"Keep your heads up and your buttons zipped." Barrett offered as his final counsel.

Ben and Tyndall spilled like eager puppies from the squad car, waving goodbyes to their Uncle Delton on the run.

"Sweet boys," Delton commented gravely.

Barrett did not reply. His mind was already turning to business. He U-turned the squad car off Main Street, headed west for Ocean.

"How'd you like to go fishing?"

"You don't fish, Bear."

"Maybe it's time I started."

There are some summer days in north Florida which greet you out of bed with a breeze that seems actually cool. Then in a couple of hours a thin overcast turns the sky to cotton, the humidity skyrockets, the sun turns into a sultry and indistinct ball, and before you can wind your wristwatch it's hotter than a fresh-fucked fox in a forest fire.

That was the kind of day which shaped up, now, over Esther's Marina. A raft of wooden piers moored a variety of pleasure craft, mostly powerboats, beneath a dull overcast. The sun baked the water vapor trapped below like a microwave. Nothing seemed to move on land, not even insects. And the water looked as featureless and dull as a slap of slate.

Barrett idled his squad car in the marina's caliche parking lot.

"You need to wait here." Barrett killed the engine.

"If I don't die of heatstroke."

"Turn on the A.C. if you have to."

Barrett left the keys in the ignition.

"I guess I don't have to tell you not to steal the car."

"Well, it wouldn't hurt," Delton replied mischievously and Barrett had to smile.

The man had his moments.

"I'll try and make it quick." Barrett patted the .38 parked in its holster.

"You gone fishing with *that*?" Delton's eye narrowed.

"Corrie said something about a boat. Splinter Townsend's?"

"Splinter's, yeah."

"Man can't afford child support but he pays cash for a boat. Sound right to you?"

"You aren't fishin', Bear, you're guessin'. Throwin' a line out there. Hoping somethin'll strike."

"You could be right," Barrett admitted.

"Well, I hope you get lucky," Delton declared.

Barrett rolled down his window. Got out. He walked slowly, deliberately, in a line for the harbormaster's office, making sure his shield was displayed prominently from the leather flap strapped to his belt. No one appeared at the tin shed's narrow veranda to greet the detective. Barrett strolled up to a screenless window. At first he didn't recognize the gnarled and bearded, white-haired old coot propped with a Pepsi before a box fan inside.

"That you, Barrett?"

"Yes, sir."

"Don't you recognize me, son?"

"I don't think so, sir."

"English class. Eighth grade."

"My Lord, is that you, Mr. Hilton?"

"In the flesh—The Old Man by the Sea."

Barrett did remember Daniel Briar Hilton, of course, the controversial and demanding English teacher whose Northern roots, transplanted in the recently integrated South, earned him the love of a few students and the hatred of the entire school board. Briar Hilton was the only person in the region who refused to use Barrett's sobriquet. It was always "Barrett," or, occasionally—when he'd screwed up—"Mr. Raines."

"'Theseus and the Minotaur.'" The onetime teacher stood to

greet his former pupil. "'Member that paper you wrote for me? That's when I knew Deacon Beach was going to have to revise its opinion of black intellect. Or rather," he corrected himself, "that's when I hoped that they would."

Barrett remembered "Thorny" Hilton as the first educator, black or white, who seemed genuinely interested in what he had to say. Mr. Hilton was a teacher who knew how to listen. He was a teacher passionate about literature and learning. He was also one of those rare pedagogues who could bring a dim and distant past gloriously to life.

"Look at the blinds." Hilton had begun his lecture on the classics by jabbing a finger at the huge Venetian blinds which hung in a classroom built during the Roosevelt administration.

"Those aren't blinds, anymore, people. Those are sails!

Black sails will signify that Theseus, son of King Aegeus, has failed to kill the Minotaur. White sails mean he has succeeded.

"Imagine the father, there, sleepless in our cloakroom. Just over there! Agonizing over what will happen once the cruel King Minos drops his only son into the labyrinth—the labyrinth from which no man, or woman, has ever returned."

Barrett read the legend over and over. The Minotaur—what a fascinating monster! Half man. Half beast. The head of a bull. The claws and teeth of a lion. And there was Theseus, trying by killing the monster to save the fourteen Athenians who were sacrificed every seven years to propitiate Minos's rage over the murder of his own son.

Barrett had especially liked the part about the girl. Ariadne gave Theseus a ball of thread to trace his way out of the labyrinth and a dagger with which to kill the Minotaur.

A piece of thread and a dagger! What flimsy, desperate weapons to oppose a monster like that! Barrett would imagine himself so armed, fighting the Minotaur. Some days he would imagine himself giant and fearless in the labyrinth. On others he was a puny thing, terrified before the beast that made his people into slaves.

But determined, always, to kill it.

And growing up, Barrett felt often like Theseus must have felt, an unknown prince lately come to claim what should have been his for the taking. But there were always Minotaurs to kill—always! And they were always hidden in impossible mazes and you were never given more than a thread, more than a dagger to find and kill the thing that would not let you be free.

There was no one to help. No one to stand beside you. You had to do it all yourself.

And even if you were successful, even if you killed the Minotaur and lifted the curse from your race you could almost bet that coming home someone would forget to raise the white sails. And your father seeing sails that were, after all, black, would cast himself in grief onto boulders which bounded the sea.

But he couldn't take time to kindle those memories now. Today he was with Mr. Hilton seeking a different kind of monster.

"I need to look at one of your boats, Mr. Hilton," Barrett explained.

"You mean search one, don't you?"

Barrett had been prepared to bulldoze or bullshit the sot who usually sat half-asleep beside the pier.

Not with Mr. Hilton, though. He just couldn't do it.

"Yes, sir," Barrett replied. "I'm here for a search."

"Got a warrant?"

"No, sir, I don't."

The retired schoolteacher regarded Barrett a long moment.

"Is this related at all to the Walker case?"

"I'm not supposed to tell you that, Mr. Hilton. But then again, I'm not supposed to be going onto boats without warrants, either."

The old man grunted over his soft drink.

"They've got you between a rock and a hard place, don't they, son?"

"If I'm not careful they do." Barrett allowed a puckish grin.

The former teacher took another long pause over his soft drink.

"Well, it turns out I was just about to call you, Barrett."

"How's that, Mr. Hilton?"

"Saw something suspicious out there," the teacher said without even glancing out the window. "On the pier.

Looked to me like maybe somebody who's not supposed to be here boarded one of our boats. Now, being harbormaster, I am required to report things of that nature. Am I not?"

"It would be prudent, yes, sir."

"I suppose it's a good thing you dropped by then." Barrett's favorite teacher smiled. "Saves me a phone call."

"Thank you, Mr. Hilton. Thanks much."

"A word of caution."

"Yes, sir."

"In the real world the hero doesn't always kill the Minotaur."

"I'll keep that in mind, Mr. Hilton."

The older man produced a pair of keys.

"It's the BayLiner out front. Slip Seventeen."

Barrett knew enough about boats to know that this one hadn't been bought on a mechanic's part-time salary. Even used, this craft was going to run thirty grand, Barrett figured. Maybe more. And this boat was rigged for deep water. Looked to have extra fuel tanks up top for her twin inboards. Barrett recognized a Loran which was without doubt slaved to the autopilot prominent at the helm.

Lots of mahogany and teak. Lots of nice brass which Splinter wasn't polishing all that well.

Let's see what's below, Barrett said to himself.

Barrett inspected the surprisingly flimsy lock which secured the boat's cabin. It always amazed Barrett how boats and planes, always expensive toys, were for the most part secured with twenty-dollar locks. Even so, Bear was glad to have Splinter's spare keys; he did not want to have to force an entry. The first key didn't get him in; it was probably for the boat's ignition. The second slipped in easily.

Barrett glanced over his shoulder to scan the marina. Nobody around. Well. In for a penny, in for a pound. Barrett slipped inside Splinter's cabin and closed the door behind him.

The interior was well appointed and surprisingly well maintained. Probably where Splinter gets his poontang, Barrett decided. The galley was larger than Bear expected. He checked the refrigerator. Running! And ice in the freezer. A certain urgency took hold then. There had to be some kind of internal power source running that fridge. Bear couldn't believe Splinter would leave the boat's generators running unless he intended to come back within some relatively short period of time to his floating love grotto. He wondered if there was any way Mr. Hilton could warn him if Splinter showed up.

Maybe. Maybe not.

'twere best done quickly, Bear quoted silently and began to rifle Splinter's cabin. He searched the galley's cabinets, the overheads, the bunks. He looked for compartments built into bulkheads or furniture. Hollow spots. The kind of places druggies typically created for their contraband.

He turned, then, to the entertainment section.

Splinter had an enormous flat-screen television and tape deck built into the cabin's forward wall. Stacked in carousels on either side of the telly were dozens of videotapes.

Barrett scanned the labels. Most were feature releases or selections of pornography.

Hello!

Barrett found a separate drawer slipped in beneath the TV. There were maybe half a dozen tapes sequestered in that drawer. A couple were wrapped in rubber bands and labeled with strips of adhesive tape.

See what we got here.

Bear leaned over to power the tube's VCR. A couple of seconds of leader jumped into images from a handheld camera. Hard to see at first. Barrett could make out a bed. Lots of mirrors. And voices almost extinguished beneath a boombox and Jimi Hendrix.

"Purple Haze." Bear knew that one.

The camera jerked past the bed and the mirrors a couple of times before it settled, finally, and focused slowly on—

Ramona Walker.

She was naked and magnificent and straddled over a bottle of black-label bourbon. Splinter Townsend, bare himself to the shorts, shouted approval from the boom box. An unseen cameraman laughed hugely. His proximity to the videocam's mike momentarily drowned out what the players were saying.

But then the words came back.

"You ain't gonna do it," Splinter was yelling. "Goddammit, woman, you *cain't* do it!"

Ramona teased the bottle with her vagina. She took in a deep breath. Her belly sucked in flat and smooth beneath high, high breasts. Down she went. Down over the bottle.

She squatted there, contracted about the neck of the bottle. And then she stood. The cameraman zoomed in. The whiskey bottle hung from her like a breeched calf.

Splinter held out his hand.

"Gimmee it."

"Take off your shorts," Ramona commanded.

When he did Ramona dropped the bottle into Splinter's open hand and took him down to the carpet.

"Rockabye baby!"

She rode on top. In command. Splinter humped half drunk and ecstatic beneath. He was already coming.

She didn't even slow down. Auburn hair fell over rock-hard nipples.

Back she leaned. Back—!

Barrett killed the tape.

Why did it bother him so much to see this? What business was it of his if Ramona wanted to walk that walk?

He hit the rewind. Went over the interior one more time. Nothing of interest in the shelves beside the TV. Some decent whiskey.

Barrett was about to go when he hit the jackpot. He was just following the antennae wire, really. The wire that led from the tube to, Barrett presumed, some receiving body on the exterior. There was a panel there, concealed by the carpet. Snugged in with a wing nut. Probably just a cavity for the spare wire and cable. Maybe an access to the generator. Barrett grunted.

But it was best to check.

Barrett unscrewed the nut which secured the panel, popped it free, plunged his arm inside up to the elbow.

And came out with a wad of cash.

Twenties and fifties were bound with hundred-dollar bills inside. A shot of adrenaline jolted straight to Barrett's heart. Barrett plunged his arm back in again, reached as far down as he could—it was something different, this time, that greeted his touch. Something cool. Something metallic.

Barrett took a grip—

And pulled an Uzi submachine gun fully armed from the receptacle secreted away below Splinter Townsend's cabin.

What to do now?

Barrett knew in his gut that he had found confirmation of his brother's story, confirmation that Delton desperately needed to gain credibility. But even with an initial excuse to enter the BayLiner, Barrett knew full well that he was not legally entitled to the products of his search. No court would allow a search as extensive and invasive as the one Barrett had just completed. A judge might buy the idea that you went onto a boat checking for burglars. He wouldn't for an instant buy the idea that once on board you could take the damn thing apart.

If the cash and guns on Splinter's boat were to have a chance in hell of being allowed as evidence, Bear knew they would have to be discovered pursuant to a legally warranted search. But even if he should manage to return with an airtight warrant, Barrett also knew he would have to conceal the extent of his initial exploration. Otherwise whatever was found during his second assault would be seen as the fruit of a prior and illegal search and would be thrown out of court.

Barrett's heart was thudding in his chest.

He would say he entered the boat at the harbormaster's request. Hilton had seen someone suspicious and given Bear the keys to the boat. He went in. Saw nothing. Came back out. That's a story that would stand up. It would cover Barrett. It would cover Rawlings, too. Maybe.

What Barrett was contemplating was not by the book. He wasn't about to rationalize that. And he wasn't about to justify his actions by bitching about rules of evidence or the shackles which the Warren court put on cops. Barrett knew what he was doing. What he didn't know, and what he was trying hard not to think about, was whether he was doing it because he absolutely had no other way to pursue Ramona's killer, or because it was the only shred of hope which he saw for exonerating his brother.

It was time to pee or get off the pot.

Barrett stowed the Uzi back into its hiding place. Replaced the cash, the panel and wing nut—

Click!

And jerked his .38 free as he hit the deck!

It was only the VCR. Ramona's steamy tape was now fully rewound. An automatic eject slid the tape from the VCR's jaws.

Barrett's gun trembled in his hands.

He holstered the weapon. Switched off the VCR.

Should he leave the tape?

Barrett hesitated a long moment.

And slid the black plastic inside his jacket.

Delton had for a change done exactly as his younger brother instructed. He had remained in the car, rolled down the windows to catch whatever breeze was available, and tuned in some Marvin Gaye on the squad car's FM radio. He was tempted to run the A.C. but was afraid the engine might overheat, so...Marvin Gaye would have to do. "I Heard It Through the Grapevine."

Nodding half asleep with the radio blaring, Delton unfortunately was not hearing anything. Had he been less tired or listening to elevator music Delton might have heard the distinctive crunch of tires on crushed rock, might have looked then out of simple curiosity or boredom into the rearview mirror to see the nondescript van which pulled to a halt directly behind the squad car.

But the day was balmy. The music was loud. Delton didn't see anything.

Barrett did. He spotted the van coming into the parking lot almost immediately upon negotiating the short leap from the Bay-Liner's deck to the pier. He saw the van. He saw twin doors pop open like bat's wings. He saw two Latin men dressed too well step outside. Shirts and ties, slacks and jackets. And Barrett knew, even before the pair strolled to either side of his dozing brother, that these suits were there to kill him.

"*Delton!*"

Barrett drew his revolver on the run.

The killers slipped sawed-off shotguns almost casually from beneath their jackets.

"*Deltoooooon!*"

A twelve-gauge blasted Delton awake. A second explosion dissolved the squad car's rear window into shards of glass and buckshot. Delton hit the floorboard and turned the ignition key in one fluid movement—

Jammed the accelerator full to the floor—

And slammed the tranny to reverse.

The cruiser leaped backward like a cannon torn loose from its moorings on a man-of-war.

"Jesus, *Delton!*"

Delton launched the squad car straight back at the twin gunners. They leapt, each to a side—

No good.

Delton hit the brakes and wrenched the wheel. Two tons of car slid sideways. The cruiser caught Hernando's men hip-high, one near the front bumper, the other near the rear. Doc would say later their spines had snapped like pretzels. And just to make sure, Delton went ahead and slammed the would-be assassins like rag dolls into their van.

Chapter nineteen

Smoot Rawlings had read Barrett's report and he was not happy.

"*What in hell were you DOING out there?*"

"I had a hunch," Barrett replied as calmly as he could to his chief.

"Hunch! Half the *goddamn* marina shot to shit! Not to mention two dead wetbacks!"

"They were after Delton."

"*I don't give a damn who they were after, YOU shouldn't have been there!*"

"I couldn't get a warrant for that boat. You know that."

"Right! So the way it works, Bear—you don't have a warrant, you don't go in. Not without exigent circumstances."

"I had a circumstance."

"What you had was old man Hilton. An' if you're not real careful some lawyer'll destroy that fine little fabrication in just about the time it takes a fart to fly out a flea's ass."

"I needed to look. You tryin' to tell me you never went looking?"

"Not for straws I didn't, no. And in my judgment that's what you were doing out there, Detective. Looking for straws."

"Those killers straw men, Chief? For who?"

"Prob'ly somebody's husband."

"That's not my judgment."

"It's your judgment that's in question, Barrett. With your brother. On the boat. Seems to me you're losing your—objectivity."

"Objectivity?"

Barrett was driven to the point of distraction. If an attempted murder wouldn't get Delton some credibility what would?

He took a deep breath.

"What if I told you I saw something on that boat?"

"Oh, God, I don't wanta know."

"Just a hypothetical, Chief."

"Sure it is."

"Suppose I told you that there was cash on board? Lots of it?"

"Just lying around, that it? For any son of a bitch to see?"

"It's only hypothetical."

"Right. And what else did you, hypothetically, see?"

"An Uzi. Just like Snake's. And then there's this tape."

Barrett slid the cassette out of his jacket.

"Doesn't look too hypothetic to me," Rawlings said drily. "What is it?"

"Donkey show. Ramona and Splinter. Plus a cameraman."

Rawlings's jaw locked tight.

"First off, Detective: If a court ever finds out how you got this information they'll never let you use it. But number two: Even if they did? You're gonna need a lot more than three consenting adults and two rifles to make me or anyone else believe that Ramona was selling guns!"

"Somebody tried to kill Delton today. Do you believe that?"

"Lots of people are after Delton. You and me between us couldn't count 'em all."

"There's got to be a connection," Barrett insisted.

"If there is, it's gonna be Taylor's job to find it."

"Taylor? It's *my* case, Chief."

"Now let me set you straight: *Your* case is the homicide of one white female Ramona Walker! That business at the marina, *whatever* it is, is outside your purview, do you understand, Detective? It is *not* part of your goddamned case!"

"Chief—"

"At ease!"

Barrett felt hairs tingle at the nape of his neck.

Smoot Rawlings was furious now, fighting hyperventilation.

"Did it ever occur to you that maybe—just maybe!—that business down at the marina was nuthin' more than some pissed-off somebody tryin' to get revenge for what he's pretty damn sure Delton did to Ramona Walker? Say, Bear? Did that possibility *ever* occur to you? Or are you just a little too close to see?"

Barrett didn't answer. What was the point?

Smoot Rawlings practically threw Barrett's report in his face.

"This is unsatisfactory. I want it rewritten. I want a statement from old man Hilton. And I want it today."

"Yes, sir."

"And next time you feel the need to look someplace, Detective Raines, you get yourself a warrant! I don't want every goddamn piece of evidence we get on your brother thrown out because you got a hard-on at a peep show!"

Barrett fought the sudden, white fire which exploded in his gut. He could have slugged Smoot, then. He could have dragged the fat bastard out of that chair and wrung his neck like a chicken.

"Now give me that tape."

"Excuse me?"

"You heard me," Rawlings bit off. "Give me the god-damn tape."

Barrett handed over the video.

"Nobody's indispensable, Barrett," came the growl across the hardwood. "Not even you."

"I understand, Chief." Barrett acknowledged the threat calmly. He'd had a feeling Rawlings wouldn't back him up.

That's why he'd made a copy of the tape.

Barrett sipped a Budweiser as he slumped in one of the twins' back-yard swings. The Bud was still beaded with condensation even though the sun had long set below the bay's indigo horizon. Barrett was still chafed by the ass-chewing he'd gotten in Smoot's office. Nothing he'd done on Splinter's boat seemed sufficient to account for the chief's volcanic reaction. Even more unsettling was Rawlings's reaction to the attempt on Delton's life. Here you have a shotgun assault that should have prompted a priority investigation and yet Smoot's response was to send Taylor Folsom and a print kit out to the dead men's van at the marina while he stayed at the station to ream Bear's ass. It didn't make sense.

Other things didn't make sense, either. Wasn't it time, Barrett had asked his chief, to get the boys from Florida's Department of Law Enforcement involved in this investigation? Wouldn't it be a good idea to contact the Bureau of Alcohol, Tobacco and Firearms regarding the potential for federal violations? Smoot said *"No!"* loud and clear to both suggestions. Barrett ached to find some cause for Rawlings's behavior which was not nefarious. And then it came to him.

It was Ramona.

One of the things that made her special was Ramona's ability to make every man she met believe he was her one and only. How many times had Smoot Rawlings been under Ramona's spell? Seen her? Smelled her? Felt her hands lightly brush the inside of his thigh?

Barrett belatedly realized that Smoot could have carried a torch for Ramona half his life. He certainly had feelings for her. Desires, surely. Or fantasies. And then along comes the Bear. Gives his chief a choice. Either believe his Helen of Troy is a tramp. Or believe that the nigger suspected of brutally murdering her is trying to save his ass by wrecking her reputation. Wasn't hard to see which choice would win out.

The tape was the final straw. Barrett hadn't thought that one through, had not imagined how Smoot would react to finding out that the woman of his dreams was dirty. Barrett pressed the beer to his forehead. Smoot couldn't afford to believe that Delton was telling the truth. Because if he did, everything he'd ever felt for Ramona Walker would have to be a lie.

It supplied further reason for Rawlings to keep outsiders away from the investigation. It explained his recent foot-dragging, his anger. It also told Barrett that, for the present at least, he was very much on his own.

Barrett placed the cool aluminum of his beer to his temple. He was trying hard not to communicate his anxieties to his brother. It was hard to know how much to tell Delton. Hard to know if he should tell him anything at all.

Delton nursed his own Bud alongside his brother. They sat side by side, did Barrett and Delton, on homemade swings secured by yellow nylon line to the smooth limb of a magnolia that spread overhead. A uniformed police officer stood vigil with a shotgun at the pines which bordered Barrett's lot. A pair of squad cars cruised the streets; their side-mounted torchlights cut swaths across the garden and lawn.

Conspicuous surveillance, Barrett had asked of the men at the station. Protection. Somebody tried to kill my brother.

Barrett just wished he knew whether it had anything to do with Ramona. Delton pawed at the perspiration stinging his eyes.

"Ain't it hot?"

No reply from Bear at all. No indication that he'd even heard the lame attempt at conversation.

"I'm sweatin' like a bored chigger in a nigger's navel," Delton tried again. Nothing. Delton took a long pull of beer. "You're the only one believes me. Aren't you, Bear? The only goddamn one. And now your ass is in a sling." That got through.

"What're brothers for?" Barrett smiled ruefully.

"Guess I wouldn't be the best to ask."

"Just another memory, Delton. That's all."

Delton considered that one over a pull or two.

"...Thing is, you get right down to it, memories are all we got. Am I right?"

"I don't know," Barrett replied. "Maybe."

Delton swirled his beer in a maelstrom about the bottom of its can.

"'Member when Old Man Suggs threw me outta shop? You remember that?"

"Weren't you building a bomb or something?"

"Inside a lamppost. Old bastard shit his britches."

Barrett laughed. He didn't want to, but he couldn't help it.

"He put you on suspension for that, didn't he?"

"Mmmhmm. I tried to get him back. Tried to stick one of his tires. Damn thang blew up in my face."

"They took you to the hospital." Barrett nodded with recollection. "I thought you were gonna die."

"Naw." Delton drained his brew. "Too damn mean to die."

Barrett could not quite bring himself to disagree. For a little while neither brother said anything. Just creaked back and forth on their swings.

"Not fair, is it, Bear? You did all the work. I got all the glory."

"And the girls, damn your hide." Barrett tried to interject some levity. "Always the woman killer."

"Yeah," Delton admitted that assessment as a matter of fact no less demonstrable than the humidity.

"But there was one girl I always wanted. Always. Never even got close."

"Really? Who was that?" Barrett perked up.

"You know her."

"Hell I do."

"She was Homecoming Queen. 1983."

Barrett turned to his brother in genuine astonishment.

"Laura Anne?!"

Delton smiled at Barrett's surprise.

"People always give me credit for being the Romeo. But the only lady I ever felt like could make me decent, hell—I never had a chance in the world of gettin'. That's 'cause you got her, Bear."

Barrett sat stunned beside his brother.

"Well, I'll be damned," he finally managed.

Delton crushed his can on his knee.

"She is special, is Laura Anne. Man'd be a damn fool to let that go."

Barrett tipped his own beer back. Finished the last, warm, amber drops.

"Guess it's about time we turned in."

"Sure." Delton was rising from his swing when Barrett placed a hand, briefly, on his brother's shoulder.

"Thank you, Delton. Thank you a lot."

Hernando regarded Frank Sienna from his familiar position at the long-dead diner's solitary table.

"Life with you is getting more complicated, *compadre.*"

There was no sun to display constellations through the roof at this hastily scheduled meeting. It was very late. There was nothing to see by except the moonlight that struck obliquely from the water and passed through the abandoned diner's unscreened windows to reflect dimly off long-dead images of singers and movie stars.

"I'm not used to paying for jobs that don't get done," Sienna responded to the Latin.

"I lost two good men trying to take care of your problem."

"*Our* problem, Hernando. The problem is ours."

"Perhaps it should become yours only."

"What the hell's that supposed to mean?"

"Maybe you should kill this cop's brother yourself. Maybe you should kill the cop. His family. Anything with a tongue."

"Now, that'd be real smart."

The Latin shrugged. "Maybe I should find another supplier for my weapons."

"I've got half a million rounds in transit for you, Hernando. That's merchandise you're getting on *credit*, need I remind you?"

Hernando patted the broad tip of his tie damply to his forehead.

"Y'know"—Sienna settled back—"I'm beginning to think maybe you're not as big a player as you'd like me to believe, Hernando. Maybe not a serious customer after all."

"I will need a thousand weapons in the next six months," the Latin informed him coldly.

"I can supply them," Frank said.

Hernando smoothed his tie. "When do I see the ammunition?"

"Week from tomorrow. Half a million, made-for-war bullets. Nine-millimeter. And I'll expect cash on delivery. *Compadre.*"

Hernando leaned on the table.

"And what are you going to do about this black man, *amigo*? Hmm? How do you plan to protect our investment?"

Sienna smiled.

"You'll see when you get here."

The television glowed, an electronic furnace in Barrett's bedroom. The flickering images cast shadows over Laura Anne's face and breasts and hips. Over her legs, long and tawny.

Barrett regarded his wife from a pillow at the foot of the bed. She pulled a sheet to her neck.

Which allowed Barrett's attention to return to the tape that flickered on the TV screen.

"Pretty kinky." Laura Anne squirmed in the bed.

"It's tame compared to a porn tape." Barrett shrugged.

"Thing is, I wouldn't know any of the people on a porn tape. *This...*" Laura Anne shivered. "I don't want to remember Ramona like this. I don't want *you* remembering her like this. The woman's entitled to her privacy, seems to me. Even dead! And here you are, a peeping Tom! What gives you the right, exactly?"

"I'm trying to find a killer."

"And you think a smut tape's gonna help?"

"I *don't know*, Laura Anne. That's why I have to look."

Barrett's wife distracted herself with one of the boys' activity books; she was trimming a page for the family scrapbook. Barrett took a quick glance.

The whole page was shot like BBs with numbered dots. Barrett loved connecting those dots with the boys. In some books, the easier ones, you could tell even without connecting the dots that, once joined with crayon or pencil, this picture would be a horse or that one a wheelbarrow. The ones Barrett preferred, though, and the ones favored by Ben and Tyndall, gave no hint at all of what they were to represent.

Barrett could distinguish even at a glance little Ben's straight, carefully wrought lines from Tyndall's crooked ones. The particular aggregate of lines and dots which Laura Anne now slipped into her scrapbook turned out to be a pair of dinosaurs. Barrett wondered briefly if these were to be the representative images for his children. He played with the idea briefly until something less pleasant in the here-and-now brought him back to the tape which unreeled on his television.

Ramona laughed pale and naked into the camera. Long, auburn hair. A sheen of wet beaded on her belly and breasts. She turned for the camera.

You could bend a nail on that butt, Barrett thought to himself.

And watched Splinter hump beneath.

"Any word on the jury?"

Barrett knew Laura Anne was trying to lure him back to the scrapbook.

"Roland figures the grand jury's gonna return an indictment tomorrow," Barrett assented dully. "Murder One they're calling it. Open and shut. I keep hoping there's something in here'll help Delton."

"Then Delton is a man in great need." Laura Anne went back to her labor.

Barrett stabbed suddenly at the VCR with its remote.

"There. See there?"

The deck buzzed to hold a picture in freeze-frame. Barrett pulled Laura Anne to the TV.

"See that? In the mirror. Man holding the camera's wearing a tie."

Not a large image in the frame. But definitely there. A tie stretched up the cameraman's wide belly and sweat-stained shirt. A pin anchored the tie above a monogram.

"Can you make it out?"

"Too small." Laura Anne shook her head. "But I don't see how a tie helps anything."

"Doesn't look right." Barrett stretched his neck. "Man wearing a tie in a situation like that. It's out of place."

"Maybe it was Snake Adders," Laura Anne suggested.

"Snake never wore a tie in his life," Barrett replied.

"Maybe they hired somebody to make the tape."

"Nuh uh. This wasn't planned. Dollars to doughnuts it started out a poker game. Just cards first. Then things get hot. Somebody drags out the video-cam. Katie bar the door."

"Even if you *knew* I still don't see how it'd help Delton," Laura Anne said stubbornly.

"Turns out Splinter served a hitch in the marines," Barrett began. "So did Snake. They both like guns. Like to own 'em. Shoot 'em. Makes sense, I guess. But they both have money they shouldn't. That *doesn't* make sense. And one other thing they held in common—"

"Ramona." Laura Anne laid the scrapbook aside. "Held literally in her case."

"Right you are," Barrett agreed. "So let's suppose Ramona was in bed with these guys for guns as well as sex. Something goes wrong. Somebody has a reason for wanting her dead: She wants more money. She wants more control."

"Or maybe she's cheating," Laura Anne offered. "Holding money back."

"Sure." Barrett nodded quickly. "Could be anything. The point is: Somebody besides Delton *could be* Ramona's killer. But to *prove* that I have to know exactly how Ramona was involved. She sure as hell didn't know anything about Uzis."

"She knew about money," Laura Anne came back. "Maybe she put up the cash for somebody else to buy. Maybe that's how she got started."

"Good woman, that's exactly what I think." Bear climbed into bed beside his wife. "But she must have done a lot more."

"Like what?"

Barrett settled onto the sheets. "Well. Suppose you're selling something you shouldn't. Drugs, guns, stolen cars—anything. If you're rich, nobody's gonna notice ten or twenty thousand extra dollars floating around. But if you're not rich, what do you do?"

"You sit on it?" she guessed.

"You make it clean," he answered. "You make the money look like legitimate profits from some reputable business. But to do that you need a business that deals a lot in cash. A bar, say—"

"Or a restaurant!"

"You got it." Bear nodded. "Gun money goes into Ramona's restaurant—comes out on the books like steak and lobster. In fact, I'm guessing that Ramona probably wasn't one of the original runners. My guess is she was recruited because somebody saw her place as an easy way to launder money."

"Have you tried this out on Smoot?" Laura Anne asked.

"Can't yet." Barrett shook his head sleepily.

"Why not?"

"Because for this to work, Snake Adders and Splinter Townsend would have to be tied to the restaurant. Partners or something. They weren't."

"You're sure of that?"

"Absolutely. Taylor checked."

"Did he check other businesses?"

"What other businesses?"

Barrett was suddenly wide awake.

"I don't know." Laura Anne shrugged. "But just because Snake and Splinter aren't partners in the restaurant doesn't mean they couldn't be partners someplace else. Does Ramona have businesses someplace else?"

"I don't know."

"Why don't you ask her accountant?" Barrett's wife suggested simply and Bear saw a whole mess of disconnected dots suddenly connecting with razor-straight lines.

"Oh, my God."

"Bear—?"

Barrett kissed Laura Anne quickly on the lips.

"You're a smart one, you know that?"

"Bear! Where're you going?"

"I'm gonna grab some shit for brains."

Detective Raines grabbed the gun in his closet.

"And then I'm going to work."

Chapter twenty

The housewarming had about run down by the time Barrett arrived at the Boatwrights' new home. Barrett had to admit it was a nice place. Close to four thousand square feet—somebody at the church reported that fact as if whispering parameters for classified technology. There was a lot of brick, a lot of bathrooms, and a big veranda which stretched on pylons over the bay.

It was late by the time Barrett got there. The dozens of well-heeled family, friends, and clients who had come to congratulate Martha and Ferris on their seaside mansion had dwindled to a trickle of thoroughly sober holdouts.

"Ready to go in?" Dick asked from his side of the cruiser.

"Wait 'til everybody leaves," Barrett replied. He didn't want to make a scene. He didn't want to embarrass the Boatwrights or give Ferris an excuse to become defensive. And so Barrett waited with Dick as the party inside wound down. It gave him some time to think. To look. This was truly the Big House which Barrett saw sprawled along the water, and Bear could not help but remember, as he waited patiently in his cruiser, that his own grandfather had waited outside a similar home that Ferris's grandfather had erected not far from this place and three decades earlier.

Old Man Boatwright had built that first large house on a swell of land beside his mill. He had warmed that earlier mansion, had the Old Man, on a bitter cold November evening. The white sawyers and foremen had trekked in stiffly with the men whose office positions gave them an automatic invitation to that housewarming. The black workers congregated beneath the brittle stars over a picnic table spread with scraps from the Big House. They warmed themselves over a lightard stump which Barrett's grandfather had dragged up to kill the chill. Warmed themselves in the year's first frost as the white folks were warmed effortlessly inside.

"Looks like it's petering out." Dick Hanson cut that memory short.

Barrett rolled down his window. Doc Hardesty was making his goodbyes at Ferris's new front door. So was Hoyt Young.

"Wouldn't normally picture Hoyt at a housewarming," Barrett grunted.

"Maybe he's got religion." Dick grinned.

The last couples bade their farewells. Barrett grabbed the briefcase propped on the center console.

"Let's go."

Ferris saw Barrett strolling up the walk. It was a sinuous walk, lit with amber courtesy lights, like a runway. Ferris had been particular about the monkey grass that bordered the walk. The occasional clumps of juniper. The crepe myrtle that shaded the front door's generous foyer.

Ferris was always particular about things like that. He liked to think that he had an artistic sensibility. Martha stood beside him, now, at their massively overwrought entrance.

"Ferris, is that a nigrah man on our driveway?"

"It's Barrett, Mother. And Dick Hanson, I believe."

"I don't remember an invitation for *them*."

A few seconds later the black man and his partner were actually inside. They had been greeted profusely and rudely at the door.

"I'm sorry you're having to come out so late," was how Martha managed it.

"Well, I didn't want to interrupt the party."

Barrett smiled while looking straight at Ferris.

There was all sorts of greenery inside. Planters of ferns and ligustrum hung from enormous cypress beams above a tiled floor. An interior door almost as heavy as the bulkhead out front closed off a study which exited immediately off the foyer. A living room spread lavishly beyond.

Martha dished out a smile to show Barrett in.

"Things are such a mess now. I wish you could have come earlier."

Barrett resisted the temptation to tell Martha that she definitely would not have wanted to have seen him earlier on her very special evening.

The guests who had come early had obviously been well fêted. Barrett could see from the door tables which spread salads and melons and pigs-in-a-blanket, sea bass and snapper and shrimp. There were enough leavings of barbecued ribs and brisket to have produced cardiac arrest in a mastodon.

"Won't you have something, Bear?" Ferris's voice squeaked through a triple chin. And was that a twitch just now from those malformed fingers? "Got plenty to eat. Sure you won't?"

"Just some time," Barrett replied.

"Surely."

"Prob'ly ought to be private," Barrett said.

"Everyone needs some privacy." Ferris's smile was brittle on his face. "Now and then."

"Is this a study right over here?" Barrett pointed to the oak door closed off to the side.

Ferris's face darkened.

"The study, yes. Well, I suppose that would be excellent for a private conversation."

"Ferris…?"

"It's all right, Martha. Just business, I'm sure."

The cypress beams which supported the living room's airy ceiling carried straight through to Ferris's comfortably appointed study. Sailing tackle draped from the beams. Blocks and pulleys. A jib. An anchor. A stained-glass seascape bordered the picture window which overlooked the winding walk out front. A second large, uncluttered window gave a view of the bay. Venetian blinds were lowered to half-mast on both windows; Barrett couldn't help noticing when he first followed Ferris into the study that the blinds were black.

He had also noticed the photographs. There were photos everywhere. Still shots of the bay and marine life, of landscapes and land animals. One photo offered a timed exposure of a hummingbird in flight.

"You've got a real vocation," Dick Hanson remarked before they got down to business.

"Avocation, really," Ferris had replied.

Ferris couldn't manage modesty even when he tried. And Barrett would agree that there was much to see in those pictures on the wall, but right now Ferris's feeble art was drowned by something raw and real which glowed like phosphorous on his television screen. The study's TV and VCR faced a fragile Victorian desk and a pair of Chippendale chairs. Ferris perched on the edge of his seat. Barrett popped in the videotape and watched the accountant as Ramona Walker played to the camera off-screen.

Voluptuous. Naked. Framed in a room filled with mirrors.

Barrett noticed Ferris kept fidgeting with the pin which anchored his omnipresent and outsized tie.

"Where'd you git this, Bear?" the big man squeaked.

"How it works, Ferris—I ask the questions. You answer. For instance: You ever take videos at a sex party?"

"At no time."

The fat rolled in waves from his jaw to his neck.

"You sure about that, Ferris?"

"It's immoral." Boatwright had to tear his eyes away from the screen. "Disgusting."

"You're lying, Ferris."

Ferris turned to face him, then, his eyes buried in their massive skull like pissholes in a snowbank.

"What you doin' to me, Bear? What you doin'?"

"Take a look." Barrett snapped open his briefcase.

There were perhaps a half-dozen glossies inside. Black-and-whites. Eight by ten. Blowups.

"Not as refined as your work, Ferris—" Barrett laid the photos out for inspection one at a time, "—but for our purposes, it'll do. What do you see here, for instance—hmm? Right here. In the mirror."

The chair groaned as Ferris leaned over.

A portion of a man's tie was enlarged so that it filled the glossy's eight-by-ten boundary.

"We got it off a mirror," Barrett explained. "Then we blew it up. What say, Ferris? What's holding that tie onto that gut you see right here?"

A Mason pin anchored the tie. The monogram was bright in silver on a turquoise face. Much larger, now. Easy to see.

FB

"I need some water."

Ferris Boatwright tried to rise from his chair. His knees buckled.

"Here you go."

If Hanson hadn't been there to help catch the big man, Barrett was sure, Ferris would have collapsed to the floor.

"Easy, now. Easy."

They eased Martha's husband back into his chair.

"Why you doin' this to me? Why?"

"We know Ramona was cleaning cash through the restaurant, Ferris. She was a sharp lady. Sharper, I think, than most of us gave credit. But she wasn't any math major. And she wasn't an accountant. That was your job, wasn't it?"

"I don't know what—"

"You bullshit me, Ferris, I'll play that tape in court. Nothing private about that, is there? All your holy-rolling friends'll get to see.

Your clients will see. Your goddamn Sunday school suckasses'll see. Your wife!"

"I want to see my lawyer," Ferris croaked like an oversized bullfrog.

Time to ease up.

"Give me a little information maybe you won't need a lawyer," Barrett told the fat man. "But that's a maybe. It's up to you."

"This is blackmail!"

"Giving evidence to a police officer is not blackmail, Ferris. Now, what in the *hell* have you been covering up?"

Ferris took a long time to reply.

"Ask Sienna."

"Frank Sienna?"

"That's right." Ferris nodded. "He's the man behind it."

"Behind what?"

"Contraband of some sort." Ferris waved his pie-sized hand vaguely.

"'Of some sort'—what the hell does that mean?" Bear demanded.

"I don't know." Ferris's head swiveled inside his shoulders. "I didn't want to know. When Ramona first came to me I was very clear about that. It was my job to clean the cash—not to know where it came from. I wanted no connection with the actual operation. And none with her partners."

"Sienna know you're involved?"

"Sienna knows everything," Ferris spit out.

Barrett took out his spiral pad.

"How many partners are we talking about here?"

"Besides me, four. Snake Adders, Splinter Townsend, Hoyt Young—"

"And Frank. Got it." Bear made the note. "How many businesses were actually cleaning money?"

"Several." Ferris massaged his temple. "Restaurant, of course. Bar. Bowling alley. And a laundromat over in Lake City."

"All cash?" Barrett asked briskly.

"Naturally." Ferris offered a wan, evil smile. "Wouldn't work otherwise, would it?"

Barrett snapped his pad shut.

"There's a lot to cover here, Ferris. We're gonna need a statement."

"Right now?" Boatwright seemed surprised.

"Or I could arrest you for juggling books," Barrett offered. "Or peddling porn. How 'bout murder?"

"No!" Ferris was suddenly agitated. "I swear to God!"

"I'll settle for a statement," Barrett said quietly. "Let's go."

Ramona's accountant clamped pale hands onto the arms of his expensive antique chair.

"I have friends to think about, Bear! Family!"

"I've got family, too," Barrett reminded Ferris quietly. "Including one who's out on bail. Sorry, Ferris, murder's got to take the door prize. Even at a housewarming."

Barrett led Ferris out of the study. Martha met them wringing her hands.

"Ferris, what is it? Is there anything wrong?"

"Nothing, honey. Don't make a fuss."

Martha turned to Barrett. "Where are you taking my husband?"

"Just to the station, Martha. Have him back in a couple of hours."

"Can't it wait?"

"No," Barrett said firmly.

"Ferris, are you under arrest?" Her voice rose urgently. Shrill.

"Martha, take it easy. We just need a statement, is all."

"A statement? What does that mean?"

"Don't make a fuss, Mama," Ferris said, but would not meet her eyes.

"He's just helping us out, Miz Boatwright," Dick offered. "It's routine."

"Routine!"

She spit as she turned to Barrett. "Time was, you wouldn't be inside my house!"

"Martha—!" Ferris interceded weakly.

"Time was, you wouldn't wipe your feet on my driveway!"

Barrett regarded her calmly. "Times change, Martha. You'll just have to get used to it."

Barrett stepped past Ferris to open the too-large door which led outside. That was all the diversion Ferris needed. The huge man slammed Barrett through the foyer, out onto the front steps.

"Ferris!" Martha screamed. But Ferris was already back inside his study.

"Dick?"

"He's locked in, Bear."

Barrett pushed past Martha to the study. Tried the door uselessly.

"Ferris!" Martha screamed again. Barrett pounded the oak once, hard, with his fist.

"Ferris, this won't do any good. Ferris?"

"What's happening?" Martha wailed. She was panicked now. Pleading. "What's he doing in there?"

"Watch her for me, Dick."

Barrett drew his .38. Fired four rounds into the lock.

Martha screamed.

Barrett and Dick kicked together, hard. Kicked again.

The door would not budge.

"Oh my God!" Martha covered her face with her hands.

"Is there another way in?" Barrett shouted. "Martha!"

"You go to hell!" she snarled.

Barrett shoved past Ferris's wife. Out the front door.

"What do you think you're doing?" She ran after him.

Barrett plunged left off the steps into a hedge of shrubbery and soaker hose. There was the study window, bordered with stained glass and azaleas.

The Bear wrapped his jacket around his hand.

"What is he—!" Barrett crashed through the picture window

and followed its shards into Ferris's study. He was just in time to see
Ferris Boatwright place a revolver to his temple.

"Ferris, *don't!*"

An explosion. The big man's head jerked back as if kicked. Ferris dropped like a sack of meal beside his custom-made desk. Martha's
scream rose high and frozen. A long, terrified lamentation—

Barrett rushed to the deacon's side beneath Martha's high shriek.
He could see the matter that oozed from Ferris's brain. He could see
the blood that spread like a stain about the man's great head. And
he could see something else.

Dozens of photographs spilled from Ferris's desk onto the
floor beside Martha's husband. They were carefully composed, these
photos. All in color. And all of Ramona. Alive. Naked. Teasing. Full-
breasted and shameless.

"Call 911, Dick!"

Barrett swept the photos aside, dropped to his knees beside
his one-time schoolmate. He would do everything he could to save
Ramona's accountant. But Barrett knew, even as he labored, that Ferris Boatwright was dead.

Chapter twenty-one

Ferris Boatwright's suicide set off a bombshell of speculation in Deacon Beach's small community. Channel 7 and Stacy Kline beat the drum looking for rhymes and reasons. And because Ferris was politically active, his death made a regional splash, too. There was even a network truck down from Tallahassee. It wasn't long before reporters linked Boatwright's suicide to Barrett's murder investigation. Bear normally didn't like having media sniffing over his cases but he had to admit that, in this instance, it could be a help.

"Too many eyes looking now for Smoot and Roland to just convict Delton out of convenience," Barrett told Laura Anne. "There's evidence now that doesn't square with their initial assumptions. Roland knows he's not gonna be able to skate through this case anymore; he's going to have to actually prove Delton guilty in court. And he can't pretend that Delton's lying about the guns."

An irony in the sudden, auspicious turn of events was that Barrett could not convey any of this good news to his brother. He could talk to Laura Anne. But to Delton, Barrett could offer only the vaguest of encouragements. Maybe this morning's get-together would change all that.

Barrett had asked for an early meeting. The chief was there with his coffee and a folder thick with Barrett's detailed report. Roland showed up on time. Barrett noticed that the miniblinds which hung like sails to shield Smoot's office from the early sun were ivory-white.

Might there be some hope at last for Delton?

"He's played us straight all along." Barrett laid out his brother's case for Smoot and Roland. "He told us Ramona was running guns and she was. Sienna's the point man. He's the one who gets the weapons. He's the one recruited Splinter and Hoyt for the heavy work. He brought Ramona in later to launder the profits."

"Who recruited Ferris?" Roland frowned.

"Ramona. She had the leverage."

All three men glanced toward the photos confiscated from the Boatwrights' elegant new home.

"We know the players in this thing," Barrett went on. "We know that Splinter and Snake and all the rest created limited partnerships for themselves in a dry-cleaning business in Lake City, a bowling alley, and a bar."

"All cash-heavy businesses," Roland had to admit.

"And all owned by Ramona Walker." Smoot reviewed the folder on his desk.

"But you still don't have anything here that'll stand up in court," Roland cautioned. "And even if you did, what's gun-running got to do with Ramona's murder?"

"Maybe she wanted more of the pie," Barrett said expansively. "Maybe she wanted out. I don't know. But I'm telling you this: Delton Raines did not kill Ramona Walker. It was one of her partners."

"Maybe Ferris killed her," Smoot suggested. "That'd explain the suicide."

"No." Barrett shook his head.

"Something drove him to it." Roland jabbed with his pen.

"Guilt," Barrett replied. "And humiliation. The man cleaned dirty money! He took dirty pictures! Sooner or later one or the other would show up in public, Ferris knew that. I think he was afraid of

Sienna, too. Matter of fact I think it was Sienna tried to kill Delton the other day. Or kidnap him, I haven't figured which."

"So your lead suspect is now Frank Sienna?"

Barrett shrugged. "He's a place to start."

"This is too damn much conjecture." Roland shook his head. But his voice lacked conviction.

Barrett leaned forward. "Remember what Ferris said? 'Ask Sienna. Sienna's the man behind it.' Well, take a look at this."

He dropped a fax onto Smoot's polished desk.

"List of gun dealers. Pennsylvania. Specifies the guys and gals who lost their license. Wanta guess who's in here?"

"Frank Sienna," Smoot chewed.

"That's right," Bear affirmed. "'Cording to the folks up there, Frank came to Pennsylvania from the marines. Combat all the way. Got home, he started a gun shop. Ran the place less than three years when they pulled his papers—Bureau of Alcohol, Tobacco and Firearms. When I called BATF they didn't even know Frank was down here."

"This is a lot of shit you're laying on us, Bear."

"Shit happens."

"I go to trial in two weeks!"

"We got the wrong man, Roland. Give me a couple of weeks I think I can prove it."

"You can get a warrant for Splinter's boat right now." Smoot nodded glumly to the folder. "What you got from Ferris ties Splinter in directly to the operation. Judge Blackmond'll grant a search. And this time it'd be legal, Bear."

"There's nothing on that boat now, you can bet." Barrett shook his head. "We've waited too long."

"Well, then," Roland interjected. "How do you plan to prove anything?"

"Delton's told us from the beginning there was a buy coming down. He believes the buyer is from somewhere in Latin America. There's been more than one transaction with this buyer, apparently. My guess is he's somebody Frank and the boys want to cultivate. If

they're gonna score with this guy they've got to move their merchandise quickly. We need to be there when they do."

"Not gonna be easy." Rawlings was shaking his head. "They've
got to know we're looking."

"Maybe we can change that," Barrett responded quickly. "Make
Frank and what's left of his boys a little more comfortable."

"How you plan to do that?" Smoot asked.

"We can use Delton."

Barrett watched for Roland's reaction. He didn't expect the
prosecutor to embrace the suggestion right away. He just hoped
Roland wouldn't reject it outright.

"Use Delton." Reed gnawed on the cap of his pen. "How?"

Barrett smiled. He had them now.

"You boys ever play poker?"

A green-visored lamp hung on a brass chain over poker cards and
whiskey. But it wasn't Ramona's place. Poker had moved to Frank
Sienna's condo not long after Ramona was killed.

"Less attention we draw to ourselves the better," Frank told
his players.

Well, they were getting a hell of a lot of attention now.

Hoyt Young's hands quivered more than usual over the ivory
chips which Frank substituted for greenbacks at his marble inlaid
table. Splinter stared blankly over his toothpick to a fan of cards.

"What's the problem, Splinter?"

"Closer we get to payday the more people get killed. First it
was Ramona. Then Snake. Now Ferris."

"Don't worry about Ferris."

"I worry," Hoyt spoke up querulously.

"Don't," Sienna commanded. And then, more reassuringly, "By
the time anybody straightens out all the kinks Ferris put in those
books, we'll be rich and gone."

"You sure about that?" Hoyt clearly hoped that Frank was.

"You know, Hoyt, sometimes you're a pain in the ass."

The doorbell chimed. Hoyt jumped.

"Jesus Christ, it's the pizza," Sienna growled.

"I'm not hungry."

"I am. Go get it."

Hoyt left the table. Splinter was still scowling.

"Play or fold, Splinter?" Sienna inquired without interest.

"You don't tell us everything, do you, Frank?"

"What's that supposed to mean?"

"Why'd you have me clean out the boat? Why so quick?"

"Let's just say I had a feeling."

"Feeling, hell. What was Bear doin' out there to begin with?"

"You know as much about that as I do, Splinter."

"Bullshit. You know something. And you're not telling me."

"I tell you everything you need to know. Now. Play? Or fold?"

"Frank—" Hoyt's voiced whined in.

"Put it anywhere." Sienna didn't look up from his cards until the pizza dropped hot into his lap.

"The hell?"

Frank Sienna threw the pizza to the floor—

And found Delton Raines standing beside his table.

"'Lo, Frank."

"He just walked in!" Hoyt wailed. "He just—"

"Shut up, Hoyt," Sienna snapped. And then, to Delton, "You got balls, boy. I do give you that."

"Just saw the delivery. Thought I'd make myself welcome."

"You're not."

"Frank." Delton smiled warmly. "You try to kill a man, you got to be nicer than this!"

"Was that—?" Splinter stalled. "Was that *you*, Frank?"

"Shut up," Sienna snarled.

Splinter did. But not Delton.

"You gotta keep your boys better informed, Frank. Didn't you tell 'em I was blackmailing Ramona? Or din' you want 'em to know?"

"I didn't know myself," Sienna replied. "Not for certain, anyway."

"Ramona sure as hell did!" Delton cackled.

"She didn't get the chance to tell me." Sienna regained his cool. "She was going to, I'm pretty sure. But then you killed her."

"Man's innocent until proved guilty, Frank." Delton toyed with an ivory chip. "You know that."

"How much does he know?" Hoyt floated the question.

"I 'bout know it all." Delton kept his eyes on Frank.

"How much did you tell the cops?" Sienna asked flatly.

"Nothing." Delton shrugged. "Don't get me wrong, I *could* have tol' 'em every little thang. The guns. The launderin'. The spick—"

"So why didn't you?"

"'Cause you all are a moneymaking proposition, Frank. And I want to be a partner."

Sienna tapped out a Marlboro. Snapped his Zippo open— Semper Fi.

"Partner, huh? That's pretty ambitious for a man headed to the electric chair."

"I'm not goin' to any chair besides this one."

Delton took Hoyt's at the table.

"Only way you're gonna beat the griddle is to jump bail and go to Cuba!" Splinter chortled.

"Don't have to do no jumpin'." Delton smiled. "Roland's gonna drop the case."

"That's a crock." Sienna got rid of a card.

"He's got to." Delton dealt Frank a card before he discarded one of his own. "Barrett's done messed up so bad! Half the evidence is inadmissible. And all that blood work? Lab fucked it up."

"Sure they did." Sienna's eyes were bright.

"Fucked it up big-time," Delton assured him. "Judge Black-mond tol' Thurman we could move for a mistrial first day."

"I don't believe it," Splinter interjected without conviction.

"Be in the paper tomorrah." Delton displayed his hand for Frank. "Read 'em an' weep."

"I'll read 'em all right," Sienna snapped. "But nothing in the paper means you partner with *me*. Every man here earns his keep. Every man contributes. What can you do for me, Delton? Besides shut your trap?"

"I can get information," Delton replied.

"I've forgotten more about guns and buyers than you'll ever know." Sienna waved him off.

"How 'bout the cops, Frank?" Delton countered. "You got a pipeline to *them*?"

"What the hell is he talking about?" Hoyt was alarmed.

"Hoyt—" Frank turned to the younger man. "Make yourself a drink."

And then to Delton—

"I'm listening."

"I been living with Bear, you know that. We talk. I find out things. I found out, f'r instance, that Bear knows Ferris was cleaning money. He knows you're a partner, Frank. You and Ramona and Splinter-brain. You, too, Hoyt. Seems like y'all got yourself into a number of cash-heavy enterprises."

"How about the guns?" Sienna asked warily.

"He suspects. Thanks to you, Splinter."

"Fuckin' nigger, I didn't say a goddamn thing!"

"He broke in your boat, jerk-off. Found some cash. Found that Uzi you hid, too. Under the TV?"

"See why I had you clean it out?" Sienna regarded Splinter mildly. "I knew the bastard wasn't out there to catch a tan. You dumb son of a *bitch*."

"Anybody could have a gun!" Splinter protested.

"Lucky for you Bear didn't have a warrant," Delton observed.

"He find anything else?" Sienna turned his attention back to Barrett's brother.

"Home movies." Delton grinned. "Splinter and Ramona. Cops call it 'Pencil Dick.'"

"Fuckin' nigger!"

Splinter launched across the table. Delton caught him in one huge hand, smacked his head like a gourd against the table. Splinter slipped to the floor.

But came up cursing with a knife. It was a switchblade. Long. Ugly.

"Man's got hisself a frog sticker," Delton commented casually.

"You ever cut up on anybody, Splinter? I mean, anybody could cut back?"

"I'll cut your ass, you black son of bitch!"

"You come over here with that pissant tickler." Delton seemed actually to enjoy the prospect. "I'll take it away and then I be usin' it—now hear me good, white boy—to worry yo' *nuts* off."

"Put it away, Splinter," Sienna said sharply.

"Fuck you!"

"I said, *put it away.*"

Frank Sienna trained a .45 automatic steadily on Splinter's chest. Townsend wavered just a moment. Folded his knife. Put it in his pocket. Sienna engaged the safety on his .45. Turned to Delton.

"How much time do we have?"

"Not a lot. Bear tol' me he was going to Judge Blackmond end of the week. Show him what-all he got from Ferris."

"I knew something was wrong!" Hoyt wrung his hands. "Goddammit, I knew!"

"Give it a rest, Hoyt," Delton said calmly. And then to Sienna, "He's not ready to move yet."

"When's he gonna be?" Sienna asked the question calmly.

"I'd say a week before he knocks on your door. Maybe two. But that's all. You got something hangin', you're gonna have to move."

"I don't trust this son of a bitch." Splinter spat it out like venom.

Sienna didn't reply right away. He took a seat at the table, gathered the cards. Shuffled the deck.

"What about it, Frank?" Delton smiled. "We playin'? Or do you wanta fold?"

Delton emerged not many minutes later into the cool lights which framed Frank's condominium complex. Palm trees not native to the region swayed their fronds in a gusty breeze off the water. Delton stumbled past the kidney-shaped pool and adjoining spa to reach Water Street.

He turned down that asphalt ribbon and past the gate which advertised "SeaCrest Condos" above a plaster dolphin. A brisk walk took Delton to a connecting blacktop road. Delton was only on Vineland a few seconds when an unmarked van pulled out from a shelter of cabbage palms to take up a position behind him.

He was perspiring heavily. He checked a newly purchased watch on his wrist and picked up his pace along Vineland.

The van closed in from behind.

Delton reached inside his shirt.

The van accelerated quickly. Delton turned to meet the headlights now turned on full—

Brakes locked!

"Jesus!"

The van's side door banged open. Barrett waited inside, framed by a courtesy light.

"Goddammit, Delton, you keep that thing *on*."

"Sorry," Delton apologized as he untangled himself from the microphone and transmitter which still clung to a strip of adhesive taped to his washboard abdomen.

"How'd I do?"

"Get in." Barrett offered a hand to his brother. "Hear for yourself."

A couple of new faces inhabited the chief's office with Roland Reed and Barrett. Coast Guard Commander Henry Sykes shared the chief's space with veteran agent John Lancaster from the Bureau of Alcohol, Tobacco and Firearms. Their attention centered on a tape recorder at Smoot's antique desk.

A spool of magnetic tape told it all:

"…Okay," came Sienna's voice from the recorder. "We play."

"I'll be damned." Roland shook his head.

"When's the gig?" Delton's voice.

"Thursday," Sienna answered tinnily. "Two A.M. No sooner. No later."

"What happens then?" Delton inquired from the tape.

"We meet Hernando," came Sienna's answer. "Introduce him to our new partner."

Barrett switched off the tape.

"You think they'll buy that ruse about a mistrial?" Commander Sykes directed his question to Bear.

"I can have Roach leak the story to Stacy Kline. By noon tomorrow everybody'll think Delton's scot-free. That's when I'd like Agent Lancaster to take over."

"We'd continue to have the detective's brother undercover," Lancaster elaborated. "Where Delton goes, we'd go. What we hope, of course, is that he'll take us to the guns. Perhaps even to the buyer."

"What's the downside for us?" Smoot put that question.

"A big one right up front," the agent replied directly. "Sienna might decide that Delton is too much of a risk. He might kill him."

"Or worse." Barrett nodded. "I've already decided it's too risky for Delton to wear a wire this time around. So we're going to bug Splinter's boat. We can protect Delton so long as they're docked. Once they're underway, though, if something goes wrong, it'll take some time to get on board."

The commander cleared his throat. "For the record: I don't know if I could ask my brother to go into a situation like this."

"He can go on that boat or face the electric chair," Barrett responded stiffly. "That change your opinion, Commander?"

Rawlings offered a caution. "Delton may help us nail some gun runners, Barrett, and still be Ramona's killer. If he is—"

"He'll go to the chair anyway," Roland promised.

It was the first time that Roland had admitted he was going for the death penalty. Barrett responded very quietly—

"All I'm asking for is a couple of weeks. Just some time to follow this thing. See where it leads."

"Still sounds like a fishing expedition to me," Smoot groused.

"We've got to fish or cut bait," Barrett replied. "There's nothing in between."

It was his chief's decision now. Barrett saw Rawlings hesitate. He leaned closely, privately to the older man's ear.

"I said I'd need your trust, Smoot. Well. Here we are. What about it?"

Chapter twenty-two

Barrett spent the rest of that week coordinating phone calls and paperwork between the Coast Guard, the county sheriff, the Florida Highway Patrol, and BATF. He hadn't known for sure whether Rawlings would approve an undercover effort of any kind. But by promising to leave Florida's Department of Law Enforcement out of the operation, the Bureau of Alcohol, Tobacco and Firearms gave Smoot the assurance he wanted that his turf would not be invaded by Tallahassee.

It wasn't a concession Barrett liked, but it was a price he was willing to pay. By Thursday everything was set to go. That afternoon Delton got the call that Frank wanted a Friday meet. Barrett came home to find his brother throwing perfectly spiraled passes to Ben and Tyndall. The boys leapt like deer to catch the pigskin, their shouts sweet and high and innocent. Even Laura Anne smiled from her kitchen window.

Barrett waited for supper to finish. Waited for the boys to bathe and brush their teeth and hear their stories before he took Delton outside to go over the details of what had been planned on his behalf.

It was late by the time they got out to the swings. They just sat there for a while, propelled in gentle arcs beneath the magnolia. A thick fog clung to the ground warm and wet to writhe in tendrils around the stakes which propped up Laura Anne's tomatoes. It was a heavy night, the kind of night that when you breathed deeply it seemed that syrup ran down your throat and spread through the capillaries of your lungs. The moon shone dimly through the clouds that scudded above the magnolia's flat and heavy leaves, its pale contribution to vision coming in measured bursts like a headlight shuttered dimly through the windows of a passing train.

A uniformed officer patrolled Barrett's backyard with a shotgun. A pair of squad cars from the county joined the local cruisers that patrolled the street.

"How much time?" Delton asked his brother.

Barrett checked his watch.

"Just about twelve hours."

The only thing they knew for sure was that Delton was to meet Sienna on Splinter's boat at precisely ten o'clock Friday night. Delton believed Sienna planned to meet his Latin buyer somewhere on the coast. Perhaps make a delivery. Barrett hoped that was the case. His plan was simply to follow Splinter's BayLiner wherever it went. With luck they could nail Sienna and "the spick" at the same time.

But any operation like this was risky. Especially on the water.

"You can still back out, Delton," Barrett told his brother. "You can call the whole thing off."

"No, I can't."

"I just don't want you to worry," Barrett said lamely.

"Be a damn fool to worry," Delton grunted. "Now bein' scared—that's somethin' different."

"I'm scared, too," Barrett confessed.

Barrett lipped a cigarette from its pack, lit it, and passed it to Delton.

"Come a ways, haven't we?" Delton accepted the cigarette. "Come a good ways in just a couple of weeks."

"A ways, yeah." Barrett inhaled deeply.

"In case things go bad..." Delton began.

"Nothing's going bad."

"I know. But just in case…"

Delton slipped an envelope from his shirt.

"What is it?" Barrett asked.

"Inside," Delton replied.

Barrett opened the envelope to find a single photograph inside. It was a high school graduation. Class of 1979. A stiff, pale principal presented an eager, young, and black Valedictorian to his community.

"Where in hell?" Barrett was amazed.

"Found it with my things." Delton shrugged. "Mama musta took it. Y'see, Bear? She was proud of you. I was, too. I din' say nuthin', I know. I was a asshole. But I was proud."

Barrett cradled the photograph in his hands.

"I'm gonna be there for you, Delton."

"I know you will, bro."

The nylon ropes squeaked pale and yellow as vines on the limb above. There was in Barrett for the first time in a long time a feeling of symmetry. Of balance. Two brothers on their swings.

Perfect synchrony.

Back and forth.

A dense fog clung to the marina's dock like a second skin. Hoyt Young and Splinter Townsend huddled against the chill on the pier beside Splinter's boat. Headlights drew their attention. A brand new Buick rolled to a stop in the marina's caliche lot. A door opened and a man stepped out. The car's headlights framed Frank Sienna briefly before the car's timer shut them off. Frank checked the lot briefly. A couple of pickups nosed emptily beneath a street light. Nothing else. Sienna strolled to the pier.

Taylor Folsom triggered a radio from a shrimp boat that bobbed one slip seaward from Splinter's BayLiner.

"Fisher to Control," the junior detective whispered, his caution unnecessary. No one could hear Taylor or the other two officers surveilling from inside the shrimper's cabin.

"Go ahead, Fisher," Agent Lancaster's voice returned over the static.

"We've got Subject Number One arriving and headed for Number One transport," Taylor came back.

"That's a roger and confirmed."

John Lancaster trained a pair of binoculars on the pier. He could see Frank Sienna follow Splinter and Hoyt onto the BayLiner's deck. So could Smoot Rawlings and Barrett Raines. The three law enforcement officers observed Splinter's boat from a Boston Whaler lying dead and dark in the water barely fifty yards off the pier at the bay's first buoy. A second Whaler, also under Lancaster's command, carried a SWAT team alongside. Both Whalers were rigged with twin two-hundred-horse Mariners. Both were equipped with Loran and GPS and both carried radio-direction-finding equipment tuned to the frequency of the bug which had earlier in the week been planted on Splinter's boat.

Delton's undercover conversations had given Lancaster's bureau the justification needed to obtain court orders that allowed the homing device and bug to be planted on Townsend's BayLiner. Lancaster and his team would not only be able to follow the cabin cruiser surreptitiously, they'd be able to hear everything Sienna and his players had to say once they were below deck to Splinter's toy-filled cabin.

It was Friday night. Game night. All the players were there. All except Delton.

"Where in the hell is he?" Smoot growled and Barrett knew that he was once again being held responsible for his brother's behavior.

"I told Roach to send him early," Barrett told his chief confidently, though in truth he was scared to death.

What if something had gone wrong?

What if Delton had panicked?

Or worse—what if he'd simply skipped? That would be just like Delton: Put Barrett and half the region's law enforcement on the water, coldcock Roach, and head for fucking Mexico.

Barrett tried not to think about that last possibility. He had put a lot of eggs in this basket. If things didn't work out Barrett knew that it wouldn't be Delton who caught the real shit at the station house; it would be the Bear.

"He's got a couple of minutes." Lancaster's calm, steady voice was a godsend.

"Should have been here early, though."

"He'll be here," Lancaster said and Barrett wondered how a man who was almost a total stranger could be so sure.

"One thing I'd like to request. Just in case things get really busy," Barrett said quietly.

"Certainly." The bureau's agent nodded.

"I've got to make a murder case around these bastards." Barrett met Lancaster's eye. "I need these people alive."

"I'll play it any way you like." Lancaster smiled. "Unless somebody's life is threatened. Bets are off after that."

Barrett exhaled a barrel full of air.

"Yes, sir, I understand. Thanks very much."

"Got a lot at stake here, don't you, Detective?"

"I didn't when I started," Barrett replied ruefully.

Lancaster lifted his head sharply. "Ah. Bingo."

Barrett scrambled for a pair of binoculars. Lancaster had brought both night-vision and ordinary optical glasses. With the ordinary opticals Barrett could see Delton. He walked tall and casually, framed by the lights which spilled from lamps set in posts along the pier, toward Splinter's boat.

"It's Delton."

Smoot seemed disappointed.

Somebody stepped off the BayLiner onto the pier.

Barrett rolled in a sharper focus. Took just a second. For a moment he couldn't make out much. But then the escort from Splinter's boat strolled back up the pier and Barrett could see that Delton had been greeted by Frank Sienna.

A short call from Taylor confirmed Barrett's more distant assessment.

"Subjects One and Two on the pier," Taylor called in. Thank God, Barrett thought to himself. But aloud, to Smoot, he simply said, "Well, Chief. I guess he's still playing straight."

Chapter twenty-three

Delton Raines could see Frank Sienna waiting for him in a perfectly circular pool of yellow light. A naked bulb set in a cedar post beside Splinter's boat cast the pale circle like a lasso around Sienna. Delton casually strolled into that noose himself.

"Evenin', Frank."

Delton had purposefully dressed like a pimp. A satin shirt was loosely bloused and laid open to the navel. Parachute slacks followed the ripples of Delton's massive thighs. Patent leather lace-ups stretched over his oar-sized feet. Sienna was dressed as usual in an open collar shirt, worn blazer, and slacks. Delton wondered if the eyes that he had been told were somewhere around him watching could see Sienna as well as he could. He hoped so. He hoped they could draw a good bead.

"Delton, how are you?"

"Could use a smoke."

Frank snapped out his Zippo like a switchblade, tapped out a Marlboro.

"Nice night for a ride," Delton commented as he lit up.

"Slight change in plans."

A powerful Evinrude coughed suddenly to life. A low, feral kind of rumble. And then a low-slung Renegade slipped jet-black from a pier opposite Splinter's BayLiner. A froth of saltwater bubbled from the prop as the craft crossed quickly over.

Hoyt Young throttled back the engine. The bubbles ceased suddenly. Splinter Townsend tossed Frank a line.

"After you." Sienna held the tie-down but significantly did not lash it secure.

"What's wrong with Splinter's boat?"

Delton's cigarette glowed more brightly for a moment.

"In *there*." Sienna put his Zippo in his blazer pocket and came out with the .45.

Delton snapped his cigarette into the water; Barrett could see it through his binoculars. It reminded him of a comet, a tiny arc of fire pulled into a Jovian deep.

Taylor's voice broke over the radio. "They've got another boat!"

"*Stand by,*" Lancaster ordered sternly. And then to Barrett, "It's a fast one. Goddamn, it's a Renegade!"

"Got her. Dark, too, dammit, not gonna be easy to follow. You think we've been spotted?"

"No." Lancaster shook his head. "I think Sienna's just being cautious. But then, it's not my brother he's got out there."

"What you gonna do, Bear?" came Smoot's question.

Bear appealed to the BATF agent for an opinion.

"We can pretty well contain them inside the buoy," Lancaster said slowly. "But if they get out around the coast in that thing, in the fog…"

"Can't you stay with them?"

"We can run with him, yeah, *if* we can see him. Problem is, without the transponder we're going to have to track visually. That's not going to be easy to do in this soup and it's going to be a lot tougher to do it without being spotted."

"Goddammit."

"Let's go in now," Smoot urged. "Stop 'em at the pier."

"We stop them now, we've got nothing," Barrett grated.

"Except your brother," Lancaster observed drily.

"Please advise, sir," Commander Sykes's voice now broke in over the radio.

"Stand by, Seaside," Lancaster responded with protocol and then turned to Barrett Raines.

"It's your call, Detective."

Barrett could feel every eye on the boat on him. He could feel every thought. Was the Bear gonna risk frying his brother's ass just to bust a case?

But Barrett knew that if he didn't bust this case, his brother's ass would fry for sure. In the electric chair.

"Stay with the boat," Barrett blurted out. "Stay with him!"

Lancaster fired his Whaler's twin Mariners to life.

"No lights," he reminded the SWAT leader on the Whaler's twin.

Hoyt Young was running the Renegade without lights. Two hundred twenty-five horsepower launched the coal-black craft like a dart past the first buoy. Delton strained hard to look straight ahead. Barrett was out there somewhere. Somewhere on one of those dark, empty-looking fiberglass shells. The speedboat's twenty-four-foot composite hull slapped down hard on the swells. Delton pitched forward. Splinter had just finished wiring Delton's wrists behind his back. Made it hard to balance as the boat slammed like a supercharged surfboard through the swells.

Sienna rode the Renegade steady as a rock. The .45 had not wavered from Delton's belly button since they'd come on board. Delton could feel his heart hammering inside his chest.

"Why don' you just shoot me here?" Delton shouted above the wind, the water, and the Evinrude.

"Need to work a while, first." Frank's voice was almost lost in the wind.

"Work?" Delton at first honestly did not discern his meaning.

Frank smiled.

"See what you told the cops!"

Delton's pulse leapt with the horses coursing over the water.
"I tol' 'em not jack shit."

It was hard to shout and look fearless at the same time. Especially pounding into the brine at fifty miles an hour with your wrists wired behind your back.

A grin split Sienna's face like a pumpkin.
"You got balls, stud? Well—we're gonna see!"

Barrett knew from the buoys that they were out of the shallows. The water would not be so warm out here. There was a sudden break in the fog. It was like flying out of a cloud at sea level. Barrett shivered in the suddenly cooler air which swept, now, at fifty miles an hour over his face. Lancaster had opened the Whaler's twin throttles wide, and still the dark dart before them seemed to slip further ahead with each jarring concussion of the Whaler's broad, heavy hull into the water.

That went on for four, five minutes. It was like chasing a phantom over the water. And then they plunged back into fog.

When they came out there was nothing.

No boat in sight.

Lancaster shouted to Barrett, "I can't see a thing!"

"We can't stop!"

"We've lost him, Detective."

Lancaster radioed briefly to the trailing Whaler. Both craft wallowed to a halt in heavy swells.

Barrett's heart froze. They couldn't stop! Not now!

"What was that last buoy?" He scrambled to keep a coastal chart flat beneath the windscreen.

"Number fourteen," Lancaster replied. "And heading almost due south."

"South?" Barrett jerked erect. "Inside the buoy? Give me a light."

Lancaster obliged. Even so, it was not easy to follow a chart with a flashlight on a pitching boat. But Barrett had a feeling. Something he really didn't need the chart to see.

"What is it?" Lancaster was at his side.

"He's not heading for the gulf!"

A frenzy of flashlights, then, as Smoot Rawlings crowded with Barrett and Lancaster over the charts.

Barrett turned to his chief.

"We should've known when they pulled up with the run-about—he never meant to go for deep water!"

"Don't see how that helps much." Smoot shook his head. "There's a hundred goddamn miles of shallows. Hell, he could be goin'—"

"Here!"

Barrett jabbed a finger onto the chart.

"Gull's Point! They're headed to Gull's Point."

"You're guessing." Smoot was unconvinced.

"It's a condemned beach." Barrett turned to Lancaster. "Texaco used it years ago to warehouse chemicals. Whole place turned toxic. They had to shut down the beach, buy out all the businesses. And it's right here—three clicks south of the buoy."

"That's five miles of coast at least." Lancaster scanned the chart.

"And we've got fog," Smoot pointed out. "Hell, you could walk right up on something and not find it."

Barrett felt an ice pick in his stomach. *I told you I'd be there for you, Delton, and I don't even know where you are.* He turned desperately to Lancaster.

"Gull's Point—it's gotta be! Have Taylor and Sykes help us search along the coast. I'll tell Roach to put every cruiser he can get on the beach."

Lancaster hesitated over the chart.

"Have you got a better idea, Agent Lancaster?" Barrett hardened. "'Cause I sure as hell don't."

Lancaster triggered his radio.

"Control to Team. Control to Team. We've got a place to look, people."

Chapter twenty-four

Sienna was impressed. It had taken nearly half an hour, once they got Delton off the boat, to secure him for his interrogation. Delton had fought like a madman for fifteen, maybe twenty minutes. Fought well, too, for a man with his wrists wired behind his back. And then, of course, once they'd finally gotten Delton tied down, Hoyt and Splinter wanted to work a little bit.

That had taken another ten minutes or so.

Delton never told them to stop.

Almost as if he was buying time, Sienna thought, grinning.

But time eventually ran out.

Splinter was nursing a cut lip and what looked suspiciously like a broken hand. Hoyt was clutching both knees. Sienna had taken some licks, too.

Delton was beaten to shit. Face and scalp cut. Eyes and cheeks bloated. The spick was hugely entertained. He was waiting with a pair of bodyguards to take revenge on the nigger man who had killed two of his shooters. It was a pleasure, once Delton was bound and helpless, to turn the guards loose.

But Sienna hadn't let them do much. He didn't want to kill

the bastard, after all. Not yet. And so Hernando waited eagerly for Sienna to get on with the rest of the show.

Barrett's brother was pinioned with hemp and wire to one of the only two chairs which remained in the long-dead diner. The chair had been firmly lashed to one of the dozen or so crates of ammunition which were stacked in a virtual wall along the bar. A South Korea bill of lading pressed against the back of Delton's head was stained with blood.

All Delton could see was Perry Como smiling at him from a frame on the wall, and Rita Hayworth stretched invitingly along the length of her pinup.

"You sick fucks."

Delton spit blood from his mouth and nostrils.

"All you have to do is tell us what you told your brother, Delton." Sienna unsnapped the cover from a leather carrying case.

"I tol' you. I din' tell him *jack shit!*"

Delton was frightened now, Sienna was sure. Whatever adrenaline had rushed into the bastard's frame had been depleted during his furious thirty minutes of resistance.

"You know what this is, don't you, Delton?"

Sienna pulled an odd-looking contraption from the leather case.

"Got this little rig in Lake City," Sienna went on. "Army surplus. It's a telephone, Delton. Field telephone. Very old fashioned. You turn the crank here—"

Frank demonstrated with a twirl of the wrist.

"Damn thing juices up the lines for miles."

The onetime marine took out a pair of wire cutters, and began to calmly strip the insulation from the phone's heavy wires.

"'Course, we're not calling long distance, are we, Delton? No. I think we'll stay local."

"*I din' tell him nuthin!*"

Sienna smiled.

"You think you've got your rocks off before, Delton? Wait'll you try this. Splinter…"

Splinter Townsend kneeled at Delton's crotch. Opened his knife.

"Guess you made the chair after all."

Splinter ripped upward savagely with his blade. Delton choked off a scream. But it was his trousers, only, that opened up to the twin electrodes that Frank held closely for his inspection.

"First question: Are you stooging for the cops?"

"Would I have come to you tonight if I was doing that, Frank? Huh? That's *crazy!*"

"How crazy, Delton? Talk to me. Save yourself some time on the phone."

Dick Hanson led a convoy of cruisers down Farm-to-Market 172 to the Old Beach Road. The asphalt meandered along the coast here, sometimes coming close to the water. More often it ran a quarter mile or more distant from a shore which varied from cypress swamp to sand dunes.

"I want intervals of half a mile," Hanson called out over the radio as men stumbled from their cars to cover the beach.

Dick took a pair of bolt cutters to the corroded fence which barred his way.

CONDEMNED BEACH, the sign read. DO NOT ENTER.

Dick cut the chain which was padlocked to the steel-mesh barrier. "I'm on the beach," Dick reported as he returned to his cruiser.

* * *

Barrett was still on the water. Lancaster had slowed the Whaler to a crawl. The fog poured in, now, like dry ice in a monster movie.

"We could be right on top of them," Smoot repeated himself nervously, "and never know it."

"Heard anything from Taylor?" Barrett asked Lancaster.

"No. It's been over half an hour. What kind of places were built along this stretch?"

"Piers, warehouses, for the most part," Barrett answered.

"How many locations are we going to have to search? Ten? Twenty?"

"We only need one," Barrett replied.

"Say, Bear!" Smoot pointed his arm like a javelin off starboard.

And there it was.

"I'll be damned," Barrett whispered. "That's Key's Diner."

Both Whalers dropped their engines to an idle. The combination of sea breeze and water could cover the engines' low stutter, Barrett knew. But they were so close! The Renegade was moored barely a spit away at the dead diner's skeleton pier. The speedboat, however, was not the boat Smoot had initially spotted.

What had drawn Smoot's attention was much, much larger. The Renegade bobbed like a toy, in fact, beside the other vessel, which was moored rock-solid at the end of the pier. This was a Cadillac, Barrett knew—a Grady White. Forty-five feet of very serious ocean-going vessel. He could see a radar mounted above its flying bridge. He could only guess at the inboard engine and fuel capacity which tucked below. But about the cargo...

"Looks like a gunboat to me." Lancaster eased his Whaler into reverse.

"Maybe," Barrett replied. "But right now I'm worried about Delton."

"Well, then." Lancaster reached for the radio. "Let's hit the beach and get him out."

Chapter twenty-five

It seemed to Barrett that the assault team was taking forever.

Lancaster didn't want to risk a sentry seeing the Whalers come onshore so he ordered both Whalers to backtrack a good hundred meters downwind of the diner before they beached. Then the swats debarked with their m-16s and Mac-10s, radios, and medical kits. Barrett hauled his shotgun out of the boat, made sure his .38 was securely holstered, then followed Lancaster's team to the cover of the dunes where Lancaster assigned approaches, positions, and radio cues to his team.

Then they had to actually reach the diner unobserved. Thankfully, a rare series of sand dunes provided perfect cover. Barrett could see team members zigzag like sand flies to take positions around the pier and diner. Another age passed as quietly radioed communications flit briefly back and forth.

A mumbled confirmation came, now, into the mike clipped at Lancaster's shoulder.

"Are we ready?" Barrett asked anxiously.

"Almost."

That's when they heard Delton's scream. It was a high, horrible, hopeless confession of agony that rose over the crash of water and wind.

"*Delton!*"

Barrett was halfway over the dune before Lancaster knocked him down.

"*You want your brother alive?*"

"You know I do!"

"Then let me do my job."

"Hurry, John. For God's sake!"

Delton Raines writhed in his chair before the smiles of singers and starlets and interrogators. The captured man's arms and legs danced crazily over feces and urine and electrodes. And then, mercifully, Delton's head lolled back.

Sienna slapped him hard. No response.

He slapped him again.

"Will he talk?" The "spick" didn't seem to care much.

"My guess is he doesn't have anything to say," Sienna replied. "Of course, you keep this up, a man will say anything you want."

"Then I kill him," the Latin man said.

"Business, first," Sienna replied. "Then pleasure."

Splinter and Hoyt displayed their Uzis behind Sienna. Hernando's bodyguards moved to cover their patron. Sienna lighted a cigarette over the crated ammunition.

"Half a million rounds. Signed, sealed, and delivered."

"It will serve a good cause."

"Fuck the cause, Hernando. I want the cash. Right now. Or you can shove these babies up your ass one round at a time."

The Latin never lost his smile. "I have two men. Well trained."

"I have two marines. Scared as hell."

Hernando frowned over the odds. A long sigh hissed from between his lips.

"Very well." The Latin man abruptly dropped a wad of well-greased bills onto the crate.

"Two hundred fifty thousand dollars American. You can count."

"Yes, I can." Sienna pocketed the cash first, then nodded to Delton Raines. "You can pick up the garbage on your way out."

Delton groaned from his chair. A swollen eye fluttered open just in time to see the Latin accept an Uzi from his bodyguard.

Sienna smiled over Delton.

"So long—partner."

Hernando pulled back the Uzi's bolt. Leveled the weapon. And all hell broke loose.

The front door exploded off its hinges. Barrett Raines rushed inside with a pair of agents to see his brother beaten to shit, wired by the balls, and roped onto half a million highly explosive rounds of ammunition.

"Deltooooooonnnn!"

Hernando turned his weapon from Delton to Barrett.

Bear's shotgun took out the well-dressed Latin's liver and lungs with a single, magnum-loaded shell.

Splinter and Hoyt hosed down on team members who flanked Barrett's charge through the front entrance of the diner. Hernando's bodyguards cut loose at a pair of SWAT members whose assault came through windows along the side. The interior rocked with the near-constant explosions of automatic weapons. Barrett could feel the concussions in his bones.

A bodyguard went down with one of Lancaster's men.

Lancaster himself came through the kitchen firing short sharp bursts.

The second bodyguard went down.

Then Splinter caught a ribbon of slugs in the bowels.

Hoyt went down screaming, his taped weapon firing on full automatic.

Sienna scrambled to the bar's cover behind the ammo.

"Delton!"

Barrett rushed forward to his brother—and Frank popped up over the bar. Barrett saw the small, dark tunnel of an Uzi's barrel.

And Delton watched his brother take a burst of nine-millimeter full in the chest.

"*Barrett!*" Delton cried out in a horrible, strangled scream.

Sienna dropped behind the bar again. Behind Barrett, behind Delton, and behind a rampart of ammunition.

"*Live rounds hold your fire,*" Lancaster commanded.

A pair of agents rushed to flank Frank Sienna on either side of his high-explosive shield.

"This is Agent Lancaster of the Bureau of Alcohol, Tobacco and Firearms. Come out now with your hands behind your head or—"

"*Grenade!*"

A sharp, white explosion knocked Lancaster and his remaining men off their feet. The diner was sheared with shrapnel. Dust and debris came crashing down.

And then a second grenade lobbed lazily to follow the first.

Frank Sienna dove out a window behind the bar just as his number-two grenade ripped through the diner's interior. The building seemed to dissolve for a moment in a haze of dust and darkness. Then came a ball of fire. Sienna went flat on the sand outside. There might be sharpshooters covering the diner's exits. But the carnage inside had forced Lancaster's shooters to give up their positions— Sienna spotted a pair as they raced in to support those members already inside.

Still better be careful, though. There might be one or two who'd stayed at home.

Frank crawled away from a wooden building that was now swollen with flames. Twenty yards down the beach he crawled. Thirty. Another explosion rocked the beach.

Frank knew this one wasn't a grenade.

Five hundred thousand rounds of nine-millimeter *Parabellum* lit up the beach. The rounds sprayed indiscriminately, a Fourth of July of high explosive. Sienna kept his head down. Into the dunes, now. The dunes would offer him cover. After that he'd hit the highway.

A pair of sharpshooters dragged Barrett and Delton from the diner only moments before the interior turned into a conflagration. Lancaster made it out on his own.

"Medic!"

He directed a SWAT member to Barrett Raines. Delton was frantic.

"Bear, you there, buddy? Bear?"

The medic reached down. He stripped the Bear's shirt off his chest—and there, snugged in beneath, was a bulletproof vest.

It was the same vest that had hung untouched in Barrett's closet for five years. It was well broken in, now. A shield of Kevlar ripped with slugs.

Barrett groaned painfully.

"Bear?" Delton's eyes widened as if his brother had emerged from the tomb.

"Easy, easy. I'm fine." Barrett shook his head groggily. And then to the medic, "Help *him*. He's the one who's hurt."

Another explosion sent sparklers into the air. Barrett turned to Lancaster.

"Where's Sienna?"

"We'll get him."

"Get me a cruiser." Barrett clutched his ribs.

"You're not going anywhere, Detective."

"Get me a cruiser!"

Frank Sienna slipped almost a half-mile through the dunes before he began the shallow ascent which would lead him off the beach and onto the ribbon of asphalt road which teased the beach.

Frank was breathing like a boxer in a fifteenth and furious round. Hard fuckin' work slugging it through the sand. Especially when you'd gone about half the way on your belly. Especially when you smoked. But there was only one more dune left. Frank glanced back toward the direction of the beach. You could still hear the report and ricochet of exploding ammunition.

Frank smiled. That should keep the bastards occupied. Sienna checked the wad inside his belt. It was all there. A quarter of a million dollars. He had the money. He had a plane waiting not four miles inland. By sunrise he'd be halfway to Belize.

Just one more dune. It was a steep one. Frank could feel his legs going to rubber with the recent strain of the ambush, the explosions and fire, the flight.

Just think about Belize. The town, the river, the country: only one name—hell anybody could remember that!

Sienna knew the highway was somewhere just ahead. He might have to cut the fence to get through, or climb it, but it was there!

He was just staggering the last few feet for the top of the dune when an engine's roar came suddenly over the sounds of wind and surf. What was it? A boat? A helicopter?

But the engine sound hadn't come from the sky or the sea. It came from the land. A siren wailed to join an engine screaming like a demon. Barrett Raines launched a police cruiser over the dunes like a tomahawk and framed Frank Sienna squarely in his halogen lights.

Sienna threw up a hand to fend off the glare and emptied his .45 into the charging squad car. Glass and metal flew over the beach, the cruiser slid sideways—

The engine died as the squad car crashed into the dune.

Frank fumbled for a new clip as he stumbled over to finish off the job.

The cruiser's door hung open. Where was the cop?

Frank was just set to pop a new clip into his .45 when a familiar voice froze him on the sand.

"Drop the gun, Frank."

Barrett Raines rose like a phoenix from the sand, his service revolver fully loaded and trained dead-center on Frank's torso.

The former marine regarded Barrett's handgun. "I thought I pickled you pretty good."

"Laura Anne's been tryin' to make me wear a vest for years," Barrett said almost conversationally. "You prob'ly did break a couple of ribs. Wanta try for more?"

Barrett pulled the hammer of his Smith & Wesson to single action.

Sienna tossed the .45 over the hood of the car.

"It was Delton, wasn't it? He ratted us out."

"Yes, he did." Barrett eased the hammer down.

"Cocksucker."

That's when Barrett let him have it. A fistful of .38 right in the nuts.

Sienna dropped like a sack to the sand.

"Delton's still my brother. Cocksucker!" Barrett hissed into the gunrunner's ear. "Which puts him *way* ahead of you."

Chapter twenty-six

By the time all was said and done the Bureau of Alcohol, Tobacco and Firearms figured that half a million rounds of ammunition had been detonated in the abandoned diner, a fact confirmed by Frank Sienna during his interrogation.

Also confirmed, this time by BATF, was the fact that the Latin buyer was Hernando Gonzales, a citizen of Mexico wanted by authorities in that country on counts of kidnapping and murder. Turned out that Señor Gonzales was a major player in the resale of weapons to gang members and drug runners along Florida's east coast.

His "cause," it seemed, wasn't what one could call political in nature.

The whole gun-running operation was unraveling even before Lancaster began Sienna's interrogation. The IRS didn't take long to look at Ramona Walker's enterprises; their audits confirmed that her various books were cooked. Ramona and her players were estimated to have laundered a million and a half illegal dollars in the previous year. A cache of unregistered Uzis was found in a U-Lock-It near Walker's coin laundry in Lake City, and Frank Sienna's prints were all over the place.

Barrett had busted the man who ran the guns.

Now he was going to nail the son of a bitch who killed Ramona Walker.

It was a sweet interrogation.

"All right, all right!" Sienna waved off his attorney.

There was a crowd of folks in the interrogation room.

Smoot was there. Roland Reed. Lancaster. Everyone who only days before had wanted no part of Barrett's investigation now jostled for a ringside seat.

Everybody wanted to be in at the kill.

Sienna was desperate. Barrett had obligingly provided Frank nicotine and caffeine in quantity; their effects had by now combined with the night's activity to bring Sienna close to that ragged edge where he might, just might, make a mistake.

"You're in deep, deep, deep shit, Frank." Barrett wasn't about to let up.

"Don't say anything more, Frank," the attorney advised unctuously.

"That's right, don't," Barrett said softly. "'Cause this way I don't have to worry about Roland pleading you to a Murder Two, or maybe even a manslaughter. This way I get to watch you fry in the chair, Frank."

"Goddamn you," Sienna rasped. "I told you I ran the guns. I bought the guns. I sold the fuckin' guns. But Ramona Walker—why in hell would I kill her?"

"My guess is she got greedy," Barrett responded. "Or maybe she got scared."

"Last time I saw that woman she was at the restaurant."

"No, Frank." Barrett smiled as he shook his head. "You knew Delton was going to be at Ramona's. You probably saw him go in. You certainly waited 'til he left. That's when the dog came out—"

"Bullshit!"

"And after the dog—you killed her."

Barrett recognized what he saw in Sienna's eyes. It was craft. And it was hatred.

Barrett wondered briefly how this piece of shit would hold up under a field telephone.

He fought off those feelings.

"I was nowhere near that house," Sienna was saying. "How the fuck could I have killed the woman when I wasn't even there?"

"Say you were never there?"

"You deaf? Or am I stuttering?"

"Just want the record clear, Frank. You're telling me you never went out to Ramona's home at any time from ten that night until six the following morning?"

"I played some cards. I went home. That's it."

"I see," Barrett said.

And then reached beneath the table.

"Recognize these, Frank?"

Barrett displayed a plastic evidence bag. A pair of shoes were tagged inside. Low-quarter loafers.

"Whadda you want with my shoes?" Sienna asked suspiciously.

"Blood. That's what happens when you kill somebody, Frank. You walk around. Get blood on your shoes."

The color bleached suddenly and completely from Sienna's already-white face.

"You were smart enough to wipe your prints inside. And the lab says the shoes were cleaned, too. But not well enough."

Barrett smiled.

"All we need for the DNA's a smidgeon, Frank. A gnat's ass will do. And we found a hell of a lot more than that."

"Frank." The attorney's voice was rising. "Don't say anything!"

Sienna was breathing heavily, now. Like a boxer.

"I went by, all right?"

Barrett didn't say a word.

"Ramona told me there was something with Delton. Some problem. I was worried; I wanted to talk! But she was *dead* when I got there! I swear to God!"

"Seems like I've heard that before." Barrett was cold as ice.

Then he nodded to Prosecutor Roland Reed.

"You can have him anytime you like."

Barrett left straight after the morning's interrogation to visit his brother. Delton had been admitted to a Taylor County emergency room after his ordeal. There was a lot of superficial damage but, aside from some dental work and cracked ribs, Delton had escaped obvious injury. However, the doctors were still very concerned about internal bleeding which might yet show up as a result of Delton's vicious beatings and electrocution. When Barrett called concerning his brother the doctor on duty told Bear it would be best for Delton to remain a day or two for observation.

Barrett arrived at his brother's pastel, semiprivate room to find Delton already dressed and checking out.

"Don't you think you're rushing this just a bit?" An intern withheld a clipboard.

"I'm fine." Delton waved impatiently. "Just let me sign the damn papers."

"H'lo, Delton."

Barrett stood at the door with a bouquet of flowers.

"Bear."

Delton seemed embarrassed, though it was hard to judge expression through the swollen and misshapen mess that was his face.

"I came to visit," Barrett said simply.

"You know me, Bear." Delton scratched his signature on a release form. "I never was much for hospitals."

"Doc said you'd need a couple of days' rest." Barrett tried not to sound too bossy.

"I'm fine." Delton stuffed his personals into an overnight bag. "Got a little jumpstart is all."

"I see. Well." Barrett set the carnations on the bed. "Roland's dropped all charges against you. It's official. Thought you might like to know."

"I reckon I ought to thank you." Delton tried to smile.

"No need." Barrett shook his head.

"Well. Thank you anyway."

Delton zipped his overnight shut.

"Delton—" Barrett stalled out.

"What is it, Bear?"

Barrett started again.

"You think we can get together?"

"Together?"

"Maybe have you back to the house," Barrett rushed. "Have dinner or something? Ben and Tyndall think you're some kind of hero and Laura Anne, well, it's like you said. She's worth seeing anytime."

"Maybe later."

Barrett placed a hand lightly on his brother's arm as the injured man shouldered toward the door.

"We got something started the last couple of weeks, Delton. Be a shame to let it die."

"You're right, Bear. But to be honest, right this minute? All I can think about's gettin' outta here."

Barrett turned to the intern.

"Is he ready?"

"I can't stop him." The doctor-to-be shrugged indifferently.

"Okay, then."

Barrett offered his brother his hand. Delton took it briefly, awkwardly.

"Be seein' you, bro," Delton said.

And then he was gone. Not a backward glance as Delton strode with barely a limp out the door, past the nurses' station, and on to freedom.

Barrett followed at a distance, just to make sure Delton was really as fit as he seemed. Bear reached the hospital lobby to see his brother burst into a waiting morass of cameras and microphones. Smiling. Confident. Handsome even with a broken face. Barrett was surprised to see Corrie waiting in the lobby, desperately provocative in a rag-thin dress. Delton pushed a path to his "ex" as if he had been waiting for her forever, bent her back for a deep kiss, and held it until the last flashbulb from the last camera had exploded.

Barrett passed through the gathered press and people as if invisible.

All the men and women around him who in previous weeks had been consumed with Ramona's murder and who had excoriated Barrett for believing his brother now seemed never to have been interested in anything except Delton's triumphant exoneration. It was as if his brother had managed in midlife to score one more fantastic touchdown.

Barrett reached the lobby's exit without a single microphone extended for his comment. Even Stacy Kline didn't notice.

It had always been that way.

Bear went home that night to the boys and Laura Anne. There should have been some satisfaction at the end of this investigation. Barrett had, after all, solved a difficult puzzle. He had balanced his duty to community and family and had persevered. But there was no sense of satisfaction for Barrett as he sat at the table with his family. Not even a sense of relief. What Barrett did feel was a kind of tension. Of foreboding.

Laura Anne offered a blunt diagnosis.

"You're still worried about what Delton'll do next."

Barrett was too tired to say she was unfair. Too tired to point out that not only had Delton been cleared, but that he had taken great risks to aid a difficult investigation and had paid a terrible price for his cooperation. Surely there was cause in all this for celebration. Surely.

But there didn't seem to be.

Barrett returned to his desk at the station later that night. He couldn't sleep. You'd think that as exhausted as Barrett felt he could drop off to neverland in a heartbeat. But it didn't usually work that way. Frequently, after a long and arduous investigation Barrett was like a watch wound too tightly. It'd take a while to unwind. He'd be better off doing paperwork and basking in the congratulations, sincere or otherwise, of the uniforms and personnel who passed by his desk than lying sleepless in his bed at home.

By eleven the squad room was deserted. Barrett nodded, half-asleep at his GI-issue desk. A single photograph lay on top of the official forms which were ignored beneath: A high school principal presented a young valedictorian to the smiles and scowls of a still-divided community.

Barrett pillowed his head with his hands. His back was to the door. He didn't see and did not hear the familiar intruder who wandered, smiling vacantly, past Roach up front and into the squad room.

It was the station mascot, in a sense—the station vagabond who now shuffled purposefully to Barrett's desk. Blondie carried a garbage bag filled with soft drink cans, as usual. But there was something else this evening, something unusual which shared company with the aluminum inside Blondie's bulky bag.

Blondie reached down into his bag, deep down as he walked to Barrett's back.

And pulled out a knife.

It was a crude thing. Ugly. A long, hand-honed blade.

A handle wrapped in tape.

Blondie leveled the weapon and marched resolutely for Barrett's undefended spine.

Barrett's chin slipped from his hands to the desk. He jerked awake—pivoted—

And found a knife in his face. Barrett froze on his seat. Not a sound in the squad room. Not a movement. Not even the stir of a fan.

"Got some cans for you, Blondie," Barrett spoke slowly.

"No, boss. Not tonight. Tonight I got somethin' for *you*."

The knife stayed level on Barrett's throat. Bear felt the familiar bulge of his revolver holstered uselessly on his shoulder. But if he could pivot quickly, get an arm on the knife—

"It's for you, Bear," Blondie said abruptly and presented the knife, handle-first, with a proud smile.

Barrett could feel the fortieth or fiftieth rush of adrenaline for the day jolt through his system.

"You just scared the pee-whining pee out of me, Blondie!"

"I found it," the homeless man went on as if Barrett hadn't said a thing. "Down to the mill."

"Did you hear what I said? You just—"

"It's a good knife," Blondie offered hopefully. "It's home-made."

Barrett found himself suddenly riveted on the crude weapon which the simpleton had just placed on his desk.

It was a weapon made by hand. A length of filed metal tapered to an ugly point. Newly oxidized rust had just begun to intrude on a sharp blade. A length of adhesive tape wound about the handle. Barrett retrieved a pencil from his desk, turned the knife over. Something then caught his attention. Something just below the crude handle.

"Where'd you say you got this thing, Blondie?"

"Ditch. Down to the mill."

It was an etching which caught Barrett's attention, a set of letters and numbers which had been drilled or scratched just below the blade's soiled handle. Barrett knew that the two letters which seemed to stare up at him belonged to the knife's maker. The two numbers, Barrett was certain, signified the year during which the weapon had been fashioned. It was the same year, in fact, that the blade's crude craftsman was to have taken a football scholarship at Florida State University.

Barrett took another look. There it was. It wouldn't go away—

D.R.–77

Chapter twenty-seven

It was about twenty minutes after eleven and Roach MacGuire had just about finished the last touches on his latest war against the cockroaches of North Florida when Barrett came beating feet past the front desk.

"Goddamn, where's the fire?"

"Got a perpetrator loose, Roach. I need an APB."

"Yes, boss. Who for?"

"Delton."

"Say again?"

"You heard me—Delton Raines. And tell 'em he's dangerous."

"Christ Almighty, Bear—?"

"Just do it, Roach! And get hold of Judge Blackmond, too. Tell him we've got new evidence. Tell him Roland's gonna want a new indictment and *be nice*, you hear? I don't want this thing thrown out of court because I forgot to kiss somebody's ass."

"Roger. And where're you headed?"

Barrett checked his weapon at the door.

"Hell, if I don't change."

*   *   *

Barrett monitored his cruiser's radio on the way out of town. It should have been a peaceful evening. Heat lightning flickered in sheets over the horizon. There was a nice breeze off the gulf.

But the narrow two-lane which Barrett turned onto now was hemmed in at each side with pine and palmettoes. There was only a milky ribbon of sky overhead and Barrett knew it was much too late to see flights of heron winging above the blacktop which he now traversed at eighty miles an hour.

He remembered the turnoff. It came almost five miles out of town, past the Old Town Road and past the third pale half-moon of sand that marked the mailman's familiar detour to the few isolated and insignificant mailboxes that punctuated the passage between Deacon Beach and Corrie Raines's trailer.

He killed the lights and engine once he made out the trailer's silhouette in its isolated hammock, and rolled to cover behind the girls' tire swing.

He gathered his flashlight and unsnapped his .38 at its shoulder holster.

The screen door banged open, then, and Corrie came outside to her car, a gaudy, plastic laundry basket balanced on her ample hip. The trunk lid yawned open like a rusty jaw. The rest of the ancient Toyota was already packed to the gills, and Barrett knew it wasn't because Delton's ex-wife was out to do a carload of laundry.

"Going someplace, Corrie?"

She jumped like a startled deer as he stepped from the shadows.

"You shouldn' be here!" She dropped the basket. *"You got no right!"*

"Oh, I've got the right," Barrett assured her. "How you gonna close that trunk, anyway? Clothesline or something?"

"You better go!"

It sounded to Barrett like she was trying to warn him.

Of what?

"Maybe I better go inside," he suggested easily. "See can I find something to tie down that trunk."

"I don't need no help!"

"Maybe not." Barrett shrugged. "But Delton needs help, doesn't he, Corrie? And he's getting it from you."

"There you go on Delton!"

She began to laugh, a high, false, nervous kind of laughter. Barrett scanned the trailer briefly for lights. Or an opened window.

"How much money you got saved up at four sixty-five an hour, Corrie? Three, four hundred dollars? That's all he wants—a little cash. And a lot of distance."

"You don't know!" She wasn't laughing, now.

Barrett decided to push.

"Soon as Delton gets you out of the county he's gonna put every dime you earned in his pocket and leave you in a ditch. That's if you're lucky."

"I don't know what you're talking about," Corrie mumbled.

"I think you do." Barrett closed the distance that remained between them. "All Delton has to say is, 'Let's go.' And look at you, Corrie, you're packing."

"Why not?" she snapped. "Couldn't be worse than here."

"Yes, it could," Barrett told her. "Look at this picture. *Look at it.*"

Barrett pulled a photo from inside his jacket and shoved it into her face. A dead woman stared from the picture under Barrett's flashlight. Ramona's emerald eyes glowed still in a face shattered like broken pottery.

"Jesus." Corrie tried to turn away.

"Delton killed her, Corrie." Barrett kept the photo in her face. "He cut her. He raped her. And he'd do the same to you, too. Just as soon as spit."

"You bastard!"

"Why don't you ask him yourself?" Bear suggested.

"You never quit, do you?"

"And ask him about that knife he threw away. In the ditch. Oh, it's the weapon, all right. Handmade. Delton always was good with his hands."

Corrie glanced nervously to the trailer.

"Delton knew she was running guns. That's all there is to it!"

"Delton knew Ramona was running guns," Barrett agreed. "But that is definitely not all there is to it. Y'see, half a truth is the best kind of lie there is. And Delton's a damn good liar."

"Wouldn't have much on you, then, would he?"

"Why don't you ask him, Corrie?" Barrett egged her on. "What are you afraid of?"

"Not you," came the voice from behind.

Barrett whirled instinctively away from that familiar voice, went for his gun—

And caught a baseball bat right across the chest.

Barrett cried out with a kind of lightning that started in his still-cracked ribs and landed in his lungs. His arms went suddenly numb. His revolver cartwheeled lazily to land practically at Corrie's feet. Delton Raines kicked the flashlight casually away. Raised the baseball bat that looked like a stick in his hands.

Barrett pulled his hands over his head.

Delton whipped the bat down for a second blow to Barrett's already-fractured ribs.

Barrett screamed. Open. Unashamed. Delton smiled viciously over his kid brother.

"Couldn't leave it alone, could you, Bear?"

He jammed the bat into Barrett's kidney. Bear arched his back in agony, his feet kicking the sand in quick, futile spasms.

"Noooooo!" Corrie jammed her fists into her mouth.

"Shut up," Delton ordered her. "Fetch me that gun."

"No, Delton," she wailed. "You don' need to!"

"Don't tell me what I need. Fetch the damn gun!"

"What about...Ramona, Corrie?" Barrett wrapped his arms around his torso for protection. "Ask...ask him about the Boss Lady!"

"You din' do nuthin' with her, Delton! Tell him you didn't!"

"She got what she deserved."

Delton tested the bat's balance.

"Was she still alive when you screwed her, Delton?" Barrett gasped. "Or did you wait 'til she was dead?"

Delton kicked him across the face before he turned once again to Corrie.

"*I said, gimme that gun!*"

"No!"

"They cain't prove anything." Delton stepped away from Barrett and toward Corrie.

She picked up the gun.

He kept coming.

"That's right, now gimme. Just gimme here."

She cocked the revolver and raised it. The barrel weaved back and forth like a cobra.

"Put it down."

She wouldn't.

"Down, Corrie!"

Barrett fought to widen the scarlet tunnel that closed ever smaller in a circle before his eyes.

"You did rape her, didn't you?" Corrie was sobbing. "An' you killed her, too!"

"You'd of killed her if you had the chance," Delton replied. "Said so a million times."

"But you *wanted* her, you bastard! In *bed!* I wasn't good enough! You wanted *her!*"

"Hell…"

Delton seemed to think it was a joke.

"If I hadn't of fucked her, somebody else would."

The gun jumped in Corrie's hand. Barrett heard the sharp, always unexpected detonation. He saw Delton drop the bat, saw him stagger with the impact of a slug.

But then Delton gained his balance. He lowered his head like a fullback and crossed the few feet between himself and Corrie in a heartbeat. A ham-sized fist swatted the revolver away; Corrie's second shot went wild.

And so did Delton.

He hit Corrie as if she were a linebacker, right below the sternum, and then he drove her up—

And broke her back on the rusted hood of her own car.

She didn't cry out. She just slid, legs limp, to the ground.

"Delton?" She raised an arm in supplication.

The revolver waited in the sand. Delton gathered it easily. "Might as well kill two birds with one stone." He smiled at the mother of his children as he pulled back the hammer.

"Delton, no!" Barrett croaked from behind.

The cylinder began its deliberate, irrevocable rotation—

"*Noooooooooooo!*" Barrett Raines threw himself bodily at his brother. Delton swiveled to meet the new target. But Bear made it inside his brother's mighty arms. Two skulls smacked sickeningly as the Bear drove his brother over Corrie's body and onto the hood of her car. Delton's hands danced on the hood. Danced crazily, as if scratching some horrible, unseen insect. But it wasn't an insect.

Barrett pulled himself off his brother's chest.

A knife remained there, buried to the hilt. It was a homemade knife. You could see the tape, black and uncompromising, which wrapped around the handle. Barrett trapped the dancing hands which tried to pull the knife free. Delton struggled to purge the steel in his chest. Barrett would not let go. There was a last, furious embrace.

Delton relaxed suddenly, abruptly.

"I'll be...God-damned."

His head slapped back onto the sheet metal like a slaughtered beast. The knife stood like a crucifix in his heart.

Barrett cradled Delton's head in his hands. And then he cried. A lifetime of sorrow and fear and anger mingled tears with blood on the rusty shield which in earlier ages would have borne Delton a hero back to his people. But not in this age. Not in this place. Barrett had solved the maze, survived the labyrinth, and killed the Minotaur, but there would be no relief for himself. And none for his people. Barrett Raines emptied his soul over his brother's body.

Unrestrained.

Unconsoled.

And unheard.

Epilogue

Barrett awoke to find a nurse checking a tube which was attached to a needle above his wrist. "It's just an i.v., Officer Raines." She smiled. "You're doing fine."

Barrett descended then like Orpheus to a world of darkness. When he awoke again Smoot Rawlings was standing beside his bed.

"You stayin' up this time?"

"Try me."

Smoot nodded and cranked Barrett half-erect in his bed.

He looked like a mummy, wrapped in tape from navel to neck. "You gonna be all right?" Smoot asked doubtfully.

"I'm the wrong man to ask right now." Barrett groaned.

"You'll mend." An orderly came in with irritating cheer. "Just need some rest, is all."

"I'd rather sleep," Barrett croaked.

"Somebody here to see you, first."

"Can't it wait?"

"No, it cannot," Laura Anne said from the door.

Her hair fell loose and free and black. And beautiful.

"Look at you." Barrett smiled weakly.

"Look at *you*," she teased.

Smoot followed the orderly out of the room. Laura Anne crossed to her husband's side. Her lips trembled beneath eyes clear as amber.

"I always wondered how I'd feel if something like this happened to you."

"How *do* you feel?"

"It hurts!" A tear ran smoothly down her high-yellow cheek. "It hurts so much!"

"It sure as hell does," Barrett agreed.

And she laughed. Laughter through the tears.

"I'm 'bout ready for that vacation," Barrett whispered.

"I've heard that before."

"No." Bear shook his bruised head. "It's time—past time! We've got a few memories left to make. Don't you think?"

She leaned over her husband.

"Why don't we see?"

A tender kiss warmed quickly. He reached for her hair. It fell like a curtain—

It took a while for Barrett to mend well enough to go anywhere. But within the week he was discharged. He got home to find a letter waiting from the Bureau of Alcohol, Tobacco and Firearms. Something about a citation for valor. John Lancaster made the recommendation. The letter suggested that Barrett might want to attend a formal ceremony in Tallahassee.

He didn't reply.

There were other things needed doing.

A month after Bear's hospitalization the Raines family could be found making memories on Fort Walton Beach. Ben and Tyndall spooned moats around a tremendous display of sand castles. Laura Anne sipped iced tea with Barrett on deck chairs set beside a cherry-red convertible. It was the wreck, the Chevrolet Malibu, renewed now and restored.

A pier marched from their picnic lunch into the Gulf of Mexico. Gulls dived for the sandwiches and deviled eggs which Laura Anne spread on the sand. It wasn't particularly hot; the sun was not so angry this time of year. And the breeze was cool. The sky spread overhead like a gentle quilt of the softest blue. Somewhere near the horizon you could see a catamaran tacking home with a distant wind.

The sails, Barrett was relieved to see, were white.

Acknowledgments to the First Edition

One of the most pleasant moments in this work is the time I now take to thank those who helped bring this book to press. It gives me much pleasure to thank P.J. Coldren, a Michigan reader who took great initiative to bring the manuscript of this novel to St. Martin's Press. I have Ruth Cavin to thank next, not only a brilliant and indefatigable editor, but a gracious champion of writers everywhere. Marika Rohn also worked hard on this book, as did Elizabeth Shipley, Margaret Longbrake, and Henry Yee. I was greatly encouraged early on by a number of talented and loyal folks in Los Angeles; thanks so much Karen, Jacqui, and Russel, and my favorite advocate, Shelley Surpin. Thanks go also to Russell Mobley, a disabled lawman in northern Florida; and to my classmates Randy Hethrington and Robert K. Livingston for giving me a living library of information related to anything outdoors or Floridian.

It's with special pleasure that I get to thank my wife, Doris, daughter, Morgan, and son, Jack, for their unselfish and enduring encouragement. Thank you, guys.

And thanks finally and always to my readers.

About the Author

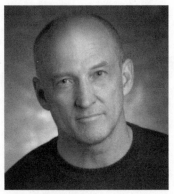

Darryl Wimberley

Darryl Wimberley is an author and screenwriter who resides with his family in Austin, Texas.

The fonts used in this book are from the Garamond family

Other works by Darryl Wimberley
available from *The* Toby Press

A Tinker's Damn

Dead Man's Bay

Kaleidoscope

The King of Colored Town

Pepperfish Keys

Strawman's Hammock

The Toby Press publishes fine writing,
available at leading bookstores everywhere. For more
information, please visit www.tobypress.com